OF this tenth volume of the *Storisende Edition* of the works of JAMES BRANCH CABELL fifteen hundred and ninety copies have been printed, of which fifteen hundred and fifty are for sale in the United States and England

This copy is number 1305

STORISENDE EDITION · X

SOMETHING ABOUT EVE

*"I was afraid, because I was
naked: and I hid myself"*

Something About Eve

A Comedy of Fig-Leaves

BY
JAMES BRANCH CABELL

ROBERT M. McBRIDE & COMPANY
NEW YORK · · · MCMXXIX

AUTHOR'S NOTE

IT MAY *be recalled that in " The Line of Love "
the life of Manuel was traced through some three
centuries of journeying, down to the introduction of
that life into the Musgrave family; and that there we
paused, temporarily, because the history of all the
Musgrave descendants is elsewhere recorded, in
" The Musgraves of Matocton," with tolerable
completeness. You may read also in " The Musgraves
of Matocton " (p. 205) of how, in 1773, the daughter of that same Gerald Allonby concerning whom
you have heard somewhat in " Gallantry " eloped
from Torwood Manor with her remote kinsman,
Theodorick Quentin Musgrave, then the lineal head
of the American Musgraves. Now it is with their
eldest son that the Biography deals in " Something
About Eve," — with that Gerald Musgrave to whom
alike through his father and his mother the life of
Manuel was thus transmitted in the nineteenth
generation.*

*About this Gerald Musgrave I have made a book
for two main reasons. He alone of all the American
Musgraves had a career of which " The Musgraves
of Matocton," in its leisured dalliance with dates and
legislative services and epitaphs and war records,*

speaks no word. It speaks, instead, of Glaum's scho-lastic career in the body of Gerald Musgrave. My second reason is, that this Gerald, alone of the Ameri-can Musgraves, adopted toward life, howsoever bunglingly, the poetic attitude, concerning which both John Charteris and I have already remarked somewhat more than suffices.

For now, in this tenth volume, the Biography re-verts to the clan of old Madoc, who was neither chivalrous nor gallant, but merely a poet, — a never-idle " maker "; and to whom all human life afforded, in the ultimate, only the raw materials which his half-tranced imaginings might remake into something more comely, more symmetrical, and more diverting. Gerald Musgrave alone of the sober-minded Musgraves was of this clan. Gerald Musgrave turned inevitably, neglecting all else, toward this or that rather beautiful idea to play with. And the history of Gerald Musgrave, therefore, sets forth how he failed, as most and perhaps all poets fail, to reach Antan.

You have already seen, in the Author's Note to " The High Place," with what diffidence, inasmuch as nobody appeared to perceive that " The High Place " possessed a rounded and jealously ordered plot, I myself was compelled to point out the fact. Here arises an even less graceful necessity. " The High Place " was so liberally assailed, it was so

AUTHOR'S NOTE

mauled and clapperclawed and spewed at, that its per-
petrator might with decorum feel privileged, in mere
self-defence, to dwell upon such subaltern merits as
the book appeared to him, even so, to display. But
"Something About Eve" fared more happily. It was
abused in a moderate number of not at all moderate
reviews, of course, for being indecent, and for being
a repetition of "Jurgen," and for not being a repeti-
tion of "Jurgen"; but that was to be expected, irre-
spective of the book's contents. . . . I remember too
that Henry Seidel Canby, of the Literary Review,
thought poorly of this book at some length: but al-
most immediately Dr. Canby was out with an article
in which he ranked his assistant editor, Mr. Christo-
pher Morley, with Goethe and Shakespeare, and thus
made Mr. Morley and myself feel quite comfort-
able. . . . So, upon the whole, "Something About
Eve" was favorably treated. I have not any valid
complaint to advance as to its reception, either as lit-
erature or as merchandise. Yet one discovers, in look-
ing over the hundreds of reviews accorded to "Some-
thing About Eve," a fact which does seem mildly
disconcerting: it is the fact that no reviewer, and so
far as I know, not any reader, evinced the least glim-
mering of perception as to what was the book's theme
and object.

To be sure, the Washington Post did raise this
exact question, and did settle it, at least to the review-

er's satisfaction, in a manner so succinct that the en-tire review may here be quoted:

" The author could have had but one object in view in writing this book, — to prove that a book of about 350 pages can be written without containing a single idea. He calls it a ' Comedy of Fig Leaves.' A comedy implies some humor, but there is no humor in this book. There is nothing about Eve, and nothing about fig leaves, even materially or metaphorically."

That is all which the Post had to say as to " Something About Eve." Yet I do not think that this sum-mary, howsoever candid, is wholly true. Nor do I think the more general finding — that " Something About Eve " concerns man's aspirations as they are at first hampered, and at last foiled, by his womankind, — to come very much nearer to the book's actual theme than did the Washington Post.

For to my mind it is sometimes plain that Ger-ald's failure to reach Antan was caused by no woman's beguilements. What detained him, when there re-mained no impediment between him and his goal, I would suggest to have been, perhaps, his own nature. Here are the woman and the child and common cor-dial human living: yonder in Antan is but ambiguity, it may be very glorious, it may be merely lethal. All news as to Antan, let it be pointed out, comes always to Gerald Musgrave from sources rather more than suspect. Meanwhile, here, upon Mispec Moor, stays

[xii]

AUTHOR'S NOTE

that which is familiar and most dear. Man — being what he is, — requires no persuading to remain where love attends him. The gods and the great myths go by, toward, it may be, concerns which are more lofty and more magnanimous: but man remains, of his own choice, and, be it added, because of all the wisdom that living has ever taught him. There are, it is said, those exceptional men who adventure very gloriously into Antan. Yet this rumor, too, comes always from ambiguous sources. It is merely certain that in the while of Gerald's tarrying with his Maya no human being, of either sex, went beyond Mispec Moor. And, in Gerald's case at least, it seems fairly certain also that not Maya detained her husband within arm's reach of the goal of all the gods of men, but the lucky fact that upon Mispec Moor Gerald Musgrave had found what contented his nature. There was not any need to journey farther.

Antan remains, they say, the home of all true poets. Yet no man is entirely a poet. A part of him is a husband, a part is a father, for example; and with these considerable fractions of a man's being, Antan has no concern, and Antan proffers to them no allure. It results that, although, as even a myopic Rossetti has observed, so many men are poets in their youth, yet, with age, and with the accompanying growth in complexity of each man's nature, all men, and most certainly all poets, fail more or less completely as poets. I would but point out that to fail as a poet may

[xiii]

very well be to succeed as a human being. Gerald did not reach Antan: yet he gained, so far as he could discover, the most nearly satisfying prizes which human life affords. He, in any case, was not ever so discourteous as to blame upon any woman the outcome that he attained to no more: and I conjecture that you and I may here with profit emulate him in chivalry. . . . Instead, the enemy was within: and instead, for all that I know, the enemy turned out, in the end, to have been a benefactor,——within of course those brief and not over fertile fields wherein beneficence, howsoever fleetingly, touches human living.

——None of which may be true, to be sure: I would but suggest that now and then this also seems, in Gerald's favorite phrase, a rather beautiful idea to play with.

THIS book was begun several years before its completion. I appear to have no note as to exactly when " Something About Eve " was started: but it was already an aging and much interlined manuscript when, in 1923, Guy Holt compiled his Bibliography of my writings, and in that opus duly listed " Something About Eve " among my forthcoming works. The chief difference between the present book and the form which this tale retained for years was that, in the earlier version, the story passed straightway from Gerald's departure from out of human living

[xiv]

to his meeting with Maya. There was, that is, in the earlier version nothing corresponding to Chapters V–XXII, but instead only a gap which I meant by and by to fill in, and never did bridge over in the tale's first form. Nor did the missing matter then appear especially important, because to me the real theme was always just the story of Gerald's contented stay upon Mispec Moor, with the gods and the myths of men passing onward to an ambiguous fate which he elected not to provoke for himself.

In any event, I became dissatisfied with the tale, for one reason and another, and the manuscript of this first version was burned in the spring of 1925. Gerald Musgrave seemed now at one with his near kinswomen, Wilhelmina Musgrave and Cynthia Musgrave, and with Hugh de Lusignan, and with George Bulmer, whose partially completed histories had all ended in the hall fireplace at Dumbarton Grange: and I turned to " The Silver Stallion," and afterward to " The Music from Behind the Moon." Yet all the while this red-headed Gerald Musgrave, whom I had first met in the pages of " The Rivet in Grandfather's Neck," retained an obscure footing in the very back of my mind. Thence he, as one who foreknows the outcome, appeared to regard me with an air of amiable and mildly humorous mockery which became more and yet more familiar. Meanwhile that ruthless bust of Æsred which Edmond Amateis had made for me, out of a bit of marble from Nero's Golden House, stayed in my writing-room: and she too appeared to regard me with a sort of sullen expectation. The two of them, in fine, seemed bent upon my writing "Something About Eve."

So I came back to Gerald Musgrave, after all, in the July of 1926. I found, in Cayford Cottage, just such a cottage as Gerald inhabited; I found, in appraising the vista from the porch of that cottage, a fair duplicate of Antan, in Pembroke, Virginia; and I found too that Gerald Musgrave's life history had become very easy to write. There was, now, no difficulty whatever about it: and the tale flowed onward without any stop, — with Nero sauntering into the story, as an affair of course, — and it seemed rather to complete itself, at last, in the June of 1927. I do not assert that this is the best of my books: but I am sure that, after the first false start, "Something About Eve" is the story which I wrote with the largest portion of ease and zest.

*I*T WAS *published in September 1927. To my chief collaborator was then paid the tribute of illustrating the large paper edition with a picture of that bust of Æsred which had both chaperoned and allured me through the book's writing.*

..But again I found that, as had been the case with "Figures of Earth," so here my first conception of "Something About Eve" seemed to have been ob-

[xvi]

AUTHOR'S NOTE

scured beyond human discovery in the completed book. To me this was always the story of Gerald's stay upon Mispec Moor: to a troublingly large number of my readers, I found, it was, instead, the story of Gerald's journeying toward Mispec Moor, and of his adventuring with Evadne and Evasherah and Evarvan and Evaine, with all the latter half of the book figuring as a relatively unimportant epilogue. And I find, to this day, that notion is prevalent.

Now there are several ways of explaining this. One is, that the material with which I finally filled in the years-old gap in Gerald's history happened, somehow, to be superior in quality to the remainder of the book, which corresponds to the story as I first shaped it. Of that possibility I am no judge. A rather less flattering explanation is, that few readers got farther than the middle of the book.

But I think this shift in emphasis is, rather, to be accounted for by the fact that to the immature-minded any reference to sexual matters is impressive beyond its rational weight. Given a book in which there is one hint of the technically "indecent," it is that single passage which the mentally immature, howsoever staid and gray, will remember, whether with sniggers or with indignation, long after the rest of the book is forgotten. I recall a queer instance of this in the reception accorded to Hugh Walpole's "The Young Enchanted," in which novel a four-letter word, thitherto — to purloin a phrase from

AUTHOR'S NOTE

George Jean Nathan, — " more intimately associated with latrines than with literature," occurred just once, and promptly became the pivot of any general discussion of " The Young Enchanted." I reflect, too, that, while the texts of Rabelais and of Apuleius are customarily printed in full, the sole passages actually read therein by the most of us are the same. . . . And I deduce it is natural enough that to many of my readers this book must always appear to be an account of Gerald Musgrave's temptation by various women, and of his edifying resistance to all temptation. Yet I repeat, nevertheless, that, so far as I am concerned, it stays the history of his resting upon Mispec Moor, to his ruin as a practising poet, but to his enlargement as a human being.

James Branch Cabell

Richmond-in-Virginia
September 1928

[xviii]

CONTENTS

PART ONE

THE BOOK OF OUTSET

PART TWO

THE BOOK OF TWILIGHT

PART THREE

THE BOOK OF DOONHAM

PART FOUR

THE BOOK OF DERSAM

[xix]

CONTENTS

PART FIVE

THE BOOK OF LYTREIA

PART SIX

THE BOOK OF TUROINE

PART SEVEN

THE BOOK OF POETS

PART EIGHT

THE BOOK OF MAGES

[xx]

CONTENTS

PART NINE

THE BOOK OF MISPEC MOOR

PART TEN

THE BOOK OF ENDINGS

PART ELEVEN

THE BOOK OF REMNANTS

PART TWELVE

THE BOOK OF ACQUIESCENCE

THE ARGUMENT OF THIS COMEDY

Set forth as clearly as discretion permits, for the
convenience of the intending reader

These shadows here are subtle: for they wait
Like usurers that briefly lend the sun
Disfavor and a stinted while to run
With flaunting vigor through life's large estate
Of fire and turmoil; or like thieves that hate
No law-lord save the posturing of desire
With genuflexions where dejections tire
The fig-leaf's trophy with the fig-leaf's weight.

Yes; they are subtle: and where no light is
These tread not openly, as heretofore,
With whisperings of that at odds with this
To veil their passing, where a broken door
Confronts the zenith, and Semiramis,
At one with Upsilon, exhorts no more.

PART ONE

THE BOOK OF OUTSET

" Wheresoever a Man Lives, There
Will be a Thornbush Near His Door."

1. How the Tempter Came

FOR some moments after he had materialized, and had become perceivable by human senses, the Sylan waited. He waited, looking down at the very busy, young, red-haired fellow who sat within arm's reach at the writing-table. This boy, as yet, was so unhappily engrossed in literary composition as not to have noticed his ghostly visitant. So the Sylan waited. . . .

And as always, to an onlooker, the motions of creative writing revealed that flavor of the grotesque which is attendant upon every form of procreation. The Sylan rather uneasily noted the boy's writhing antics, which to a phantom seemed strange and eerie. . . . For this mortal world, as the Sylan well remembered, was remarkably opulent in things which gave pleasure when they were tasted or handled, — the world in which this pensive boy was handling, and now nibbled at, the tip-end of a black pen. Outside this somewhat stuffy room were stars or sunsets or impressive mountains, to be looked at from almost anywhere in this mortal world, — which would also afford to the investigative, who searched in appropriate places, such agreeable smells as that of vervain and patchouli, and of smouldering incense, and of hayfields under a large moon, and of pine woods, and the robustious salty odors of a wind coming up from the sea.

[3]

Likewise, at this very moment, you might encounter, in the prodigal world outside this somewhat stuffy room, those tinier, those mere baby winds which were continually whispering in the tree-tops about this world's marvelousness now that April was departing; or you might hear the irrationally dear sound of a bird calling dubiously in the spring night, with a strange and piercing sweetness; or, if you went adventuring yet farther, you might hear the muffled, small, delicious voice of a woman who was counterfeiting embarrassment and pretending to disapprove of your enterprise. . . . Outside this book-filled room, in fine, was that unforgotten mortal world in which any conceivable young man could live very royally, and with never-failing ardor, upon every person's patrimony of the five human senses.

And yet, in such a well-stocked world, this lean, red-headed boy was vexedly making upon paper (with that much nibbled-at black pen) small scratches, the most of which he almost immediately canceled with yet other scratches, all the while with the air of a person who is about something intelligent and of actual importance. This Gerald Musgrave therefore seemed to the waiting, spectral Sylan a somewhat excessively silly mortal, thus to be squandering a lad's brief while of living in vigorous young human flesh, among so many readily accessible objects which a boy like this could always be seeing and tasting and smelling and hearing and handling, with unforgotten delight.

But the Sylan reflected, too, a bit wistfully, that his own mortal youth was now for some time overpast. It had, in fact, been nearly six hundred years since he had been really young, a good five and a half centuries since young Guivric and his nine tall comrades in the famous fellowship had so delighted in their patrimony of five human senses and had spent that inheritance rather notably. Yes, he was getting on, the Sylan reflected; he had quite lost touch with the ways of these latter-day young people.

Yet it was perhaps unavoidable that, in the great while since he had gone about this world in a man's natural body, the foibles of human youth had become somewhat strange to him; and it was not, after all, to appraise the wastefulness of authors that you had traveled a long way, from Caer Omn to Lichfield, at the command of another Author, to put this doomed red-headed boy out of living.

The Sylan spoke. . . .

THE Sylan spoke. He spoke at some length. And the young man at the writing-table, after arising with the slight start which these supernatural visitations invariably evoked from him, had presently heard the Sylan's proposal.

"Who is it," said Gerald, then, "that tempts me to this sacrifice and to this partial destruction?"

The Sylan replied, "The name that I had in my mortal living was Guivric, but now I am called Glaum of the Haunting Eyes."

That was a queer name, and it was a queer arrangement, too, which this vague wraith in the likeness of a man was proposing, — an arrangement, Gerald Musgrave decided, which, at least, was worth consideration. . . .

For, as a student of magic, Gerald Musgrave in his time had dealt with many demons: but never had been made to him, before this final night in the April of 1805, such a queer, and yet rational, and even handsome offer as was now held out. Gerald pushed aside the manuscript of his unfinished romance about Dom Manuel of Poictesme; he straightened the ruffles about his throat; and for an instant he weighed the really quite alluring suggestion. . . . Most demons were obsessed by the notion of buying from you a soul which Gerald, in this age of reason, had no sure proof that he possessed. But this Glaum of the

[6]

Haunting Eyes, it seemed, was empowered and willing to rid Gerald of all corporal obligations, and to take over Gerald's physical life just as it stood, — even with all the plaguing complications of Gerald's entanglement with Evelyn Townsend.

" I was once human," the Sylan explained, " and wore a natural body. And old habits, in such trifles as apparel, cling. I feel at times, even nowadays, after five centuries of a Sylan's care-free living, rather at a loss for human ties."

" I find them," Gerald stated, " vast nuisances. Candor is no more palatable than an oyster when either is out of season. And my relatives are all cursed with a very disastrous candor. They conceal from me nothing save that respect and envy with which they might, appropriately, regard my accomplishments and nobler qualities."

" That has been the way with all relatives, Gerald, since Cain and Abel were brothers."

" Still, but for one calamity, I could, it might be, endure my brothers. I could put up with my sisters' voluble and despondent view of my future. I might even go so far in supererogation as to condone — upon alternate Thursdays, say, — a chorus of affectionate aunts who speak for my own good."

" The first person, Gerald, that pretended to speak for the real good of anybody else was a serpent in a Garden, and ever since then that sort of talking has been venomous."

" Yet all these afflictions I might," said Gerald, — " conceivably, at least, I might be able to endure, if only the pursuit of my art had not been hampered, and the ease of my body blasted, by the greatest blessing which can befall any man."

[7]

" You allude, I imagine," said the Sylan, " to the love of a good woman? "

" That is it, that is precisely the unmerited and too irremovable blessing which may end, after all, in reducing me to your suggested vulgar fraction of a suicide."

Now Gerald was silent. He leaned far back in his chair. He meditatively placed together the tips of his two little fingers, and then one by one the tips of his other fingers, until his thumbs also were in contact; and he regarded the result, upon the whole, with disapprobation.

" Every marriage gets at least one man into trouble," he philosophized, " and it is not always the bridegroom. You see, sir, by the worst of luck, this Evelyn Townsend was already married, so that ours had necessarily to become an adulterous union. It is the tragedy of my life that I met my Cousin Evelyn too late to marry her. Any married person of real ingenuity and tolerable patience can induce his wife to divorce him. But there is no way known to me for a Southern gentleman to get rid of a lady whom he has possessed illegally, until she has displayed the decency to become tired of him. And Evelyn, sir, in this matter of continuing her immoral relations with me has behaved badly, very badly indeed — "

" All women — " Glaum began.

" No, but let us not be epigrammatic and aphoristic and generally flippant about a perverseness which is pestering me beyond any reasonable endurance! You know as well as I do that every pretty woman ought, by and by, to remember what she owes to her husband and to her marriage vows, and to act accordingly. Repentance when suitably timed in a liaison makes

[8]

for everybody's happiness. But some women, sir, some women stay more affectionately adhesive than an anaconda. They weep. They reply to their helpless paramours' every least attempt at any rational statement, ' And I trusted you! I gave you all! ' "

Glaum nodded, not unsympathetically. " I also in my time have heard that observation without any active enjoyment. It is, I believe, unanswerable."

Gerald shuddered. " There is, for a Southern gentleman at all events, no really satisfactory reply save murder. And against that solution there is of course a rather general prejudice. Therefore a woman of this bleating sort exacts fidelity, she makes every nature of unconscionable demand, and she pesters you to the verge of lunacy, always upon the unanswerable ground that her claim upon your gratitude, and upon your instant obedience in everything, ought not to exist. Oh, I assure you, my dear fellow, there is no more sensible piece of friendly counsel existent than is the Seventh Commandment! "

" Your aphorisms are more or less true, and your predicament I can understand. Nevertheless — "

But the Sylan hesitated.

" You also understand us Musgraves perfectly! " Gerald applauded. " For I perceive you are now about to wheedle me forward in this business by throwing obstacles in my way."

" I was but going to point out the truism that, nevertheless, it may be wiser to put up with your Eve unresistingly — "

" The name," emended Gerald, " is Evelyn."

At that the Sylan smiled. " Yes, to be sure! Women do vary in their given names. It might be wiser, then, I was about to say, for you to put up with

your Evelyn unresistingly, rather than for a student
of magic, with so little real practical experience as
yours, to go blundering about the doubtful road
which leads to Antan."

"But, sir, I have the soul of an artist! Once" —
and Gerald pointed to his manuscript, — "once it
was the little art of letters. Then, through my
acquaintance with Gaston Bulmer, who is no doubt
known to you — "

The Sylan shook his spectral head, like smoke in a
veering wind. "I have not, I believe, that pleasure."

"You astound me. I would have supposed the
name of Gaston Bulmer to be in all infernal circles a
household word, because the dear old rascal is an
adept, sir, of wide parts, of taste, and of sound judg-
ment. Then, too, since Mrs. Townsend is his daughter, he has now for some while been my father-in-law
for all practical purposes — But, where was I? Ah,
yes! Through Gaston Bulmer, I repeat, I became
initiated into the greatest of all arts. Now I desire to
excel in that art. I note that I falter in the little art
of letters, that my prose is no longer superb and
breath-taking in its loveliness, because my heart is
not any longer really interested in writing, on account
of my heart's ever-pricking desire to revive in its full
former glories the far nobler and — at all events, in
the United States of America, — the unjustly neglected art of the magician. And from whom else —
just as you have suggested, my dear fellow, — from
whom else save the Master Philologist can I get the
great and best words of magic? Do you but answer
me that very simple question!"

"From no one else, to be sure — "

"So, now, you see for yourself!"

" Yet the Master Philologist is nowadays a married man, and is ruled in everything by his wife. And this Queen Freydis has a mirror which must, they say, be faced by those persons who venture into the goal of all the gods of men — "

" That mirror, too," said Gerald, airily, " I may be needing. Mirrors are employed in many branches of magic."

Glaum now was speaking with rather more of graveness than there seemed any call for. And Glaum said:

" For one, I would not meddle with that mirror. Even in the land of Dersam, where a mirror is sacred, we do not desire any dealings with the Mirror of the Hidden Children and with those strange reflections which are unclouded by either good or evil."

" I shall face the Mirror of the Hidden Children," Gerald said, with his chin well up, " and should I see any particular need for it, I shall fetch that mirror also out of Antan. When a citizen of the United States of America takes up the pursuit of an art, sir, he does not shilly-shally about it."

" For my part," the Sylan answered, " I wearied, some centuries ago, of all magic: and I hanker, rather, after the more material things of life. For five hundred years and over, in my untroubled abode at Caer Omn, in the land of Dersam, I have reigned among the dreams of a god — "

" But how did you come by these dreams? "

" They forsook him, Gerald, when his hour was come to descend into Antan."

" That saying, sir, I cannot understand."

" It is not necessary, Gerald, that you should. Meanwhile, I admit, the life of a Sylan has no fret in it, a Sylan has nothing to be afraid of: and there is in me a mortal taint which cannot endure interminable contentment any longer. You conceive, I also was once a mortal man, with my deceivings and my fears and my doubts to spice my troubled deference to the ever-present folly of my fellows and to the ever-present ruthlessness of time and chance. And, as I remember it, Gerald, that Guivric, whom people so preposterously called the Sage, got more zest out of his subterfuges and compromises than I derive from being care-free and rather bored twenty-four hours to each insufferable day. Therefore, I repeat, I will take over your natural body — "

" But that, my dear fellow, would leave me without any carnal residence."

" Why, Gerald, but I am surprised at such scepticism in you who pay your pew-rent so regularly! We have it upon old, fine authority that for every man there is a natural body and a spiritual body."

Then Gerald colored up. He felt that both his erudition and his piety stood reproved. And he said, contritely:

" In fact, as a member of the Protestant Episcopal Church, I am familiar with the Burial Service — Yes, you are right. I have no desire to take issue with St. Paul. The religion of my fathers assures me that I have two bodies. I can live in only one of them at a time. It is, for that matter, a bit ostentatious, it has a vaguely disreputable sound, for any unmarried man to be maintaining two establishments. So, let us get on! "

" Therefore, I repeat, I will take over your natural body, just as that first Glaum once took over my body; and I will take over all your body's imbroglios, even with your mistress, — who can hardly be more tasking to get along with than are the seven official wives and the three hundred and fifty-odd concubines I am getting rid of."

" You," Gerald said, morosely, " do not know Evelyn Townsend."

" I trust," the Sylan stated, more gallantly, " to have that privilege to-morrow."

It was in this way the bargain was struck. And then the Sylan who was called Glaum of the Haunting Eyes did what was requisite.

THE Sylan who was called Glaum of the Haunting Eyes, be it repeated, did that which was requisite. . . . To Gerald, as a student of magic, the most of the process was familiar enough: and if some curious grace-notes were, perhaps, excursions into the less wholesome art of goety, that was not Gerald's affair. It was sufficient that, when the Sylan had ended, no Sylan was any longer visible. Instead, in Gerald Musgrave's library, stood face to face two Geralds, each in a blue coat and a golden yellow waistcoat, each with a tall white stock and ruffles about his throat, and each clad in every least respect precisely like the other.

Nor did these two lean, red-headed Geralds differ in countenance. Each smiled at the other with the same amply curved, rather womanish mouth set above the same prominent, long chin; and each found just the same lazy and mildly humorous mockery in the large and very dark blue, the really purple, eyes of the other: for between these two Gerald Musgraves there was no visual difference whatever.

One half of this quaint pair now sat down at the writing-table; and, fiddling with the papers there, he took up the pages of Gerald Musgrave's unfinished romance, about the high loves of his famous ancestor Dom Manuel of Poictesme and Madame Niafer, the Soldan of Barbary's daughter. Gerald had begun

[14]

this tale in the days when he had intended to endow America with a literature superior to that of other countries; but for months now he had neglected it: and, in fact, ever since he set up as a student of magic he had lacked time somehow, with every available moment given over to runes and cantraps and suffumigations, to get back to any really serious work upon this romance.

Then the seated Gerald, smiling almost sadly, looked up toward his twin.

" Thus it was," said the seated Gerald, " a great while ago at Asch, when two Guivrics confronted each other and played shrewdly for the control of the natural body of Guivric of Perdigon. All which I lost on that day, through my over-human clinging to the Two Truths, I now have back, after five centuries of pleasure-seeking in the land of Dersam. And I find this second natural body of mine committed to the creating of yet more pleasure-giving nonsense, about, of all persons, that eternal Manuel of Poictesme! I find this body also enamored of the fig-leaf of romance! "

" It may be that I do not understand your simile," said the standing Gerald, " for in the United States of America the fig-leaf is, rather, the nice symbol of decency, it is, indeed, the beginning and the end of democratic morality."

" Nevertheless, and granting all this," replied the now demon-haunted natural body of Gerald Musgrave, " the fig-leaf is a romance with which human optimism veils the only two eternal and changeless and rather unlovely realities of which any science can be certain."

" Ah, now I comprehend! And without utterly

[15]

agreeing with you, I cannot deny there is something in your metaphor. Yet I must tell you, sir, that I am perhaps peculiarly qualified to deal with Dom Manuel because of the fact that this famous hero was my lineal ancestor — "

" Oh, but, my poor Gerald, was he indeed! "

" Yes, through both the Musgrave and the Allonby lines. For my mother's father was Gerald Allonby — "

And Gerald would have gone on to explain the precise connection, of which the Musgrave family was justifiably proud. But the unappreciative Sylan who now wore good Musgrave flesh and blood had remarked, of all conceivable remarks:

" I honestly condole with you. Yet ancestors cannot be picked like strawberries. And my luck was even worse, for I was of Manuel's fellowship. I knew the tall swaggerer himself throughout his blundering career. And I can assure you that, apart from his unhuman gift for keeping his mouth shut, there was nothing a bit wonderful about the cock-eyed, gray impostor."

This was surprising news. Still, Gerald reflected, a demon did, in the way of business, meet many persons in circumstances in which the better side of their natures was not to the fore. Gerald therefore flew to defend the honor of his race quite civilly.

" My progenitor, in any event, carried through his imposture. He died very well thought of by his neighbors. That you will find to be a leading consideration with any citizen of the United States of America. And I in turn assure you that my account of the great Manuel's exploits will be, when it is completed, an exceedingly fine romance. It will be a tale which has

[16]

not its like in America. Loveliness lies swooning upon every page, illuminated by a never-ceasing coruscation of wit. Through a refreshing shower of epigrams parade the most striking and original sentiments under umbrellas of delicate phrasing. Meanwhile an exuberant fancy canters through the loftiest uplands of romance. . . . In fact, this is a story which, as you might put it, grips the reader. There is no imaginable reader but will be instantly engaged by my adroit depiction of the hardihood and the heroic virtues of Dom Manuel — ”

" But," said the really very handsomely disguised Sylan, " Manuel had always a cold in his head. Nobody can honestly admire an elderly fellow who is continually sneezing and spitting — ”

" In American literature of a respectable cast no human being has any excretory functions. Should you reflect upon this statement, you will find it to be the one true test of delicacy. At most, some tears or a bead or two of perspiration may emanate, but not anything more, upon this side of pornography. That rule applies with especial force to love stories, for reasons we need hardly go into. And my romance is, of course, the story of Dom Manuel's love for the beautiful Niafer, the Soldan of Barbary's daughter — ”

" Her father was a stable groom. She had a game leg. She was not beautiful. She was dish-faced, she was out and out ugly, apart from her itch to be reforming everybody and pestering them with respectability — ”

" Faith, charity and hope are the three cardinal virtues," said Gerald, reprovingly. " And I think that a gentleman should exercise these three, in just

[17]

this order, when he is handling the paternity or the looks or the legs of any lady."

" — And she smelt bad. Every month she seemed to me to smell worse. I do not know why, but I think the Countess simply hated to wash."

" My dear fellow! really now, I can but refer you to my previously cited rule as to the anatomy of romance. A heroine who smells bad every month — No, upon my word, I can find nothing engaging in that notion. I had far rather play with some wholly other and more beautiful idea than with a notion so utterly lacking in seductiveness. For that manuscript before you is not a legal deposition, but a romance. It is a romance such as has not its like in America. I therefore consider that I display considerable generosity in presenting you with those quite perfect ninety-three pages, and in permitting you to complete this romance and to take the credit for writing all of it. Why, your picture will be in the newspapers, and learned professors will annotate your fornications, and oncoming ages will become familiar with every mean act you ever committed! "

To that the Sylan replied: " I shall complete your balderdash, no doubt, since all your functions are now my functions. I shall complete it, if only my common-sense and my five centuries of living among the loveliest dreams of a god, and, above all, if my first-hand information as to these people, have not ruined me for the task of ascribing large virtues to human beings."

" I envy you that task," said Gerald, with real wistfulness, " but, very much as there was a geas upon my famous ancestor to make a figure in this world, just so there is a compulsion upon me. The compulsion is upon me to excel in my art; and to do this I must liberate the great and best words of the Master Philologist."

Then the true Gerald went out of the room through a secret passage unknown to him until this evening.

iv. THAT DEVIL IN THE LIBRARY

YET Gerald looked back for an instant at that
unfortunate devil, in the appearance of a
sedate young red-haired man, who remained
in the library. To regard this Gerald Musgrave, now,
was like looking at a droll acquaintance in whom
Gerald was not, after all, very deeply interested.

For this Gerald Musgrave, the one who remained
in the library, was really droll in well-nigh every respect. About the Gerald who was now — it might be,
a bit nobly, — yielding up his life in preference to
violating the code of a gentleman, and who was now
quitting Lichfield, in order to become a competent
magician, there was not anything ludicrous. That
Gerald was an honorable and intelligent person who
sought a high and rational goal.

But that part of Gerald Musgrave which remained
behind, that part which was already marshaling more
words in order the more pompously to inter the exploits of Dom Manuel of Poictesme, appeared droll.
There was, for one thing, no sensible compulsion
upon that red-haired young fellow thus to be defil-
ing clean paper with oak-gall, when he might at that
very instant be comfortably drunk at the Vartreys'
dinner, or he might be getting pleasurable excitement
out of the turns of fortune at Dorn's gaming-parlors,
or he might be diverting himself in his choice of four
bedrooms with a lively companion.

[20]

But, instead, he sat alone with bookshelves rising stuffily to every side of him, — rather low bookshelves upon the tops of which were perched a cherished horde of porcelain and brass figures representing one or another beast or fowl or reptile. Among the shiny toys, which in themselves attested his childishness, the young fellow sat of his own accord thus lonelily. And his antics, incontestably, were queer. He fidgeted. He shifted his rump. He hunched downward, as if with a sudden access of rage, over the paper before him. He put back his head, to stare intently at a white china hen. He pulled at the lobe of his left ear; and he then rather frantically scratched the interior of·his ear with his little finger.

Between these bodily exercises he, who was so precariously seated upon the crust of a planet teetering unpredictably through space, was making upon the paper before him, with his much nibbled-at black pen, small scratches, the most of which he presently canceled with yet other scratches, all the while with the air of a person who was about something intelligent and of actual importance. The spectacle was queer; it was unspeakably irrational: for, as always, to an onlooker, the motions of creative writing revealed that flavor of the grotesque which is attendant upon every form of procreation.

Yet it was upon a graver count that Gerald felt honestly sorry for the inheritor of Gerald Musgrave's natural body. For Gerald was giving up his life out of deference to the code of a gentleman with rather more of relief than he had permitted the Sylan to suspect. And the poor devil who had so rashly taken over this life would — howsoever acute his diabolical intelligence, — he too would, in the

end, Gerald reflected, be powerless against that unreasonable Evelyn Townsend and that even more
unreasonable code of a gentleman.

Nobody, Gerald's thoughts ran on, now that he
had found a rather beautiful idea to play with, nobody who had not actually indulged in the really
dangerous dalliance of adultery in Lichfield could
quite understand the hopelessness of the unfortunate
fiend's position. For in the chivalrous Lichfield of
1805 adultery had its inescapable etiquette. Your
exact relations with the woman were in the small
town a matter of public knowledge familiar to everybody: but no person in Lichfield would ever formally grant that any such relations existed. Eyes might
meet with perfect understanding: but from the well-
bred lips of no Southern gentleman or gentlewoman
would ever come more than a suave and placid,
" Evelyn and Gerald have always been such good
friends." For you were second cousins, to begin with:
and — in a Lichfield wherein, as everywhere else in
this human world, most people unaffectedly disliked,
and belittled, and kept away from their cousins, —
that relationship was considered a natural reason for
you two being much together. Moreover, every
woman in Lichfield was, by another really rather
staggering social convention, assumed to be beautiful
and accomplished and chaste. That was an assumption
which did not need to be stated: that was merely
among all Southern gentry an axiom in the vast code
of being well-bred.

It followed that, when you were once involved in
a liaison, your one salvation was for your co-partner
in iniquity to become tired of you, and to cease dwelling upon the fact that she had trusted you and had

given you all. That remained, of course, by the dictates of Southern chivalry, at any moment her privilege: but in this case the inconsiderate woman only grew fonder and fonder of Gerald, and repeated the dreadful observation more and more frequently. . . . And it remained, too, the privilege of the technically aggrieved husband to pick a quarrel with you, provided only that the grounds of this quarrel in no way involved a mention of his wife's name. Then, still by the set rules of Lichfield's etiquette, there would be a duel. After the duel you either were dispiritingly dead or, else, if you happen to be the more assuredly luckless survivor, you were compelled, merely by the silent force of everybody's assumption that a gentleman could not do otherwise, to marry the widow. To do this was your debt to society at large, in atonement for having "compromised" a lady, where, bewilderingly enough, she was unanimously granted never to have been concerned at all. For never, in either outcome, would the occurrence of anything "wrong" be conceded, nor would ever the possibility of a lady's having committed adultery be so much as hinted at in any speech or act of the chivalrous gentry of Lichfield.

Meanwhile you were trapped. There was no way whatever of avoiding that bleated, "Oh, and I trusted you! I gave you all!" You were not even privileged to avoid the woman. It was not considered humanly possible that you were bored, and upon some occasions frenziedly annoyed, by the society of a beautiful and accomplished and chaste gentlewoman who honored you with her friendship. There was, instead, compressing you everywhere, the tacit but vast force of the general assumption that your indebtedness to her could not ever be discharged in full. The deplorable — and sometimes, too, the rather dear — fond woman's inability to keep her hands off you was conscientiously not noticed. So your Cousin Evelyn pawed at you in public without an eyebrow's going up: hostesses smilingly put you together: other men affably quitted her side whensoever you appeared. Her husband was no different: Frank Townsend, also, genially accepted — in the teeth of whatsoever rationality the man might privately harbor, — the axiom that " Evelyn and Gerald have always been such good friends."

Of course, Gerald granted, this was, in the upper circles of the best Southern families, an exceptional case. Time and again Gerald had envied the dozens of other young fellows in Lichfield who were conducting their liaisons with visibly such superior luck. For the lady tired of them or, else, was smitten with convenient repentance: and these gay blades passed on high-heartedly to the embraces of yet other technically beautiful and accomplished and chaste playfellows. But Evelyn evinced an impenitence which threatened to be permanent: Evelyn did not tire of Gerald; she pawed at him; she slipped notes into his hand; she bleated almost every day her insufferable claim to upset his convenience and his comfort: and he cursed in all earnestness that fatal charm of his which held him in such desperate loneliness.

— In loneliness, because not even the lean comfort of candor, not even any quest of sympathy, was permitted you. A gentleman did not kiss and tell: he, above all, might not tell that the kissing had become an infernal nuisance. Not any of your brothers, neither one of your sisters — not even when your

[24]

indolence and your general worthlessness had reduced Cynthia to whimpering bits of the New Testament, or had launched Agatha in a chattering mill-
race of babbling maledictory vaticinations, — would
ever recognize to you in plain words that you and
Cousin Evelyn were illicitly intimate. Nor would any
of your kindred, either, ever contemplate the possibility of you yourself acting or speaking here with
common-sense, or in any other manner violating the
formulas set for every gentleman's conduct by the
insane and magnificent code of Lichfield.

For it was, after all, magnificent, in its own way,
the code by which those bull-headed Musgraves —
who shared the blood that was in your body, but no
one of the notions in your astonishingly clever head,
— along with the rest of this brave and stupid Lichfield, lived day after day, and carried genial, never-
troubled self-respect into the graveyard. This code
avoided, so far as Gerald could see, no especial mis-
doing or crime: but it did show you how, with the
appropriate and most graceful of gestures, to commit
either, when the need arose, in the prescribed fashion
of a well-bred Southern gentleman. Yes, really, Gerald reflected, that code was rather a beautiful idea to
play with. It was an excellent thing to be a gentleman: but it proved always fatal, too, in the end,
simply because no lady was a gentleman.

However, it was that poor devil in the library who
was now involved in the dangerous task of carrying
through an adultery in Lichfield after the fashion of
well-bred persons. It was in his ears that a still rather
dear but too damnably adhesive Evelyn would be
bleating every day a reiteration of the fact that she
had trusted him and had given him all. And Gerald

himself, having decorously laid down his life rather than violate this dreadful code of a gentleman, was now fairly in train to become a competent magician.

Not ever again would he sit writing among those bookshelves, engrossed, and rubbing at his chin or forehead, or scratching his head, or sticking his little finger into his ear, or restively shifting his weight from one buttock to the other buttock, in his multiform efforts to quicken, somehow, the flow of lagging thought. He would pause no more to prop his chin (with an unpleasantly moist hand, as a rule), and thus to stare lack-wittedly at one or another of the china and brass toys which he had, quite as idiotically, collected to make vivid his bookshelves. All these queer exercises, as Gerald, standing there, had seen them in the last few minutes performed by the natural body of Gerald Musgrave, did, manifestly, not constitute an engaging or a sane way of spending the evening, in a somewhat stuffy room.

No, he was now, forever, very happily done with all these forlorn gymnastics. It was only the natural body of Gerald Musgrave which henceforward would, before this commensurately irrational audience of small elephants and dogs and parrots and chickens, go through these foolish writhing antics, in that wholly nice looking young idiot's endeavor to complete the romance about Dom Manuel of Poictesme. . . . Well, one could but wish the poor devil joy of his bargain! and it no longer really mattered that all which pertained to Gerald Musgrave was rather droll, Gerald decided, as he passed out of sight of that red head bent over that incessant pen scratching.

PART TWO

THE BOOK OF TWILIGHT

*" It is Not Well to Look a
Gift Horse in the Mouth."*

GERALD descended nineteen steps; and in the dusk he found waiting there, beside a tethered riding-horse, yet another young man, with hair as red as Gerald Musgrave's own.

"That you may travel the more quickly, along a woman-haunted way, in your journeying toward your appointed goal," this stranger began, "I have fetched a horse for you to ride upon."

Yet the speaker was not wholly a stranger. So Gerald now said, "Oh, so it is you!" As a student of magic, Gerald had held earlier dealings with this red-haired Horvendile, who was Lord of the Marches of Antan.

And Gerald went on, gratefully: "Come now, but this is kind! Even as a courtesy between fellow artists, this is generous!"

"The amenities of fellow artists," returned Horvendile, "are by ordinary two-edged. And this one may cut deeper than you foreknow."

"Meanwhile you have brought me this huge shining horse, which cannot be other than Pegasus —"

"Whether or not this divine steed be that Pegasus which bears romantics even to the ultimate goal of their dreams, depends upon the horseman. It has been prophesied, however, that the Redeemer of Antan and the monarch who shall reign, after the overthrow of the Master Philologist, in the place beyond

[29]

good and evil, will come riding upon the silver stallion that is called, not Pegasus, but Kalki — "

" Oh! oh! " said Gerald; and for an instant he considered this surprising turn of affairs. To reign in Antan had, very certainly, been no part of his modest plans; but he saw at once how much more becoming it would be, and how much better suited to his real merits, to enter into Antan as its heir apparent, resistless upon the silver stallion famous in old prophecies, rather than to come as a suppliant begging for a few words.

" Prophecies," said Gerald, then, " ought to be respected by all well brought up persons. Only, does this horse happen to be Kalki? Because, you see, Horvendile, that appears to be the whole point of the prophecy."

Rather oddly, Horvendile said, " Whether or not this divine steed be that Kalki which bears romantics even to the ultimate goal of all the gods, depends upon the horseman."

Gerald considered this saying. Gerald smiled, and Gerald remarked:

" Oh, but now I comprehend you! The rider and the owner of any horse is, quite naturally, entitled to call the animal whatsoever he prefers. Very well, then! I shall christen this riding-horse Kalki. Yes, Horvendile, upon mature deliberation, I will accept the throne of Antan, without considering my personal preferences and my dislike of publicity and ostentation, in order that the prophecy may be fulfilled, because that is always a good thing for prophecies."

" Since that is your decision, Gerald, you have but, after you have paid homage here, to mount intrep-

[30]

idly. And the divine steed will carry you upon no common road, but, since he is divine, along that way which the gods and the great myths pursue in their journeying toward Antan."

"It is appropriate, of course, that I should travel on the road patronized by the best classes. Nevertheless, it would, I think, be a rather beautiful idea — "

"Nevertheless, also," said Horvendile, "and all the while that you waste in talking about beautiful ideas, there is a man's homage to be paid here; and now, moreover, at the first gap of Doonham, the Princess awaits you with some impatience. It would not be going too far to say, indeed, that she hungers for your coming."

"Come now, but the things you tell me steadily become more palatable!" remarked Gerald, as he approached the huge stallion. "Now that I have accepted the responsibilities of a throne and of all the great and best words of the Master Philologist, it would be most unbecoming for a princess to be ignored by anyone who already is virtually a reigning monarch. There are amenities to be preserved between royal houses. Very terrible wars have sprung from the omission of such amenities. So do you lead me forthwith to this impatient princess; but do you first tell me the adorable name of her highness!"

Horvendile answered, "The princess who just now awaits you is Evasherah, the Lady of the First Water-Gap of Doonham."

"I admit that the information, now I have it, means very little. Nevertheless, my dear fellow, do you direct me to the water-gap of this princess!"

"Yet, I repeat, it would be wise for you, before

departing from this place, to render a man's homage to the ruler of it."

"Well, Horvendile, the name of this tropical, damp, and this rather curious smelling country is no doubt better known to you than, I confess, it stays to me."

"This place has not any name in the reputable speech of men. It is the realm of Koleos Koleros."

At that name Gerald bowed his head; and, as became a student of magic, he courteously made the appropriate sign.

And Gerald said: "Very dreadful is the name of Koleos Koleros! Yet, quite apart from the fact that I am a member of the Protestant Episcopal Church, I owe this Koleos Koleros no homage. And I, very certainly, shall not linger to pay any, with a princess waiting for me! Rather, do I elect to pass hastily through this land of quags and underbrush, and to leave this somewhat unsanitarily odored neighborhood, in which, I perceive, misguided persons yet live — "

For these two young men were no longer alone in this ambiguous valley. Through the twilight Gerald now saw many women passing furtively toward a dark laurel grove; and from out of that grove came a queer music.

Then Horvendile spoke of these women.

VI. EVADNE OF THE DUSK

NOW all the while that Horvendile talked it was to the accompaniment of that remote queer music: and Gerald was troubled. He came, at least, as near to being troubled as Gerald ever permitted himself to do. For Gerald did not really enjoy trouble of any kind, and said frankly that he found it uncongenial.

"But these," said Gerald, by and by, "all these, my dear fellow, I had thought to have perished a long while ago."

"You travel, Gerald, on the road of the greater myths. Such myths do not perish speedily. And, besides, nothing is true anywhere in the Marches of Antan. All is a seeming and an echo: and through this superficies men come to know the untruth which makes them free. It follows, in my logic, that to-day these women are the flute-players of Koleos Koleros. They serve to-day, forever unsatiated, that most insatiable divinity who is shaggy and evil-odored, and who can taste no pleasure until after bloodshed —"

"I have read, also," Gerald broke in, with the slight smile of one who is not unpleased to display his learning, "that this Koleos Koleros is a somewhat contradictory goddess, producing the less the more constantly that she is cultivated and stirred up —"

"Oho, but a most potent goddess is this Koleos Koleros!" continued Horvendile. "She is wrinkled and flabby in appearance, yet the most stout of heroes falls at last before her. Infants perish nightly in her gloomy vaults, and plagues and diseases harbor there —"

But again Gerald had interrupted him, saying: "Yet I have read, moreover, that this modest and retired Koleos Koleros, alone of eternal beings, is ever ardent to quench the ardor of her servitors; and that — still to praise merit where merit appears, — in her untiring warfare with all men that rise up to oppose her, she displays the magnanimity to favor, and to embrace lovingly, the adversary that attacks her most often and most deeply."

Horvendile thereupon held out his hand. He showed thus the tip of his forefinger touching the tip of his thumb so that they formed a circle. And Horvendile said:

"She varies even as the moon varies. Yet equally is this divine small monster the bestower of life and of all joy; she charms in defiance of reason: and whensoever Koleos Koleros appears, red and inflamed and hideous among her tousled tresses, a man is moved willy-nilly to place in her his chief delight."

"Oho!" said Gerald, and, as became a student of magic, he also made the needful sign, "oho, but a most potent goddess is this Koleos Koleros!"

"Now, then," continued Horvendile, "all they who in this place serve eternally this most whimsical divinity are a loving and a peculiarly happy people. Their amorousness, which here is not ever blighted by shrill reprobation, has need at no time to fear

either the chastisement of human law nor the anathe-
mas of any other religion anywhere in the quiet
brakes and lowlands of the moist realm of Koleos
Koleros. For, you conceive, these feminine myths
who now are flute-players in and about the shrine of
the wrinkled goddess, and who through so many centuries have been trained in all the arts of pleasure,
came by and by into a certain confusion — "

" But what sort of confusion, Horvendile, do you
mean? For I find your speaking another sort. And I
am rather more interested in that princess — "

" I mean that their religion, which ranks pleasure
above all else, permits no man to pass by unpleased."

" Ah, now I understand you! "

" — I mean that, through the duties of their religious faith, their way of living has been given over
to an assiduous and an empirical study of all the
charms peculiar to a woman, the more particularly
as these charms are employed — "

" Let us say, in the exercise of their religion,"
Gerald suggested, " for I wholly understand you,
sir."

" It has followed that the taste of these ladies has
become more delicate. It has followed that, by force
of considering their own feminine loveliness, always
unveiled and in lively employment, and by compar-
ing it so intimately and so jealously with the loveliness of their female rivals in the service of the
wrinkled goddess, they have become connoisseurs of
the beauties peculiar to their sex. They have acquired
a refinement of taste — "

" To be refined in one's taste is eminently praiseworthy. Ah, my dear fellow, if you but knew what
shocking examples of bad taste we kings are continu-

ally encountering among our sycophants! And that reminds me, you said something about a princess — "

" — They have learned to despise the hasty and boisterous and, between ourselves, the very often disappointing ways of men — "

" Ah, yes, no doubt! " said Gerald. " Men are a bad lot. But we were speaking of a princess — "

" — And they have lovingly contrived more finespun and more rococo diversions without the crude assistance of any man. Then also they delight in playing with many well-trained pets, — with goats and large dogs and asses and, they tell me, with rams and with bulls also. The surprising and mysterious joys which blaze up among these flute-players are, thus, very violent and delicious."

Gerald said then that kindness to dumb animals was generally reckoned a most estimable trait in the United States of America. Whereas, in all quarters of that enlightened and hospitable republic, Gerald estimated, a princess —

" Yet," Horvendile went on, " these learned women do not forget, in mere pleasure-seeking, their religious duty of permitting no man to pass by unpleased. Go to them, therefore, you will be welcome. Yonder at this instant a religious festival is preparing. Yonder sweet-voiced Leucosia, who hereabouts is called Evadne, waits for you — "

" But I have not the honor of knowing this Evadne — "

" She is easily known, by her violet hair and her sharp teeth. Moreover, Gerald, her wise sisters — Telês, and Parthenopê, and Radnê, and Ligeia, and Molpê, — all these will greet you with ardor. They

[36]

will deny to you no secret of their pious rites; they will share with you esoteric joys religiously. They will incite you to perform among their choir, in the most secret shrine of Koleos Koleros — ”

“ But, really now, my dear fellow! I have no talent whatever for music. I would be quite out of place in any choir.”

“ These flute-players are very ingenious. They will find for you some suitable instrument. And there will be strange harmonies and much soft laughter at this festival: each reveller will pour out libations copiously: cups will be refilled and emptied until dawn. There will be for you perfumes and rose garlands and the most exquisite of wines and the most savory of dishes and other delicacies. The *pièce de résistance* will be served to you in nineteen ways. Due homage will be paid to Koleos Koleros.”

“ Nevertheless,” said Gerald, “ there is a phrase which haunts me — ”

“ That dusky grove of laurels yonder is the hall of this pious feast. Nothing will be lacking to you at this feast if you attend it with proper religious exaltation; and you will discover abilities there which will surprise you.”

“ Ah, as to that now, Horvendile — ! Yes, I have a man’s proper share of ability, I have quite enough ability for two persons. Nevertheless, there is a patriotic phrase which haunts me, and that phrase is *E pluribus unum.* For I have compunctions, Horvendile, which are translating that same phrase, a little freely, as ‘ One among so many.’ ”

“ It seems to me a harmless phrase even in your paraphrase. More harm may very well come of the fact that these learned ladies will endeavor to cajole you out of the divine steed, so that he may be added to their trained pets — "

" Oh! oh, indeed! " said Gerald. " But that is nonsense. The rider upon Kalki, and none other, has to fulfil that estimable old prophecy: and a deal of good such wheedlings will do any woman breathing, with a fine kingdom like that of mine set against a mere kiss or, it may be, a few tears! "

" That matter remains to be attested in due time. Meanwhile, I can but repeat that if you do not render a man's homage to the ruler of this place there is no doubt whatever that the slighted goddess will avenge herself."

" Sir," Gerald now replied, with appropriate dignity, " I am, as were my fathers before me, a member of the Protestant Episcopal Church. Is it thinkable that a communicant of this persuasion would worship a goddess of the benighted heathen? Do you but answer me that very simple question! "

" In Lichfield," Horvendile retorted, " to adhere to the religion of your fathers is tactful, and in this place also, as in every other place, tactfulness ought to be every wise man's religion. Otherwise, you will be running counter to that which is expected of the descendants of Manuel and of Jurgen; and you may by and by have cause to regret it."

But Gerald thought of his church, and of its handsome matters of faith in the way of organ music and of saints' days and of broad-mindedness and of delightful lawn-sleeved bishops and of majestic rituals. He thought of newly washed choir-boys and of his prayer-book's wonderful mouth-filling phrases, of rogation days and of ember days and of Trinity Sunday. He thought about pulpits and hassocks and

[38]

stained glass and sextons, and about the Thirty-nine Articles, and about those unpredictable superb mathematics which early in every spring collaborated with the new moon to afford him an Easter: and these things Gerald could not abandon.

So he said: " No. No, Horvendile! I pay no homage to the wrinkled goddess."

Then Horvendile warned him again, " You may find that decision costly."

" That is as it may be! " said Gerald, with his chin well up. " For a good Episcopalian, sir, finds in the petulance of no heathen goddess anything to blench the cheek and make the heart go pitapat."

Still, he looked rather fondly through the dusk. And now his shoulders also went up, shruggingly.

" Yet I concede," said Gerald, " that, howsoever firm my churchmanship, and even with a princess waiting for me, I am tempted. For yonder fluteplayer who still delays to join her companions — who are now, no doubt, already about their merry games with one another and with their trained pets, — has charms. Yes, she has charms which give my thoughts, as it were, a locally religious turn, and make the notion of joining her a rather beautiful idea. I deplore, of course, her feathered legs. Even so, she displays, as you too may observe, in her so leisurely retreat, an opulence in that most engaging kind of beauty which once got for Aphrodite the epithet of Callipygê. I contemplate, with at least locally pious joy, the curving of those reins, the whiteness and the fineness of the skin, and the graciousness of those superb contours, designed without any stinting or exaggeration, into the perfection of those fair twin moons of delight — "

[39]

But in a moment Gerald said, " Still, there is something vaguely familiar, a something which chills me — "

And Gerald said also: " Or, rather, in their so gentle undulations as she walks unhurriedly away from us, in their so amiable convulsions, — in their heavings, their twitchings, their ripplings and their twinklings, — rather, do the bewitching and multitudinous movements of those silvery spheres resemble, to my half dazzled eyes, the unarithmeticable smiling of the sunlit sea, to which, as you will remember, Horvendile, old Æschylos has so finely referred. I feel that I could compose a not discreditable sonnet to that most beautiful of backsides. There is nothing more poetical than is the backside of a naked woman who is walking away from you. Its movements awaken the yearnings of all elegiac verse. . . . And I do not doubt, sir, that the front of this featherylegged lady is fully as enchanting as the rear. Yes, I imagine that the façade too has its own peculiar attractions: and I admit, in a word, that I am tempted to confront her — "

Horvendile glanced toward the woman who alone remained within reach. " That is Evadne, who in the days of her sea-faring was called Leucosia. And it is plain enough that she waits for temptation to inflame and to uplift you into raptures somewhat more practical than all this talking."

" She waits," said Gerald, " in vain. At this distance she is a rather beautiful idea; nearer, she would be only another woman with her clothes off. Moreover, sir, I am a self-respecting member of the Protestant Episcopal Church: and besides that, as I now perceive, it is of Evelyn Townsend's figure that this woman's half-seen figure reminds me. That resemblance makes for every sedentary virtue. I have learned only too well what comes of permitting any female person to trust you and to give you all. Then, too, I am called to duties of more honor and responsibility in my appointed kingdom. And for the rest, I prefer to disappoint these ladies by failing in ardor at such a distance as will not provoke my blushes. No, Horvendile: no, I am still haunted by that patriotic phrase *E pluribus unum;* and I shall not just now presume to render a man's homage to Koleos Koleros, among quite so many flute-players. Moreover, you assert that a princess is waiting for me, to whom I prefer to present the member of another royal house in the full possession of all faculties. So I do not elect, just now, to share in these — if you will permit the criticism, — somewhat un-American methods of religious exercise. I ask, instead, that you conduct me to the impatient princess about whom you keep talking so obstinately that, I perceive, there is no least hope of my stopping you."

It was in this way that Gerald began his journey by putting an affront upon Koleos Koleros.

PART THREE

THE BOOK OF DOONHAM

" Though a Woman's Tongue be but Three
Inches Long, It can kill a Six-foot Man."

VII. EVASHERAH OF THE FIRST WATER-GAP

A GOOD-MORNING to you, ma'am," Gerald had begun. His horse was tethered to a palm-tree, and Horvendile was gone, so that there now was only the Princess to be considered. " And in what way can I be of service? "

Yet his voice shook, as he stood there beside the alabaster couch. . . . For Gerald was enraptured. The Princess Evasherah was, in the dawn of this superb May morning, so surprisingly lovely that she excelled all the other women his gaze had ever beheld. Her face was the proper shape, it was appropriately colored everywhere, and it was surmounted with an adequate quantity of hair. Nor was it possible to find any defect in her features. The colors of this beautiful young girl's two eyes were nicely matched, and her nose stood just equidistant between them. Beneath this was her mouth, and she had also a pair of ears. In fine, the girl was young, she exhibited no deformity anywhere, and the enamored glance of the young man could perceive in her no fault. She reminded him, though, of someone that he had known. . . .

Such were the ardent reflections which had passed through Gerald's mind in the while that he said decorously, " A good-morning, ma'am: and in what way can I be of any service? "

[45]

But the Princess, in her impetuous royal fashion, had wasted no time upon the formal preliminaries which were more or less customary in Lichfield. And while Gerald's patriotic republican rearing had been explicit enough as to the goings-on in monarchical families, he was whole-heartedly astounded by the animation and candor which here confronted him. There was no possible doubting that the Princess was inclined to trust him and to give him all.

" But, oh, indeed, ma'am," Gerald said, " you quite misunderstand me! "

For he had it now. This woman was uncommonly like Evelyn Townsend.

Gerald sighed. All ardor had departed from him. And with a few well-chosen words he placed their relationship upon a more decorous basis.

Now the Princess Evasherah, that most lovely Lady of the Water-Gap, was lying down even when Gerald first came to her, just after sunrise. She was lying upon a couch of alabaster, which had four legs made of elephants' tusks. Upon this couch was a mattress covered with green satin and embroidered with red gold; upon the mattress was the Princess Evasherah in a brief shirt of apricot colored silk; and, over all, was a saffron canopy adorned with fig-leaves worked in pearls and emeralds.

This couch was furthermore shaded by three palm-trees, and it stood near to the bank of the river called Doonham. And by the sparkling ripples of that river's deep waters — as the Princess Evasherah explained, some while after she and Gerald had reached a friendly and clean-minded understanding, with no un-American nonsense about it, — was hidden the residence of the Princess, where presently they would have breakfast.

" But," Gerald said, a little dejectedly, " I have just now no appetite of any kind."

" That will not matter," said the Princess: and for no reason at all she laughed.

" — And to live under the water, ma'am, appears a virtually unprecedented form of royal eccentricity — "

" Ah, but I must tell you, lord of the age, and most obdurate averter from the desirer of union with him, that very long ago, because of a girlish infatuation for a young man whose name I have forgotten, I suffered a fiery downfalling from the Home of the Heavenly Ones, into the waters of this river. For I had offended my Father (whose name be exalted!) by stealing six drops of quite another kind of water, of the water from the Churning of the Ocean — "

" Eh? " Gerald said, " but do you mean the divine Amrita? "

" Garden of my joys, and summit of sagacity," the Princess remarked, " you are learned. You have knowledge of heavenly matters, you have traversed the Nine Spaces. And I perceive that you who travel overburdened with unresponsiveness upon this road of the gods are yet another god in disguise."

" Oh, no, ma'am, it is merely that, as a student of magic, one picks up such bits of information. I am the heir apparent to a throne, I cannot honestly declare myself any more than that: and I am upon my way to enter into my kingdom, but it is not, I am tolerably certain, a celestial kingdom."

The Princess was not convinced. " No, my pre-

ceptor and my only idol, it is questionless you are a
god, all perfect in eloquence and in grace, a temptation unto lovers, and showing as a visible paradise to
the desirous. Here, in any event, out of my keen
regard for your virtues, and in exchange for that
great gawky horse of yours which reveals in every
feature its entire unworthiness of contact with divine
buttocks, here are the five remaining drops, in this
little vial — "

Gerald inspected the small crystal bottle quite as
sceptically as the Princess had regarded his disclaimer
of being a god. " Well, now, ma'am, to me this looks
like just ordinary water."

She placed one drop of the water upon her finger-
tip. She drew upon his forehead the triangle of the
male principle, she drew the female triangle, so that
one figure interpenetrated the other, and she invoked Monachiel, Ruach, Achides, and Degaliel.
No student of magic could fail to recognize her employment of an interesting if uncanonical variant of
the Third Pentacle of Venus, but Gerald made no
comment.

After that the Princess Evasherah laughed mer-
rily. " Now, then, companion of my heart, now that
you have promised me that utterly contemptible
horse of yours, I unmask you. For I perceive that
you, O my master, more comely than the moon, are
the predestined Redeemer of Antan — "

" That much, ma'am, I already know — "

" In short," said the Princess, " you are Fair-
haired Hoo, the Helper and Preserver, the Lord of
the Third Truth, the Well-beloved of Heavenly
Ones, thus masked in human flesh and in human forgetfulness and in peculiarly unhuman coldness. Yet

very soon the power of the Amrita will have bestowed unfailing vigorousness upon your thinking, and presently the hounds of recollection will have run down the hare of your inestimable glory."

" That is well said, ma'am. It is spoken with a fine sense of style. And I conjecture that, although the better stylists usually omit this ingredient, it has some meaning also. . . . Yes, you do allude to my having red hair, but the hare of my inestimable glory, which you likewise mention, is not capillary, but zoölogical, — in addition to being also metaphorical. . . . You state, in brief, in a figurative Oriental way, that by and by I shall recollect something which I have forgotten. . . . But just what is it, ma'am, that you so confidently expect me to recollect? "

" My lord, and acme of my contentment, you will recall, for one matter, the love that was between us in this world's infancy, when you did not avert from me the inspiring glances of fond affection. For you, the bright-tressed, the resplendent, are unmistakably the Well-beloved of Heavenly Ones. I perfectly remember you, by your high nose, by your jutting chin, and by the eminence of yet another feature whose noble proportions also very deeply delighted me during my visit to your Dirghic paradise, and which I perceive to remain unabatedly heroic."

Gerald, gently, but with decision, took hold of her hand. It seemed to him quite time.

Then the fair Lady of the Water-Gap, she who would have been so adorable if only she had not reminded Gerald more and more of Evelyn Townsend, began to talk about matters which Gerald, as yet, really did not remember.

She spoke of Gerald's golden and high-builded home, in which, it seemed, this Princess had trusted him and had given him all: and she spoke also of the unresisting love for mankind which had led Gerald to quit that exalted home, among the untroubled lotus-ponds of Vaikuntha, upon nine earlier occasions, and of his nine fine exploits in the way of redemption.

She spoke of how Gerald had visited men sometimes in his present heroic and elegant form, at other times in the appearance of a contemptible looking dwarf, and upon yet other occasions as a tortoise and as a boar pig and as a lion and as a large fish. His taste in apparel seemed as fickle as his charitableness was firm. For over and over again, the Princess said, it had been the power of Gerald, as Helper and Preserver, which had prevented several nations and a dynasty or two of gods from being utterly destroyed by demons whom Gerald himself had destroyed. It was Gerald, as he learned now, who had preserved this earth alike from depopulation and from ignorance, when during the first great flood the Lord of the Third Truth, in his incarnation as a great fish, had carried through the deluge seven married couples and four books containing the cream of earth's literature: whereas, later, during a yet more severe inundation, Gerald had held up the earth itself between his tusks, — this being, of course, in the time of his incarnation as a boar-pig, — and swimming thus, had preserved the endangered planet from being as much as mildewed.   •

And Evasherah spoke also of how when Gerald was a tortoise he had created such matters as the first elephant, the first cow, and the first wholly amiable woman. He had created at the same time, she added, the moon and the great jewel Kaustubha and a tree called Parijata, which yielded whatever was desired of it, and it was then also that Fair-haired Hoo, the Well-beloved Lord of the Third Truth, had invented drunkenness. There had been, in all, Evasherah concluded, nineteen supreme and priceless benefits invented by Gerald at this time, but she confessed her inability to recall offhand every one of them —

" It is sufficient, — oh, quite sufficient! " Gerald assured her, with wholly friendly condescension, " for already, ma'am, it embarrasses me to have my modest philanthropies catalogued."

Yet Gerald, howsoever lightly he spoke, was thrilled with not uncomplacent pride in his past. He was not actually surprised, of course, because logic had already pointed out that the ruler of Antan would very naturally be a divine personage with just such a magnificent past. To be a god appeared to him a rather beautiful idea. So he first asked what was the meaning of that skull over yonder in the grass: the Princess explained that it was not her skull, but had been left there by a visitor some two months earlier: and then Gerald, after having agreed with her that people certainly ought to be more careful about their personal belongings, went on with what was really in his mind.

" In any event, ma'am," he hazarded, with the brief cough of diffidence, " it seems there have been tender passages between us before this morning — "

" I trusted you! I gave you all! " she said, reproachfully. " But you, disposer of supreme delights, and fair vase of my soul, you have forgotten even the way you used to take advantage of my confidence! For how can the modesty of a frail woman avail against the brute strength of a determined man! "

" No, Evelyn, not to-night — I beg your pardon, ma'am! My mind was astray. What I meant to say was that I really must request you to desist." Then Gerald went on, tenderly: " To the contrary, my dear lady, our love stays unforgettable. I recall every instant of it, I bear in mind even that sonnet which I made for you on the evening of my first respectful declaration of undying affection."

" Ah, yes, that lovely sonnet! " the Princess remarked, with the uneasiness manifested by every normal woman when a man begins to talk about poetry.

" — And to prove it, I will now recite that sonnet," Gerald said.

And he did.

Yet his voice was so shaken with emotion that, when he had completed the octave, Gerald paused, because it was never within Gerald's power to resist the beauty of a sublime thought when it was thus adequately expressed in flawless verse. So for an instant he stayed silent.

He detained the soft and ever-straying hands of the Princess Evasherah, of this impulsive and investigatory lady, who so troublingly resembled Evelyn Townsend, and Gerald pressed these hands to his trembling lips. This lovely girl, returned to him almost miraculously, it might seem, out of his well-nigh forgotten past, was not merely intent once more to trust him and to give him all. She trusted also, as Gerald felt with that keen penetration which is natural to divine beings, to delude and to wheedle him into some material loss. What the Princess desired to cajole him out of was, perhaps, not wholly clear. Nevertheless, he felt that, in some way or another way, Evasherah was attempting to deceive him. It might be that neither her explanation as to that skull nor even her so candid-seeming adoration of his wisdom and his comeliness was entirely sincere. For women were like that: they did not always mean every word they said, not even when they were addressing a god. And so, the gods had over-painful duties laid upon them, Gerald decided.

After that he sighed: and he continued the reciting of his sonnet with an air of lofty resignation, with which was intermingled a certain gustatory approval of really good verse.

"Light of my universe, that is a very beautiful sonnet," the Princess remarked, when he had finished "and I am proud to have inspired it, and I am almost equally proud of the fact that you (through whose supreme elegance and amiable aspect my heart is once more rent with ecstasy) should remember it so well after these thousands of years."

"Years mean very little, ma'am, to Fair-haired Hoo, the Helper and Preserver, the Lord of the Third Truth, the Well-beloved of Heavenly Ones: and centuries are, quite naturally, powerless to dim my memories of any matter in any way pertaining to you. Yet affairs of minor importance do rather tend to become a bit ambiguous as the æons slip by. . . . For example, what, in the intervals between my redemptory exploits — upon mere week days, as it were, — what do I happen to be the god of?"

"That," said the Princess, "O my master, and

[53]

pure fountain-head of every virtue, is a peculiarly silly question to be coming from you, who are, as everybody knows, the Lord of the Third Truth."

"Ah, yes, to be sure, — of the Third Truth! My divine interests are invested in veracity. Well, that is highly gratifying. Yet, ma'am, there are a great many gods, and it is a rather beautiful idea to observe that, even where their professional spheres are the same, these gods differ remarkably. Thus, Vulcan is the lord of one fire, and Vesta of another, but Agni and Fudo and Satan rule over yet other fires, each wholly individual. Cupid and Lucina traffic in the same port, but not in the same way. Æolus controls twelve winds, and Tezcatlipoca four winds, and Crepitus only one wind — "

"Director of my life, and comely shepherd of my soul, I know. Few gods are strange to me or to my embraces. Many a Heavenly One has invited me to love, and I have yielded piously: my kisses have written the tale of my religious transports upon many divine cheeks."

"— And I imagine that this water from the Churning of the Ocean was not intended, in the first place, to further my apotheosis. I mean, ma'am, I do not suppose you went to the trouble of stealing six drops of the Amrita in order just to recall to me that divinity which, in the press of other affairs, I had somehow permitted to slip my mind?"

"Disposer and sole archetype of the seven magnanimities, you speak the truth. For the five remaining drops, as I was trying to tell you when you kept interrupting me, O my lord, and beloved of my heart, and joy of both my eyes, were intended for the five human senses of the young man about whom I was then rather foolish; and upon whom I meant to bestow immortality and eternal youth. The first drop, inasmuch as the Amrita confers a never-ending vigorousness, I had of course already placed. So my Father (whose name be exalted!) smote us both with lightnings, in his impetuous way, and tumbled us both from out of the Home of the Heavenly Ones into this river. My young man was thus drowned before I had the chance to confer upon him any of the favors which I greatly fear your superior strength and your pertinacity are now about to force from me — ”

Gerald replied: “ I really do think you would get on far more quickly with your story if you were to keep both of these like this. The position, you see, is much more American: it lacks that earlier air of such personal freedom as a democracy does not think well of.”

“ Light of the age, I hear and I obey. Yet all my tale has been revealed to your consideration — ”

“ Yes,” Gerald assented, “ but your history interests me far more — ”

“ Far more than what, O cruel and resplendent one? ”

“ Why, far more than I can say, of course. So let us get on with it! ”

“ But my sad history is now as refined glass before your discerning glance. It suffices to add that the immortal part of my young man was happily removed from the waters of this river, and is now worshipped as a god in Lytreia. But for me, alas! the squirrel of calamity continued to revolve in the cage of divine wrath. For, so perfectly ridiculous is the way my Father (whose name be exalted!) behaves when the least thing upsets him, that I was condemned through the length of nine thousand years to assume certain official duties in the waters of this river, in the repugnant shape of a crocodile."

But with that statement Gerald took prompt issue. "What may be your official duties as the guardian of these waters I can no more guess than I can guess how your visitors happen to be so careless about leaving their skulls behind. That really is a sort of slapdash and inconsiderate behavior which I cannot condone without considerable reflection. But I do know that the shape which I have beheld, and still see a great deal of, in nothing resembles the shape of a crocodile."

"Epitome of every excellence, and exalted zenith of my existence, that is because the nine thousand years of my doom have now happily expired. The proof of this is that already my luckless substitute arrives. We shall now behold her encounter with the terminator of delights and the separator of companions. Thereafter, when we have had breakfast, O vital spirit of my heart, whom my unmitigated love incites me to devour out of pure affection, I shall ride hence upon the horse with which you have so gallantly presented me, to enter again into the Home of the Heavenly Ones."

With that, the Princess pointed.

W ITH that, the Princess pointed. And Gerald also now looked toward the river. . . .
He viewed an unsolid-seeming world of dimly colored movings. Directly before him the deep river sparkled and rippled eastward with unhurried, very shallow undulations. But, under the sun's warmth, mists rising everywhere above the waters streamed eastward too, unhastily, and in such unequal volume that now this and now another portion of the wide landscape beyond the river was irregularly glimpsed and then, gradually but with a surprising quickness, veiled. Very lovely medallions of green lawns and shrubbery and distant hills thus seemed to take form and then to dissolve into the mists' incessant gray flowing, toward the newly risen sun. . . .

And Gerald also saw that, some fifty feet away from him, an unusually unclad, elderly woman was approaching the river bank, carrying in her thin arms a child. The woman trudged forward toward the river like a drugged person, because of the doom which was upon her.

Now this woman seemed to stumble, and she fell into the water, but in falling she cast the child from her, so that it remained safe in the coarse tall-growing grass.

The woman whom divine will had led hither to serve as a scapegoat for the Princess Evasherah proceeded to drown satisfactorily, and with indeed a sort of decorum. She sank twice, with hardly any beating or splashing of the waters, because of that doom which was upon her. The child, though, whom no long years of living had taught to accept a preponderance of unpleasant happenings, screamed continuously, in candid, mewing disapproval of divine will.

Out of the near-by reeds came a bright-eyed jackal; and it furtively approached the child.

The Princess rose from the alabaster couch and from Gerald's partially detaining arms. She stood for an instant irresolute. In her lovely face was trouble. Her mouth, a little open, trembled. Gerald liked that. Here was revealed the ever-tender heart of womanhood and the quick generous sympathy with all afflicted persons which living had taught him to look for only in the best literature.

The Princess quitted Gerald. She hastened to the river bank. The jackal backed from her, crouching in a half-circle, with bared teeth, and the reeds swallowed the beast. The Princess leaned down, and with a lovely gesture of compassion the Princess caught the drowning woman by one hand and assisted her ashore.

It was then that the Princess Evasherah cried out in wordless surprise. Then too her raised hands clenched, and her little fists jerked downward in a gesture of candid exasperation.

And then also the old woman who had but now been saved from drowning unfastened the small copper bowl and the knife which hung by copper chains about her waist. The Princess took these, she approached the wailing child, she stooped, and the crying ceased. The Princess returned to the strange woman, calling out, " Hrang, hrang! " To the gray lips of this woman Evasherah applied the blood which was now in the copper bowl, and the remainder of the child's blood she sprinkled over the woman's unveiled breasts and between the woman's legs, which were held wide apart for this fecundation.

" Hail, Mother! " said Evasherah. " All hail, O red and wrinkled Mother of Every Princess! Hail, fertile and insatiable Havvah! A salutation to thee! Spheng, spheng! a salutation to thee, and all delight to thee for a thousand years of thy Wednesdays! Drink deep, beloved and wise Mother, for an oblation of blood which has been rendered pure by holy texts is more sweet than ambrosia."

At first the elder lady had seemed peculiarly red and inflamed and hideous among her tousled tresses. Now she was placated, she panted, and her eyes rolled languorously. She began, with aggrieved reproach, —

" But, O my dearie! you have relapsed into a masculine display of clemency such as has flung away your allotted chance of redemption."

" Sorrow and mourning reside in my heart, O my Mother: my limbs are rendered infirm by remorse. For I had no least notion it was you. I thought only that some mortal woman was to take over my duties in the repulsive shape of a crocodile; and I could not bear to hear the small voice of the little child crying out as the sharp jackal teeth drew nearer, and to reflect that I was destroying two lives in order to purchase my freedom from this endless love-making and over-eating."

" But it was a boy child. Dearie, you are talking as though these sons of Adam were of real importance. And to hear you, nobody would ever give you your due credit for having piously ended the ambitions of so many hundreds of them, since you have protected the entrance to the road of gods and myths against the impudence of these romantics."

" Yet, refuge of the uplifted, and asylum of the vigorous, the persons whose blood has nourished my exile were all young men aflame with impure intentions. And a child is different. It is not right that the stainless flesh of a little boy, which is an offering acceptable to all our exalted race, should be torn by the long teeth of an undomesticated dog."

" That is true. That is alike a truthful and a pious reflection. A child is different from all other afflictions, because a child alone can always be an endless and a quite new sort of trouble. That nobody knows better than I who am the Mother of every Princess, with my daughters everywhere policing the wild dreams of men so inadequately. Yet a thing done has an end. And it may be that by and by I can get around your Father — "

" Whose name be exalted! " remarked Evasherah.

" That also, dearie, is a wholly proper observation, — though, as I was saying, you know as well as I do how pig-headed he is. Meanwhile, there is nothing left for you, for the present, save another incarnation, and another century or two of seductiveness upon the verge of Doonham."

" But I have been," observed the Princess, " a crocodile professionally for nine thousand years, for all that my chest is so delicate. The cats of conjecture are therefore abroad in the meadows of my meditation purring that this time I would prefer something a little less damp."

" Dearie, since your next incarnation is but a matter of form, do you by all means please yourself, so that you stay a destruction to young men and to their upsetting aspirations. You have been wholly inadequate this morning, I observe — "

" Why, but — " said the abashed Princess.

Her voice sank as she went on rather ruefully with a talking which to Gerald was now inaudible. He could merely see that the elder lady had hazarded a suggestion which Evasherah at once dismissed with an emphatic toss of her lovely head. He saw too the Princess place together the palms of her hands and then draw them about seven inches apart.

" Oh, fully that, at first! " she stated, in the raised tones of mild exasperation; " so that, altogether, this unresponsive person (within whose ancestral tomb may pigs propagate!) remains incomprehensible."

The old woman replied: " In any event, you have failed; but that does not really matter. He travels, you assure me, with his assured betrayer. And the road he follows, that also, is lively enough and long enough to betray him in the end. For he will meet others of my daughters; and if all else fails, he will meet me."

" The ship of my enduring resolution is not yet wrecked upon the iceberg of his indifference; and I am not through with him, by any means. I am returning to this unremunerative occupier of my couch, — for breakfast, O my Mother! "

And now the old lady answered with a mother's ever-responsive tenderness. " That is my own child. One has to persevere with these romantics, no matter how hard the task may seem. For none of us knows yet what these romantic men desire. My daughters prepare for them fine food and drink, my daughters see to it that their homes are snug, and at the end of each day my daughters love them dutifully. All things that men can ask for, my daughters furnish them. Why need so many of these men nurse strange desires which do not know their aim? for how can any of my daughters content such desires? "

" One can but summon, O my Mother, the terminator of delights and the separator of companions and the ender of all desires."

" There are other ways, my dearie, which are more subtle. That way is of the East, that way is old and crude. Still, that way also quiets over-ambitious dreaming; and that way serves."

Gerald blinked. He was a bit troubled by the matter-of-fact occurrence before his eyes of a perfectly incredible happening.

For the elder lady became transfigured. She became larger, all ruddiness went away from her, and she took on the black and livid coloring of a thunder cloud. In her left hand she now carried a pair of scales and a yardstick. Her face smiled rather terribly as she steadily grew larger. Her necklace, you perceived, was made of human skulls, and each of her earrings was the dangling corpse of a hanged man in a very poor state of preservation. Altogether, it was not a grief to Gerald when the Mother of Every Princess had attained to her full heavenly stature, and had vanished.

But the Lady of the Water-Gap was changed in quite another fashion. Where she had stood now fluttered a large black and yellow butterfly.

[62]

IX. How One Butterfly Fared

SO it was in the shape of a large butterfly that Evasherah returned toward Gerald, to careen and drift affectionately about him, in a bewildering medley of bright colors. He cried to her adoringly, " My darling — ! " He grasped at her: and she did not avoid him.

Gerald now held this lovely creature, by the throat, at arm's length. He began the compelling words, " Schemhamphoras — " And in Gerald's face was no adoration whatever.

Instead, he continued, rather sadly, " — Eloha, Ab, Bar, Ruachaccocies — " and so went through the entire awful list, ending by and by with " Cados."

His prey was now struggling frantically. The unreflective girl had not allowed for her lover's being a student of magic. And her restiveness was — well, it might be, pardonably, — a bit interfering with Gerald's æsthetic delight, now that he paused to admire the splendor of the trapped Princess's last incarnation, before he used the fatal Hausa charm.

For Evasherah's wings were of a wonderful velvety black and a fiery orange color, her body was golden, and her breast crimson. He noted also that Evasherah, in her increasing agitation of mind, had thrust out from the back of her neck a soft forked horn which diffused a horrible odor.

[63]

And those curved, strong, needle-sharp fangs which were striking vainly at him were so adroitly designed that Gerald fell now to marveling, still a little sadly, at their superb efficiency. A yellowish oil oozed from their tips. They had, he saw, just the curve of two cat claws: whensoever such fangs struck flesh, their victim's recoil would but clamp fangs which were shaped like that more deeply and more venomously; it was a quite ingenious arrangement. It perfectly explained, too, how the visitors of this soft-spoken, cuddling and utterly adorable Princess happened to leave their skulls in the thick grass around her alabaster couch.

Then Gerald said: "O Butterfly, O Gleaming One, your breakfast this day is disappointment, your fork is agony, and your napkin death. O Butterfly, repent truly, abandon falsehood, put away deceit and flattery, cease thinking about your deluded lovers even remorsefully. Repent in verity, do not repent like the wildcat which repents with the fowl in its mouth without putting the fowl down. Where now is the artfulness which was yours, where are the high-hearted, tricked lovers? — To-day all lies in the tomb. This world, O Butterfly, is a market-place: everyone comes and goes, both stranger and citizen. The last of your lovers is a pious friend, he assists the decreed course of this world."

Still, it was rather strange that the body she had chosen appeared to belong to the species *Onithoptera cræsus*, — Gerald decided, as his foot crushed the squeaking soft remnants and rubbed all into a smeared paste of blood and gold-dust, — because, of course, this kind of butterfly was more properly indigenous to the Malay Archipelago than to these parts,

[64]

over and above the fact that for any butterfly to have the fangs of a serpent was false entomology.

However, the geography and local customs and all else which pertained to the Marches of Antan were tinged with some perceptible inconsequence, Gerald reflected, as he returned to his tethered stallion. He mounted then, cheered with the yet further reflection that he had got from Evasherah the rather beautiful idea of being a god, and had got also the four remaining drops from the Churning of the Ocean. The properties of this water were sufficiently well known to every student of magic.

PART FOUR

THE BOOK OF DERSAM

" What Has a Blind Man
to Do with Any Mirror? "

NOW Gerald mounted on the stallion Kalki, and Gerald traveled upon the way of gods and myths, down a valley of cedar-trees, into the realm of Glaum of the Haunting Eyes. The land of Dersam was already falling away into desolation, because of the disappearance of its liege-lord into mortal living. And at Caer Omn, which formerly had been the Sylan's royal palace, and where Gerald got his breakfast, the three hundred and fifty-odd concubines of Glaum were about their cooking and cleaning and nursing, but the seven wives of Glaum sat together in a walled garden.

Six of these wives were young and comely, but the seventh seemed — to Gerald's finding, — as wrinkled as a wet fishnet, and as old as envy.

By the half-dozen who retained their youth, however, Gerald was enraptured. As he looked from one of them to the other, each in her turn appeared so surpassingly lovely that she excelled all the other women his gaze had ever beheld. . . . But, no! Glaum was his benefactor. Glaum at this instant, in Lichfield, was toiling away at that unfinished romance about Dom Manuel of Poictesme which by and by was to make the name of Gerald Musgrave famous everywhere. It would, therefore, never do to encourage these so shapelily and chromatically meritorious dears to follow out the dictates of womanly

[69]

confidence and generosity to the point where they could bleat about it. No, to permit them all to deceive one husband would be an unfriendly and injudicious pleonasm, Gerald reflected. And Gerald sighed whole-heartedly.

The seven women had sighed earlier. " What else is now come to trouble us? " said the wives of the Sylan when Gerald came.

He answered them, with a great voice: " Ladies, I am Fair-haired Hoo, the Helper and the Preserver, the Lord of the Third Truth, the Wellbeloved of Heavenly Ones. Yet, I pray you, do not be unduly alarmed by this revelation! I am not a ruthless deity, I deal fiercely with none save my misguided opponents. I, in a word, am he of whom it was prophesied that I, my dear ladies, or perhaps I ought to say that he — although, to be sure, it does not really matter which pronoun a strict grammarian would prefer, since in any case the meaning is unmistakable and very sublime, — would at his or at my appointed season appear, in unexampled and appropriate splendor, to reign over Antan, riding upon the silver stallion Kalki."

But the wives of Glaum seemed unimpressed. " Your meaning, sir," said one of them, " may be terrible, but certainly it is not plain."

This wife had reddish golden hair, uncovered: she wore a blue gown, so fashioned that it left her right breast wholly uncovered, also; and doubtless for some sufficient purpose, she carried an iron candlestick with seven branches.

Gerald asked, with indignation tempered by her good looks: " And do you doubt my divine word? Do you dispute my Dirghic godhead? "

Another wife answered him, a glorious dark sultry creature in purple, who wore a semi-circular crown and had about the upper part of each bare arm two broad gold bands.

She said: " Why should we question that? Gods by the score and by the hundreds, gods in battalions, have passed through the land of Dersam, going downward toward Antan, to enter into well-earned rest after their long labors in this world."

" Ah, so it appears that Antan is the heaven of all deserving gods, and that I am to rule a celestially populated kingdom well worthy of me! "

" We have not ever been to Antan. We thus know nothing of its customs. We know only that many gods have passed us, traveling upon all manner of steeds as they went down into Antan. Bes rode upon a cat, and Tlaloc upon a stag, and Siva upon a bull: we have seen Kali pass upon the back of a tiger: above our heads Zeus has gone by upon the back of an eagle, as he traveled abreast with Amen-Ra upon the back of a very large beetle. We therefore think it likely enough that you who pass upon this shining horse are yet another one of these gods. What are the gods to us, in this our season of unexampled trouble? "

Then the seven wives fell into a lamentation, and their complaining was that, since Glaum of the Haunting Eyes had left them, the sacred mirror reflected only the person who stood before it.

" And is not such the nature of all mirrors? " Gerald asked.

" Oh, sir," replied the wife who carried a bunch of keys, and who wore that unaccountable tall bifurcated orange-colored headdress, " but until yesterday ours was the mirror which showed things as they ought to be."

" And what did one discover in it? "

Now the old wife spoke. Her head was wrapped in a white turban; her face had no more color than has the belly of a fish; and a sprinkling of white hairs, so long that they had grown into spirals and half-circles, glittered upon her shaking chin. Thus was she who answered, saying, —

" To the aged, such as I have now become, the Mirror of Caer Omn reveals nothing any more: but to the young, such as we all were before Glaum left us, it was used to reveal that which may not be described."

" Then why do you not place before it some young person — ? "

" Alas, sir, but there is no longer any co-respondent youth in the mirror! "

The speaker was the brown-haired and alluringly plump wife who wore nothing at all anywhere, and whose delicious body had been depilated in every needful place.

Then the seven wives of Glaum of the Haunting Eyes raised a lament; and now the pallid sharp-nosed wife who was far gone in pregnancy, and who wore that maroon-colored headdress shaped like a cone, began to speak of the young fellows who formerly had come to them out of the sacred mirror.

She spoke of very handsome, tall, brisk, nimble, impudent young fellows, that had been always jolly and buxom and jaunty, and not ever grumpish like a husband; of over-rash young fellows who must have their flings, who stuck at nothing, who went to all lengths, who had a finger in every pie, who kept the

[72]

pot a-boiling; of what forward, eager, pushing, plodding, thwacking, negligent of no corner, businesslike, never-wearying, soul-stirring workmen they had been at every job they undertook; of what great plagues they had been, too, without the least bit of any patience or of any modesty; and of how unreasonably you missed these sad rapscallions now that there was no longer any co-respondent youth remaining in the sacred Mirror of Caer Omn.

Gerald replied: " Your plaint is very moving. I regard a mirror which begets any such young fellows as a rather beautiful idea. It is true that I am a bachelor, and therefore object to no reasonable mitigation of matrimony. But I am also a god, dear ladies, a god who brings all youth with him here in this vial."

At that the last wife spoke. Her hair was flaxen; her body was everywhere engagingly visible through her gown, of a transparent soft green tissue; she carried a small golden-hilted sword. And this wife said:

" You differ, then, from those other gods who have passed this way. No youth went with these gods, who had themselves grown old and tired and more feeble, and who journeyed toward a resting from all miracles and away from a world wherein they were no longer worshipped."

" But I," said Gerald, " I am a god who is, moreover, a citizen of the United States of America, wherein every sort of religion yet flourishes as it can never do in an effete and sophisticated monarchy. So do you show me the way to the temple of the sacred Mirror of Caer Omn! "

THE seven wives conducted Fair-haired Hoo, the Helper and the Preserver, to the Temple of the Mirror. It was the old wife who now lifted from the mirror a blue veil embroidered with tiny fig-leaves worked in gold thread. You saw then that this mirror was splotched and clouded and mildewed. It reflected sallowly a distorted and rather speckled Gerald: it glistened with an unwholesome iridescence.

Thereafter Fair-haired Hoo, the Helper and Preserver, the Lord of the Third Truth, when he had announced his various titles, with such due ceremony as befits an exchange of amenities between divine powers, moistened his finger-tips with one drop of water from the Churning of the Ocean. Upon the sacred Mirror of Caer Omn he drew with his finger-tip the triangle of the male and of the female principle, so that the one interpenetrated the other: and he invoked Monachiel, Ruach, Achides, and Degaliel.

Then there was never a more inconsequent rejoicing witnessed anywhere than was made by the seven wives of Glaum of the Haunting Eyes, now that the sacred mirror was altered, for these seven ungrateful scatter-brained women were now singing a sort of hymn in honor of the charitableness and the vigorous procreative powers of the sun.

"But what under the sun has the sun," said Gerald, a little flustered, "to do with the not inconsiderable favor which I have conferred upon this country? And do you think such anatomical details as you are singing about quite the proper theme for an opera? "

They replied: " Sir, it is obvious that you are a sun god, of the clan of Far-darting Helios and Freyr the Fond Wooer and the Elder Horus and Marduk of the Bright Glance, all of whom have ridden this way as they passed down toward Antan. Sir, it is clear that the Lord of the Third Truth, also, is a god whose mission it is to awaken warmth and humidity and a renewal of life in all that he touches — "

" But," Gerald said, " but with my finger."

" — Just as," they concluded, " you have done to this mirror. Therefore, sir, we are praising your charitableness and your vigorous procreative powers."

" Ah, now I comprehend you! Still, let us, in these public choral odes, let us adhere strictly to the charitableness! Those other solar traits I would describe as far better adapted to chamber music, in some duet form. Meanwhile, since this somewhat un-American hymn is intended as a personal tribute, I accept your really very personal arithmetic in the proper spirit, dear ladies, as a pious exaggeration. For of course, just as you say, it does seem fairly obvious I am a sun god."

Yet Gerald, after all, was now more deeply interested in that huge mirror than in anything else. He saw that the mirror which they worshipped in the land of Dersam was not in any way dreadful. If only the mirror of Freydis was like this, then every inheritance which awaited him in his appointed kingdom might well be pleasant enough.

For now the Mirror of Caer Omn shone with a

golden, clear glowing. It did not any longer reflect a distorted and speckled Gerald. It did not reflect anything. It seemed, instead, to be evolving its own mountainous strange landscape now; and everywhere, in the vague shining depths of this quaint mirror, were now appearing the most heroic and lovely beings, such as one never saw in Lichfield. . . .

BUT when three huge men beckoned to him, and Gerald had moved forward, he found, with wholly tolerant surprise, that this mirror was in reality a warmish golden mist, through which he entered into the power of these three giant blacksmiths, and into the shackles of adamant with which they bound him fast to a gray, lichen-crusted crag, the topmost crag above a very wide ravine, among a desert waste of mountain tops; and he entered, too, into that noble indignation which now possessed Gerald utterly. For it was Heaven he was defying, he who was an apostate god, a god unfrightened by the animosity of his divine fellows. He had preserved, somehow, — in ways which he could not very clearly recall, but of which he stayed wholly proud, — all men and women from destruction by the harshness and injustice of Heaven. He only of the gods had pitied that futile, naked, cowering race which lived, because of their defencelessness among so many other stronger animals, in dark and shallow caverns, like ants in an ant-hill. He had made those timid, scatter-brained, two-legged animals human: he had taught them to build houses and boats; to make and to employ strong knives and far-smiting arrows against the fangs and claws with which Heaven had equipped the other animals; and to tame horses and dogs to serve them in their hunting for food. He had

[77]

taught them to write and to figure and to compound salves and medicines for their hurts, and even to foresee the future more or less. All arts that were among the human race had come from Prometheus, and all these benefits were now preserved for his so inadequate, dear puppets, through the nineteen books in which Prometheus had set down the secrets of all knowledge and all beauty and all contentment, — he who after he had discovered to mortals so many inventions had no invention to preserve himself. Prometheus, in brief, had created and had preserved men and women, in defiance of Heaven's fixed will. For that sacrilege Prometheus atoned, among the ends of earth, upon this lichen-crusted gray crag. He suffered for the eternal redemption of mankind, the first of all poets, of those makers who delight to shape and to play with puppets, and the first of men's Saviors. And his was a splendid martyrdom, for the winged daughters of old Ocean fluttered everywhere about him in the golden Scythian air, like wailing seagulls, and a grief-crazed woman with the horns of a cow emerging from her disordered yellow hair paused too to cherish him, and then went toward the rising place of the sun to endure her allotted share of Heaven's injustice.

But he who was the first of poets burst Heaven's shackles like packthread, ridding himself of all ties save the little red band which yet clung about one finger, and rising, passed to his throne between the bronze lions which guarded each of its six steps, and so sat beneath a golden disk. All wisdom now belonged to the rebel against Heaven, and his was all earthly power: the fame of the fine poetry and the comeliness and the grandeur of Solomon was known in Assyria and Yemen, in both Egypts and in Persepolis, in Karnak and in Chalcedon, and among all the isles of the Mediterranean. He sported with genii and with monsters of the air and of the waters; the Elementals served King Solomon when he began to build, as a bribe to Heaven, a superb temple which was engraved and carved and inlaid everywhere with cherubim and lions and pineapples and oxen and the two triangles. There was no power like Solomon's: his ships returned to him three times each year with the tribute of Nineveh and Tyre and Parvaam and Mesopotamia and Katuar; the kings of all the world were the servants of King Solomon: the spirits of fire and the lords of the air brought tribute to him, too, from behind the Pleiades. His temple now was half completed. But upon his ring finger stayed always the band of blood-colored asteria upon which was written, " All things pass away." These glittering and soft and sweet-smelling things about him, as he knew always, were only loans which by and by would be taken away from him by Heaven. He turned from these transient things to drunkenness and to the embraces of women, he hunted forgetfulness upon the breasts of nine hundred women, he quested after oblivion between the thighs of the most beautiful women of Judea and Israel, of Moab and of Ammon and of Bactria, of Baalbec and of Babylon: he turned to wantoning with boys and with beasts and with bodies of the dead. These madnesses enraptured the flesh of Solomon, but always the undrugged vision of his mind regarded the fixed will of Heaven, " These things shall pass away." The temple which he had been building lacked now only one log to be completed. He cast that gray and lichen-crusted cedar log into the Pool of Bethesda: it sank as though it had been a stone: and Solomon bade his Israelites set fire to the temple which all these years he had been building as a bribe to Heaven.

But when the temple burned, it became more than a temple, for not only the flanks of Mt. Moriah were ablaze, a whole city was burning there, and its name was Ilion. He aided in the pillaging of it: the golden armor of Achilles fell to his share. In such heroic gear, he, like a fox hidden in a slain lion's skin, took ship to Ismaurus, which city he treacherously laid waste and robbed: thence he passed to the land of the Lotophagi, where he viewed with mildly curious, cool scorn the men who fed upon oblivion. He was captured by a very bad-smelling, one-eyed giant, from whom he through his wiles escaped. There was no one anywhere more quick in wiles than was Odysseus, Laertes' son. He toiled unhurt through a nightmare of pitfalls and buffetings, among never-tranquil seas, outwitting the murderous Laestrigonians, and hoodwinking Circe and the feathery-legged Sirens and fond Calypso: he evaded the man-eating ogress with six heads: he passed among the fluttering, gray, squeaking dead, and got the better of Hades' sullen overlords and ugly spectres, through his unfailing wiliness, — he who was still a poet, making the supreme poem of each man's journeying through an everywhere inimical and betraying world, he who was pursued by the wrath of Heaven which Poseidon had stirred up against Odysseus. But always the wiles of much-enduring Odysseus evaded the full force of Heaven's buffetings, so that in the end he won home to Ithaca and to his meritorious wife; and then, when the suitors of Penelope had been killed, he went, as dead Tiresias had commanded, into a mountainous country, carrying upon his shoulder an oar, and leading a tethered ram, for it was yet necessary to placate Heaven. Beyond Epirus, among the high hills of the Thesproteans, he set the oar upright in the stony ground, and turning toward the ram which he now meant to sacrifice to Poseidon, he found Heaven's amiability to remain unpurchased, because the offering of Odysseus, who was a rebel against Heaven's will to destroy him, had been refused, and the ram had vanished.

But in his hand was still the rope with which he had led this ram, and in his other hand was a bag containing silver money, and in his heart, now that he had again turned northerly, to find in place of the oar an elder-tree in flower, now in his heart was the knowledge that no man could travel beyond him in hopelessness and in infamy. He remembered all that he had put away, all which he had denied and betrayed, all the kindly wonders which he had witnessed between Galilee and Jerusalem, where the carpenters of the Sanhedrin were now fashioning, from a great lichen-crusted cedar log found floating in the Pool of Bethesda, that cross which would be set up to-morrow morning upon Mt. Calvary. Then Judas flung down the accursed silver and the rope with which he had come hither to destroy himself, because an infamy so complete as his must first be expressed with fitting words. It was a supreme infamy, it was man's masterpiece in the way of iniquity, it was the reply of a very fine poet to Heaven's proffered truce after so many æons of tormenting men causelessly: it was a thing not to be spoken of but sung. He heaped great sheets of lead upon his chest,

[81]

he slit the cord beneath his tongue, he tormented himself with clysters and with purges and in all other needful ways, so that his voice might be at its most effective when he sang toward Heaven about his infamy.

But when he sang of his offence against Heaven, he likened his hatefulness to that of very horrible offenders in yet elder times, he compared his sin to that of Œdipus who sinned inexpiably with his mother, and to that of Orestes whom Furies pursued forever because he had murdered his mother. But it was not of any Jocasta or of any Clytemnestra he was thinking, rather it was of his own mother, of that imperious, so beautiful Agrippina whom he had feared and had loved with a greater passion than anyone ought to arouse in an emperor, and whom he had murdered. Nothing could put Agrippina out of his thoughts. It availed no whit that he was lord of all known lands, and the owner of the one house in the world fit for so fine a poet to live in, a house entirely overlaid with gold and adorned everywhere with jewels and with mother of pearl, a house that quite dwarfed the tawdry little Oriental hovel which Solomon had builded as a bribe to Heaven, because this was a house so rich and ample that it had three-storied porticos a mile in length, and displayed upon its front portico not any such trumpery as an Ark of the Covenant but a colossal statue of that Nero Claudius Cæsar who was the supreme poet the world had ever known. Yet nothing could put Agrippina out of Nero's thoughts. From the satiating of no lust, howsoever delicate or brutal, and from the committing of no enormity, and from the loveliness of none of his poems, could he get happiness and real peace of mind. He hungered only for Agrippina, he wanted back her detested scoldings and inter-meddlings, he reviled the will of Heaven which had thwarted the desires of a fine poet by making this so beautiful, proud woman his mother, and he practised those magical rites which would summon Agrippina from the dead.

But when she returned to him, incredibly beauti-ful, and pale and proud, and quite naked, just as he had last seen her when his sword had ripped open this woman's belly so that he might see the womb in which he had once lain, then the divine Augusta drew him implacably downward among the dead, and so into the corridors of a hollow mountain. This place was thronged with all high-hearted worshippers of the frightening, discrowned, imperious, so beautiful woman who had drawn him thither resistlessly, and in this Hörselberg he lived in continued splendor and in a more dear lewdness, and he still made songs, only now it was as Tannhäuser that the damned ac-claimed him as supreme among poets. But Heaven would not let him rest among these folk who had put away all thought of Heaven. Heaven troubled Tannhäuser with doubts and with premonitions, even with repentance. Heaven with such instruments lured this fine poet from the scented Hörselberg into a bleak snow-wrapped world: and presently he shiv-ered too under the cold wrath of Pope Urban, bells rang, a great book was cast down upon the pavement of white and blue slabs, and the candles were being snuffed out, as the now formally excommunicated poet fled westerly from Rome pursued by the ever-present malignity of Heaven.

But from afar he saw the sapless dry rod break

[83]

miraculously into blossom, and he saw the messengers of a frightened Bishop of Rome (with whom also Heaven was having its malicious sport) riding everywhither in search of him, bearing Heaven's pardon to the sinner whom they could not find. For the poet sat snug in a thieves' kitchen, regaling himself with its sour but very potent wines and with its frank, light-fingered girls. Yet a gibbet stood uncomfortably near to the place: upon bright days the shadow of this gallows fell across the threshold of the room in which they rather squalidly made merry. Death seemed to wait always within arm's reach, pilfering all, with fingers more light and nimble than those which a girl runs furtively through the pockets of the put-by clothing of her client in amour. Death nipped the throats of ragged poor fellows high in the air yonder, and death very lightly drew out of the sun's light and made at one with Charlemagne all the proud kings of Aragon and Cyprus and Bohemia, and death casually tossed aside the tender sweet flesh — which had been as white as the snows of last winter, and was as little regarded now, — of such famous tits as Héloïse and Thaïs and Queen Bertha Broadfoot. Time was a wind which carried all away. Time was preparing by and by (still at the instigation of ruthless Heaven) to make an end even to François Villon, who was still so fine a poet, for all that time had made of him a wine-soaked, rickety, hairless, lice-ridden and diseased sneakthief whose food was paid for by the professional earnings of a stale and flatulent harlot. For time ruined all: time was man's eternal strong ravager, time was the flail with which Heaven pursued all men whom Heaven had not yet destroyed, ruthlessly.

[84]

OF THE GOLDEN TRAVEL

But time might yet be confounded: and it was about that task he set. For Mephistophilus had allotted him twenty-four years of wholly untrammeled living, and into that period might be heaped the spoilage of centuries. He took unto himself eagle's wings and strove to fathom all the causes of the misery which was upon earth and of the enviousness of Heaven. That which time had destroyed, Johan Faustus brought back into being: he was a poet who worked in necromancy, his puppets were the most admirable and lovely of the dead. Presently he was restoring through art magic even those lost nineteen books in which were the secrets of all beauty and all knowledge and all contentment, the secrets for which Prometheus had paid. But the professors at the university would have nothing to do with these nineteen books. It was feared that into these books, restored by the devil's aid, the devil might slily have inserted something pernicious: and besides, the professors said, there were already enough books from which the students could learn Greek and Hebrew and Latin. So they let perish again all those secrets of beauty and knowledge and contentment which the world had long lost. Now Johan Faustus laughed at the ineradicable folly with which Heaven had smitten all men, a folly against which the clear-sighted poet fought in vain. But Johan Faustus at least was wise, and there had never been any other beauty like this which now stood before him within arm's reach (as surely as did death), now that with a yet stronger conjuration he had wrested from all-devouring time even the beauty of Argive Helen.

But when he would have touched the Swan's daughter, the delight of gods and men, she vanished,

[85]

precisely as a touched bubble is shattered into innumerable sparkling bits, and three thousand and three of them he pursued and captured in all quarters of the earth, for, as he said of himself, Don Juan Tenorio had the heart of a poet, which is big enough to be in love with the whole world, and like Alexander he could but wish for other spheres to which he might extend his conquests, and each one of these sparkling bits of womanhood glittered with something of that lost Helen's loveliness; yet, howsoever various and resistless were their charms, and howsoever gaily he pursued them, singing ever-new songs, and swaggeringly gallant, in his fair, curly wig and his gold-laced coat adorned with flame-colored ribbons, yet he, the eternal pursuer, was in turn pursued by the malevolence of Heaven, in, as it seemed, the shape of an avenging horseman who drew ever nearer unhurriedly, until at last the clash of rapiers and the pleasant strumming of mandolins were not any longer to be heard in that golden and oleander-scented twilight, — because of those ponderous, unhurried hoofbeats, which had made every other noise inaudible, — and until at last he perceived that both the rider and the steed were of moving stone, of an unforgotten stone which was gray and lichen-crusted.

But when fearlessly he encountered the overtowering statue, and had grasped the horse about its round cold neck, he saw that the stone rider was lifeless, and was but the dumb and staring effigy of a big man in armor which was inset with tinsel and with bits of colored glass. It was the bungled copy and the parody of a magnanimous, great-hearted dream that he was grasping, and yet it was a part of him, who had been a poet once, but was now a battered old

[86]

pawnbroker, for in some way, as he incommunicably knew, this parodied and not ever comprehended Redeemer and he were blended, and they were, somehow, laboring in unison to serve a shared purpose. He derided and he came too near to a mystery which he distrusted, and which yet (without his preference having been consulted in the affair) remained a part of him, as it was a part of all poets, even of a cashiered poet, and a part very vitally necessary to the existence of a Jurgen. A Jurgen had best not meddle with such matters one half-second sooner than that dimly foreseen, inevitable need arose for a Jurgen also to be utilized in the service of this mystery, without having his preference in the affair consulted. The aging pawnbroker was a little afraid. He climbed gingerly down from the tall pedestal of Manuel the Redeemer, he descended from that ambiguous tomb upon which he was trampling, he stepped rather hastily backward from that carved fragment of the crag of Prometheus. He stepped backward, treading beyond the confines of the golden mirror which was worshipped at Caer Omn; and he was thus released from its magic.

NOW before him the mirror still glowed goldenly, and now a hunchback held out both his hands toward Gerald, whom he was trying to allure into the form and mind of this sardonic, cracker-jawed, sly knave who had such melancholy eyes. Gerald was much tempted to become this Punch, and to relive for a little the rascal's defiant and ever-restless life. And then too, behind Punch waited tall Merlin, crowned with mistletoe, he that created all chivalry, and that, being himself the great fiend's son, first taught men how to live as became the children of God. It would be quite entertaining to enter into Merlin's dark heart. Moreover, to the other hand of Punch, stood a glittering suave gentleman with a blue beard, in whose uxoricides it might be vastly interesting to share. . . .

Yet Gerald, facing these three rather beautiful ideas, was of two minds. " For I am a god, with a throne awaiting me in Antan, where all the other gods will be my lackeys, — and, for that matter, with no doubt a whole cosmos of my own twirling and burning to unheeded clinkers somewhere in space, which I ought at this moment to be looking after and embellishing. And in this particular small world which I am quitting, the powers of Heaven do quite honestly seem — when you look at them from a perhaps biased standpoint, that is, — and only to a certain extent, of course, — and if you are so ill-advised as to consider matters in a pessimistic, morbid, wholly un-American way — "

Gerald paused. He smilingly shook his red head. " No. It is far better for us gods not to criticize the handiwork of one another. So I shall without one word of reproof permit my fellows to play as they like with this planet called Earth. I shall of course, very probably, make new planets a bit more conformable to my personal fancy. But I shall say nothing about the planet I am now quitting at all likely to hurt anybody's feelings. No: I shall, rather, rely upon the appealing eloquence of a dignified silence reinforced by a decisive departure."

And Gerald said also: " As for this mirror which is worshipped in the land of Dersam, it pleases me as a toy. But I who am a Savior and a sun god with nine such very fine exploits behind me, in the way of swimming and of decimating devils, and of restoring warmth and making moons, and of really remarkable broad-mindedness as to what particular animal I may happen to look like, — I, the Helper and the Preserver, who am called to reign over the goal of all the gods of men, — why, I must necessarily lose by exchanging such a tremendous destiny for anything to be found in this mirror."

Then Gerald said: " No. I must never forget that, whether I am a Savior or a sun deity, or whether I am habitually used to discharge both functions, I in any case remain Fair-haired Hoo, the Helper and Preserver, the Lord of the Third Truth, and so on. I am a most notable figure, of some sort or another sort, in Dirghic mythology. I am the appointed rider of the silver stallion. I am destined to inherit from the

Master Philologist the great and best words of magic, and after that poor hospitable fellow's downfall it is I who am predestined to reign in his stead over the place beyond good and evil which is the goal of all the gods of men and the reward of their meritorious exertions. I cannot forsake such a fine destiny in order to play with the droll and pretty figures that move about in the depths of this mirror. And whether or not this is a mirror which I may require hereafter, when I have come into my kingdom and have resumed my exalted divine estate in my appropriate mythology, is a matter which I shall settle in due time who have all eternity wherein to do whatever I may prefer."

THEN Gerald perceived that the wives of Glaum were not yet through with their wonder-workings, for these seven women were now about a ceremony which they called Asvamedha. They led into the temple a brown horse. Before the mirror they struck down this horse with pole-axes. The tail was cut off by the flaxen-haired wife in green, and the naked wife carried it away, Gerald did not know whither. The horse's head also was severed from the body, by that wife who was with child; the head was then adorned with a chaplet made of small loaves of bread. This head was afterward impaled upon a stake and thus was set upright before the mirror, but not facing it. Then the six wives of Glaum who yet remained in the temple mixed the blood of the horse with the blood of unborn calves; they turned the stake: and they showed Gerald what he must do.

When he had obeyed, and when they had all invoked Evarvan, then the golden glowing of the sacred mirror was turned into a paler haze like that of moonshine. Out of this silvery mistiness came a crowned woman. She was clothed in white, and about her head shone an aureole.

And Gerald was enraptured. For this Evarvan of the Mirror was so surpassingly lovely that she excelled all the other women his gaze had ever beheld.

Yet somehow it was not the coloring nor the placing of her features that he was noting. Rather, he was observing himself and the thing which was happening to this careful, this well-poised, fastidious, parched, rather pitiable Gerald whom for so many years he had known. The creature had not for a great while, not since, indeed, the days of his first insanity about Evelyn, been visited by any real emotion: now, momentarily at least, he was ablaze: he was caught perhaps: and it was this imminent personal peril that Gerald was noting, aloofly, with a drugged sense of derisory exultation.

For this Gerald, as it seemed to him, had known quite well, a great while ago, before his lips had touched for pastime's sake the lips of any woman anywhere, that this woman who, it seemed, was called Evarvan, existed in some place, and waited for him, and would by and by be found. That most important fact, which a boy had known, a thriftless, very silly young man had let slip out of mind. Throughout all the twenty-eight years of his living, it seemed to Gerald, this Evarvan had been the true and perfect love of his heart's core. . . . To the extreme romanticism of this phrase he conceded a smile: that he should have concocted a phrase so abominable showed him just now to be neither fastidious nor well poised. . . . Nevertheless, here was the woman whose existence he, even in Lichfield, had always dimly divined, and of whom — he had it now, — of whom Evelyn Townsend had been a parodying shadow in human flesh. The likeness had been just sufficient to get him into a great deal of trouble. He saw that likeness now, quite plainly.

" And this woman too is going to get me into

trouble, I very much fear. For all my being cries out to her. Eh, Gerald, one needs caution here, my lad, you who find trouble uncongenial! "

Evarvan spoke. And she was speaking, oddly enough, as it seemed to him, of that Evelyn who went about Lichfield immured in the body which was a poor copy of Evarvan's body. Yet Gerald was listening hardly at all. He did not like the strong, insane and over-youthful emotions which this woman roused in him. They endangered his welfare. For this woman was awakening in him those old, unforgotten fervors which he had once felt for Evelyn Townsend, and which had betrayed him into the horrid bondage of an illicit love-affair. This Evarvan was ensnaring him, he knew, into the insanities appropriate to youth and inexperience: and such nonsense had to be controlled.

So it was half dazedly Gerald protested that — quite apart from the claims of his divine duties as a Savior and a sun god, and apart too from the obligations he was under to ascend the throne of Antan, — he could no longer endure the stupidities and the fretfulness and the jealousies of the Evelyn who had made adultery wholly unendurable.

" If she were but a bit like you, ma'am," Gerald gallantly remarked, — with somewhat increasing composure now that this woman reminded him, the more closely that he observed her, yet more and more of Evelyn, — " the case would be different."

" But I," said Evarvan of the Mirror, " will remain with you always, if you indeed desire to become my lover. For there is a way, Gerald, there is for you through my mirror's aid an open way to contentment. You shall know an untruth, and that untruth will make you free: the doings of the world, and all the bustling that is made by merchants and by warriors and by well-thought-of persons talking about important matters, will then run by you like a little stream of shallow, bickering waters: and you will heed none of these things, but only that loveliness which all youth desires and no man ever finds save through my mirror's aid. You will live among bright shadows very futilely: yes: but you will be happy."

Gerald replied hoarsely: "I desire only you. I cannot think of thrones, nor of any gods, now that you stand here within arm's reach. All my life long I have desired you, as I know now, my dearest, throughout the dreary while of over-much playing and laughter that I have lived in ever-dwindling faith I would yet win to you by and by. But now I am again as Johan Faustus, — or, rather, I am as Jurgen in that other old story, when he had come at last to Helen, the delight of gods and men: only I am more favored than was Jurgen, for my Helen speaks. . . ."

"Oh, and I speak for your own good, my darling, for there is a condition to be fulfilled before I may trust you and may give you all."

Gerald answered: "No, Evelyn, not to-night — But indeed I entreat your pardon, my dear. My mind must have been wandering. Yes, yes! as I was saying, the difference is that Helen speaks!"

"For your own good, my dearest."

"Yes; you speak, naturally, of a condition for my own good, just as Glaum hinted that so many more or less friendly persons would be doing in these parts."

"I speak, though, of a very easy condition. You

must yourself perform a tiny Asvamedha; and you must immolate before my mirror, not any really valuable horse, of course, nor even a good-looking horse, but only that hideous and wholly worthless horse which you have brought with you into the land of Dersam."

Then Gerald said: " And that is a small price to pay for the attainment of the one thing which my heart quite earnestly desires, is it not? For all my life I have hungered, as I believe that all poets hunger, for that unflawed beauty, seemingly not ever to be found upon this earth, which now stands revealed in the form of a woman, and which now speaks to me with the voice of a woman — oh, quite with the voice of a woman! — and speaks, too, for my own good. Yes, it is a small price, such as any boy of nineteen or thereabouts would pay gladly. For I must tell you, who are the delight of gods and — well! of adolescent boys, at least, in every quarter of the world, — that all this very strongly reminds me of that first sonnet which I made about you when I was a boy of nineteen."

Evarvan did not wholly conceal her uneasiness over the prospect of hearing this sonnet. But there was none the less in her voice a tenderness almost motherly now that she asked of Gerald, —

" And did you make verses, then, about me, dear, so early? "

" To prove it," Gerald replied, " I will now recite to you that identical sonnet."

And he did.

But his voice was so shaken with emotion that, when he had completed the octave, he paused, because it was never within Gerald's power to resist the beauty of a sublime thought when it was thus adequately expressed in flawless verse. So for an instant he stayed silent. He caught up the lovely hands of Evarvan of the Mirror, and he pressed them to his trembling lips.

For this beguiling bright dream was now become a snare to delay him in journeying onward to his appointed kingdom, and to betray him again into bondage to the rather beautiful ideas and tinsel notions of youth. Presently he would be seeing no more of this traitorous dream woman, who was preparing to trust him and to give him all, and who none the less was more lovely and more dear than any real thing anywhere. Afterward he would regret her, he knew: always he would regret Evarvan, among whatsoever delights they were which awaited Gerald in his appointed kingdom. Nevertheless, this dream was an impediment in the way of a Savior and a sun deity, with whose appropriate functions this dream was interfering: and the most painful duty which confronted Gerald was not precisely to be discourteous to a lady, but to discourage sacrilege.

Dismissing these cursory reflections, Gerald sighed: and he continued the reciting of his sonnet with an air of lofty resignation intermingled with a gustatory approval of really good verse.

" That," said Evarvan of the Mirror, when he had ended, " is a very beautiful sonnet, and I am proud to have inspired it. But we were talking about something else, I have quite forgotten what — "

" I," Gerald said, " have not forgotten."

" Oh, yes, now I do remember! We were talking about the lucky chance afforded you to get rid of that dreadful horse of yours."

[96]

EVARVAN OF THE MIRROR

Gerald looked for one instant at the most lovely of all the illusions he had found in the Mirror of Caer Omn. Then he began to recite the multiplication tables.

You saw that she was frightened. She said, — " Oh, and I trusted you! I gave you all! "

She bleated now; her beauty was dimmed: and she seemed just the Evelyn Townsend who had pestered Gerald beyond any reasonable endurance.

But Gerald, howsoever heavy was the heart of Gerald who quite honestly objected to being troubled by anything, went on inexorably to exorcise Evarvan with the old runes of common-sense. He spoke of the elephant that is the largest of beasts, and of the very dissimilar household economy practised by a King of Israel and by Elijah the Tishbite, and of the straight line that is the shortest distance between two points; and the old magic was potent.

Before his eyes Evarvan of the Mirror was changed. Of the degradation which was put upon her, it suffices to report that this lovely lady went backward in the course of every mortal woman's living. She passed from girlhood into a lank-legged childhood, and thence into drooling and feebly puking infancy, and after that into the shapes she had worn in her mother's womb. In the end there remained of the most dear illusion which Gerald had found in the Mirror of Caer Omn only two pink figures in the form of a soft throbbing egg and of a creature like a tadpole darting lustfully about it: and these melted back into the moonshine of the Sacred Mirror of Caer Omn.

Nor was that all. The wives of Glaum and the Temple of the Mirror and all that was about Gerald began to waver. All the material things about him showed now like paintings on a gauze curtain which was moving and crinkling in a very gentle breeze. The shaping of the six wives became longer and more attenuated: they were shaped like the shadows of women in a fine sunset. These so prettily tinted shadows strained toward the mirror and entered it precisely as you may see smoke drift toward and out of an opened window. Then all the temple followed them collapsingly, as if colored waters were running into a hole. The mirrow swallowed all. Caer Omn was gone: the land of Dersam was a ruined land without inhabitants. Afterward the pale glass blinked seven times like summer lightning, and the mirror was not there.

Gerald stood alone in the cedar-shadowed way. He was weeping quite unaffectedly. His very deepest poetic sensibilities had been touched by the rather beautiful idea that he had loved this woman all his life long, and that now he had lost her forever: but a little way behind Gerald the silver stallion stayed unimmolated, and grazed placidly.

PART FIVE

THE BOOK OF LYTREIA

*" Whether *You Boil or Roast Snow,*
You Can Have but Water of It."

GERALD passed on, riding upon the stallion Kalki, down a valley of cedar-trees, into the realm of Tenjo of the Long Nose. This was the land of Lytreia, they told him. But, here too, dejection overbrooded all, and the atmosphere was elegiac, for people everywhere were lamenting that vigor and resiliency and liveliness had gone out of their noses, so that no man in Lytreia was able to sneeze or to employ his nose in any other normal way.

" Well, now, suppose you take me to this king of yours," said Gerald, " for it may be I can re-awaken hereabouts all the lost joys of influenza."

" And who shall we say to him has come into Lytreia, red-headed and riding upon the back of this huge and sparkling horse with the splendid nose? "

" You will say to your king that this land is honored by a visit from Fair-haired Hoo, the Helper and Preserver, the Lord of the Third Truth, the Well-beloved of Heavenly Ones, as he passes toward his appointed kingdom in Antan, riding in very terrible estate upon the back of his famous silver stallion Kalki, a beast which, strictly speaking, has no nose, but only nostrils at the tip of his long, noble head."

They also seemed unimpressed. " No god is of terrible estate except the Holy Nose of Lytreia; nor do we concede the existence of any kingdom not his. Nevertheless, you may come with us."

" Upon my word," thought Gerald, " but in these parts the people pay very inadequate homage to us gods and are little better than heretics."

But he went with these over-sceptical persons quietly to their King Tenjo.

And Tenjo received the Well-beloved of Heavenly Ones more affably. First, though, the grave, white-bearded King shared with the visiting god a quite excellent dinner, which was handsomely served to them by ten pages in ermine and a seneschal in vermilion silk: not until dinner was over, and the two sat drinking their spiced wine out of gold goblets, would the King talk about his troubles. Then Tenjo complained that his nose was fallen and flabby. It was no longer worshipful. That was in all ways deplorable, said the King, refilling his goblet, inasmuch as his people worshipped a nose, and could respect no male creature who had not a large and high-standing and robust and succulent nose.

Gerald was a little puzzled, because this seemed to him a queer sort of calamity to be befalling anybody, unless it was caused by the magic of the wu. But Gerald made no comment. He asked only how this sad state of affairs had come about.

He was told that all the youth and vigor had been taken out of the Holy Nose of Lytreia, and out of Tenjo's nose, and out of the nose of every man in the kingdom, by the blighting magic of a sorceress who had lately established her residence in the tomb of King Peter the Builder.

" It is there," said Tenjo, " the veiled Mirror of

the Two Truths is hidden: but not even of that does this sorceress seem afraid."

"Nor, for that matter, am I: for I am Lord of the Third Truth. Well, it is fairly evident this woman is a wu."

",You may be right. I confess that dreadful possibility had not ever occurred to me — "

"Only we gods are omniscient, my dear Tenjo," said Gerald, kindlily. "So there is no need for any mere king to be ashamed of his human blindness."

" — Because, as I must tell you, before this minute I had not ever heard of a wu."

"You have been lucky. The less one hears of such creatures, the better for everybody. So, how is this woman called?"

"She is called Evaine," said Tenjo; "and she is called also the Lady of Peter's Tomb, now that she has taken possession of it."

Then Gerald finished his fourth goblet, and Gerald hiccoughed, and Gerald said: "Your case, my dear fellow, while perplexing, is not wholly desperate. For I bring youth with me, and I will renovate your withered noses. I am competent to deal with any wu. I give you, in fact, my divine word that you shall be rid of this wu. Yes, Lytreia shall be rid of her, even though it is necessary that to undo her hoodoo I do with due to-do woo the wu, too — "

"Would you be so kind," said Tenjo, looking troubled, "as to repeat that, rather more slowly?"

Gerald obliged him, and continued: "Yes, I assure you, upon the most sacred oath of our Dirghic heaven, — known only to the gods, my dear fellow, so that you will, I trust, pardon my not repeating it,

[103]

— that I will subject this wu and this mirror also to my divine inspection — "

" Ah, but I must tell you," said Tenjo, seeming yet more troubled, " that the man who looks into that mirror straightway finds himself transformed into two stones. For that reason it is hidden away in Peter's Tomb, and it is kept veiled, and of course no man has ever dared go near it."

" How, then, did this mirror ever manage to change anybody into two stones if nobody ever dared go near it? "

" Why, but the mirror was compelled to change them into two stones because that was the law. It was not at all the mirror's fault. Surely, you who are a god and are omniscient, and who are now nearly drunk enough to see everything double, can see that much? "

" So far as your explanation goes, I can see the mirror's blamelessness in the face of an obdurate physical law. Nor does any god object to a physical law which concerns other people."

" And they kept away from the mirror because they knew about this law. Surely, that too was natural? "

" In a way, yes. But how could they be certain about this law? "

" How could they help it, how could anybody be ignorant of one of our very oldest and most famous laws, which comes down to us, indeed, from sources so august and venerable that they antedate all history? "

" Why, then, who enacted this law? "

" How should I know, when, as I was just telling you, this law is older than any recorded history? "

" But in a thousand pounds of law there is not an

ounce of pleasure, and there are entirely too many laws," said Gerald, shaking his red head above his golden goblet rather despondently. " There is common, statutory, international, maritime, ecclesiastical, and martial law. There is the law of averages, the Salic law, and Grimm's law of the permutations of consonants. There is Jewish sacred law; there is prize law; there is the law of gravitation; there is John Law, who first developed the natural wealth of the Mississippi, and William Law, who was a great mystic. There are, in logic, the laws of thought, just as in astronomy and physics and political economy there are, severally, the well-known laws of Kepler and Prevost and Gresham. In fine, there are laws everywhere, and they are very often a nuisance. He that goes to law loses time and money and rest and friends. Law is a lottery, law is a bottomless pit, law is an ass which slaps his tail in every man's face. So it very well may be, my dear fellow, that in a world so legally overstocked this law of yours is superfluous, and therefore wrong."

But Tenjo was not convinced by Gerald's relentless logic. Tenjo said only:

" I do not any more know what you are talking about than you do. But I do know that " — here Tenjo hiccoughed, with judicial graveness, — " that it does not alter the principle of the thing."

" That," Gerald conceded, gloomily, " is true. Nothing does."

" So this mirror will continue to transform into two stones all men who look into it, although I cannot see how it matters the worth of one box of matches in hell, because so long as the law is such, no man will ever look into this mirror."

[105]

" Yet, do you but answer me this very simple question! What if some intelligent, unsuperstitious person were to look into this mirror, — and were to come back not changed into stone, and not hurt in any way, — would that not prove to you the insanity of this law? "

" Of course it would not! That would only prove the man was a liar. The plain fact of his not being changed into two stones would be legal proof in any of our courts or in any law-respecting place anywhere that he had not ever looked into the Mirror of the Two Truths."

" Oh, very well! " said Gerald. " No, thank you, my dear fellow, not another drop! Let us go to the temple! And let us each lean upon the other's arm, for your most excellent wine does not seem to have clarified anything exactly."

NOW, when the grave, white-bearded King and the red-headed god had come to the Temple of the Holy Nose, they entered it arm in arm, followed by the King's court. And when they approached the adytum, the head priestess came toward them exhibiting a cteis, or large copper comb, which she offered to Tenjo. The King accepted it, he parted her hair in the middle, and he spoke the Word of Entry.

Said Tenjo: " I enter, proud and erect. I take my fill of delight imperiously, irrationally, and none punishes."

The head priestess replied, " Not yet."

Tenjo said, " But in three months, and in three months, and in three more months, the avenger comes forth, and mocks me by being as I am, visibly; and by being foredoomed to do as I have done, inevitably."

This ceremony being discharged, they all entered the adytum, and then the three priestesses led Gerald toward the collapsed and shrivelled idol which was in the adytum. And Gerald whistled.

" — For do you call this," said Gerald, " a nose? "

" Sir," replied the priestesses, " we do. As, likewise, do all other well-conducted persons."

" Yet, I would call it," said Gerald, whose naturally fine color was now perceptibly heightened by Tenjo's excellent wine, " another member."

" Such, sir," they answered him, " is not our custom."

" Nevertheless," said Gerald, waggling very gravely his red head, " nevertheless, it is written in the scriptures of the Protestant Episcopal Church that, even as great ships are turned about in the sea's roaring main with a small helm, even so is every man guided in the main by a small member — "

They said, " Yet, sir — "

" And this member is not well spoken of by the Apostolic Fathers. This member has ruined virgins: its conquests are stained with blood: it has caused the widow to regret: it has deceived the wisest and most elderly of men. It is, in fine, a member whose blushing hue is wholly proper to its iniquitous history."

They replied, " Still, sir — "

" It is an over proud and wild member. Most justly is it written that every kind of beasts and of birds and of serpents and of things in the sea is to be tamed, and has been tamed, by human kind; but that this member can no man tame; for it is an unruly member, seeking ruthlessly its prey; a rebellious member, prominent in uprisings; a member very often full of deadly poison."

They said, " None the less, sir — "

" I deduce that this member here represented is not worshipful. I deduce that it is not well for you of Lytreia to worship this shrivelled image of a tongue, for all that you call it a nose."

They answered now: " As above, so below, saith the supreme mystic. You must understand, sir, that, while there is much piousness and wide erudition in what you tell us, yet is the word ' nose ' a word with connotations and with a decreed correspondence in anatomy — "

" I do not at all understand that saying, and so I cannot quite see your point of view. I merely know that, in consonance with the words of St. James the Just, and according to the scriptures of the Protestant Episcopal Church, this member is a tongue. And I admit that this tongue, which your heathenish up-bringing induces you to call a nose, is in a peculiarly bad way. But the divine word of Fair-haired Hoo, the Helper and Preserver, the Lord of the Third Truth, has been pledged to help and to preserve this idol. So we will see what can be done about it."

Then Gerald moistened his finger-tip with a drop of the water from the Churning of the Ocean. As the Lady of the First Water-Gap had done to Gerald's forehead, so Gerald did to the shrivelled idol of Lytreia.

It was changed. Its limpness departed; its coloring quickened; corded large blue veins, very intricately forked and branched, arose about its now glowing surface, which revealed also many tiny veins that were brightly red and astonishingly tortuous. It became enormous and high-standing and robust and succulent. It throbbed and jerked. It was hot to the touch: and the roughened cartilage of its erect tip-end now glistened with imperial purple.

And everywhere at that same instant the magic of Evaine was lifted from Lytreia, and the nose of every man regained its proper proportions and vigor. Young couples to the right hand and to the left could be seen withdrawing to sneeze in private: the girls were already producing their handkerchiefs. And

[109]

the three priestesses began to bathe the rejuvenated idol with refreshing water: they wreathed it with leaves of the Indian wood-apple; they placed before it flowers and incense and sweetmeats. Meanwhile they chanted a contented song in honor of the Holy Nose.

Tenjo and all the older lords and dowagers of Tenjo's court had kneeled in worship. Gerald only remained standing as arrogantly erect as was the idol which people worshipped in Lytreia.

"I honor in a civil way," said Gerald, "the spirit of this tongue — "

"But this," said Tenjo the King, now speaking almost peevishly, "is not a tongue. It is the Holy Nose of Lytreia."

"Do you not be flying, my dear fellow, upon the wings of bad temper, into the face of scripture and of logic! In a civil way, I repeat, I honor this member. I personally am rather fond of talking. Nevertheless, as being myself a member of the Protestant Episcopal church, and as being also a self-respecting member of the Dirghic mythology, I must decline to worship this so restive and inflammable member of any man's body."

Tenjo at that got up from off his knees. He came toward Gerald: and the white-bearded, grave King then spoke with rather less of peevishness than of compassion.

"You will regret such sayings. For that also is a law of Lytreia. However, do you now ask what you will for the vigor which you have restored to our noses, and we will gladly pay that price. Yet for the blasphemies which you have uttered in this temple the spirit of the Holy Nose will by and by be asking a price: and that price nor you nor any other lad will ever pay gladly."

Gerald replied, " For the renovation of your noses, and as a propitiatory trap for the doomed wu in Peter's Tomb, you will pay me the price of one black rooster."

" But what," asked Tenjo, " is a rooster? "

" Why, a rooster is the herald of the dawn, it is the father of an omelet, it is the pullet's first bit of real luck, it is the male of the *Gallus domesticus.*"

" We do not call a male chicken that — "

" No," Gerald assented, " no, but you ought to. And not to do so is wholly un-American."

" Yet why do you Americans call this particular bird a rooster, when everybody knows that all birds except ostriches and cassowaries roost, and that every flying bird everywhere is thus a rooster?"

" Well, I admit that we do not reason about it as you reason in Lytreia. I admit that the word ' rooster ' is a word without connotations and without any correspondence in anatomy. Nevertheless, every nation has its customs. And it is as much our well-established American custom to call the male of the chicken a rooster as it is your custom to call that thing a nose."

" But we call that a nose because it is, in point of fact, a nose. It is, as we have told you I do not know how many times, the Holy Nose of Lytreia."

Gerald was honestly exasperated by the obstinacy of the people of this kingdom.

" Even so," said he, " if you want the truth — "

He spoke then the truth about that tongue, as it appeared to him. But his remarks were lost to history through the circumstance that none of his hearers ever thought of setting them down in writing.

[111]

Instead, his hearers shuddered. They gave him a black cock, and they drove him out of that temple. It was in this way that Gerald, who had begun his journeying by denying homage to Koleos Koleros, now put an affront upon the Holy Nose of Lytreia.

NOW Gerald rode upon the silver stallion toward the immemorial, moss-overgrown tomb of King Peter the Builder, and Gerald carried under his left arm the black cock. Gerald noted, with an interest natural to any student of magic, the glorification tree which grew beside this tomb. He once more whistled meditatively. Then he hitched his shining stallion to an over-candidly carved and painted post which stood in eternal erection at the door of the tomb, and he went in.

The interior of this spacious tomb was lighted with nineteen iron lamps swung from the ceiling. Gerald thus saw, first of all, the great four-square mirror covered with a flesh-colored cloth. Before it fumed a smoking brazier; and beside this stood the appearance of a woman. To her left hand was a broad bed, and to her right, a gilded pig-trough heaped with fig-leaves. These leaves this woman was crumpling and tearing into little pieces one by one before she destroyed them in the fire of the brazier.

She heard Gerald's civil cough. She turned: and Gerald was enraptured.

For Evaine of Peter's Tomb was so surpassingly lovely that she excelled all the other women his gaze had ever beheld. The colors of this beautiful young girl's two eyes were nicely matched, and her nose stood just equidistant between them. Beneath this was

[113]

her mouth, and she had also a pair of ears. The girl was young, she exhibited no deformity anywhere, and the enamored glance of the young man could perceive in her no fault. There was, to be sure, a puzzling likeness to somebody he had once known, but Gerald's quick wits soon unriddled the mystery. This woman reminded him of Evelyn Townsend.

Nor was this all. He observed now that this woman was, just as he had suspected, a Fox-Spirit, for now from Evaine of Peter's Tomb emanated the power of her magic. That magic which overmasters all animals now smote at Gerald; and in a mildly amusing way he found its assaults really quite interesting.

"For this is the goety of beasts," he reflected. "This is the brutish half-magic of the wu which maddens men, along with all other animals in their rutting season, and robs them of self-control. This magic persuades me, almost, that I, too, am only a bundle of cellular matter upon its way to becoming manure. Yes, my life, too, at just this moment, seems but a grudged brief season of bewildered appetites and of baffled surmise such as is the life of a mortal man. I, too, seem a mere human being passing from the forgotten to the unforeseeable. Under the assaults of this small carnal magic, I seem again to go in that continuous masked loneliness which mortal persons in Lichfield and elsewhere call living. I long to put out of mind the frailness and the transiency of my hold upon living. The nonsensical notion has occurred to me that such forgetfulness may be hired by bringing the epidermis which masks me into superficial contact with the homogeneous animal matter in which hides this Fox-Spirit. . . . Yes, I am being, as it were, maddened with desire; I am very rapidly becoming the prey of this Fox-Spirit's irresistible powers of fascination, so to speak. And I find it really quite interesting to observe how this half-magic which destroys so many men now impiously strikes beyond its proper arena, at that which is divine; and how this foolish magic attempts to deceive even me, who am a Savior and a sun god."

Such were the cursory reflections which passed through Gerald's mind in the while that he said, aloud, " Good-evening, ma'am! "

The Fox-Spirit Evaine, without replying to him directly, took out of her bosom a white gem about the size of an orange. She tossed this up into the air, and caught it again. Gerald conjectured that this was her soul, but he made no comment.

He displayed to her his cock, saying, as was needful, " I entreat you to accept my rooster — "

" But what," asked learned Evaine, " what did you call this tamed descendant of the wild Bankiva fowl, — whose original habitat was in Northern India from Sindh to Burmah, and in Cochin China, and in many of the Malay Islands as far as Timor, and in the Philippines? "

" Why, in the United States of America, ma'am, we, rather more briefly, and for a variety of reasons, call this bird a rooster."

" It has been well observed," she replied, " by Pliny the Elder — a celebrated Roman naturalist, born 23 A.D., perished in the eruption of Vesuvius 79 A.D., — that every nation has its customs."

Then the Fox-Spirit dexterously cut off the head of Gerald's cock with the sacrificial ax, and turning toward the East, she spoke the needed words three times. One entered now in a scarlet coat, a yellow vest, and pale green knee-breeches. His head was like that of a mastiff, with the addition of two horns and the ears of an ass, but he had the legs and hoofs of a calf. Such was he who carried off the black cock which Gerald had brought for the Fox-Spirit's master, as a propitiatory offering and a trap.

Gerald smiled. Gerald shook hands, politely, with Evaine the learned Fox-Spirit.

" I am," said Gerald, " a god."

She replied: " I am one who serves all gods. I honor every tribe of those divine beings whose existence scholars have so variously accounted for as the products of physical and ethical and historical and etymological blunders abetted by homonymy and polonymy. But I require for my piety a honorarium."

" And what is that honorarium? "

She told him.

And as she spoke, Evaine drew near to him, and yet nearer, and she was remarkably desirable. If only she had not now reminded Gerald more and more of Evelyn Townsend, she would have been resistless.

" Very well, then! " said Gerald, affably: " you shall have that honorarium to-morrow morning if you still care to demand a reward so trivial."

Immediately afterward he said, " But, indeed, ma'am, you quite misunderstand me! "

Then with a few well-chosen words he placed their relationship upon a more decorous basis.

And Evaine the Fox-Spirit laughed. Such unresponsiveness she declared to be, when manifested by a god, wholly surprising, and comparable to the Seven Wonders of the World, namely: (1) the Pyramids of Egypt; (2) the Hanging Gardens of Babylon; (3) the Tomb of Mausolos; (4) the

Temple of Diana at Ephesus; (5) the Colossus of Rhodes; (6) the Statue of Zeus by Phidias; and (7) the Pharos at Alexandria. Yet Evaine continued, she perceived that she might trust him —

"You may do nothing of the sort! " said Gerald, decisively. "You may not even give me all. No, ma'am, it would be quite unadvisable, because, as I am forced to point out, you in your unfading youth and omniscient learning are many thousands of years older than I am in my present incarnation. Beside you, I am a mere boy. Now, it is often a great disadvantage to a boy, it is by and by a curse to him, to succumb to the loving confidence and generosity of a woman much older than himself. It is unwholesome. It is un-American."

"Is it, then, inconsistent with the manners of a continent in the Western Hemisphere — first named America by Waldseemüller, a teacher of geography in the college of Saint-Dié among the Vosges, in a treatise called *Cosmographia*, published in 1507, — for me to like you so much that I want just to touch you and be near you? "

"No, ma'am, that, I regret to say, is universal. Besides, I did not particularly mean you. I only mean that there are such women, as we both know, dear lady, who prey upon young boys. They employ for this purpose all their confidence and generosity without the least scruple. And many a hard, bitter, cynical man has originally had his faith in and his regard for everything good and holy blasted in his very first boyhood by the confiding nature and generosity of some middle-aged woman or another and her subsequent references to the advantage he took of her."

"It is possible that you speak with the clearness

recommended by Quintilian as the chief virtue of speech, — born in Spain about 25 A.D., died about 95 A.D., patronized by Vespasian and Domitian, — but it is certain that I do not understand one word of your speaking."

" — However," Gerald continued, " when a boy has a nice, clean friendship with an older woman it is one of the most valuable and helpful experiences that can come into his life. A friendship such as this appears to me a rather beautiful idea. The older woman — particularly when she is older by many thousands of years, — can teach him, as his mother out of the superficial knowledge of a callow half-century or so cannot possibly do, about women. She can inspire and direct him. She can fire his ambition. She can encourage him. She can be to him in every way a liberal education."

" Now, certainly, I shall never understand your American way of uttering so many platitudes — derived from the Greek word *platys*, meaning ' flat,' — when I was attempting to do all these things! "

" Ah, but we must keep the education entirely oral, and we must keep, too, your little hands — So, now, that is very much better! "

" It is better still to permit a wilful person to have his way, — a remark attributed to Periander, an ancient sage, and Tyrant of Corinth during the sixth century B.C., — since you elect to give me my honorarium for nothing," Evaine said, rather sulkily.

Gerald elected to do nothing of the sort. But, since his real intentions would have been an awkward matter to explain, he kept silent about them.

After that Gerald questioned the learned Fox-Spirit. She explained to him willingly enough the

laws of Lytreia and described the basket they were
found in, and she made it plain just how these laws
were enforced by a committee of midwives and stone-
masons. She spoke of the magic she had put upon
Lytreia. She spoke of Tenjo, telling how in the prime
of his youth he came to be called Tenjo of the Long
Nose; and her statistics were remarkable. She talked
then about the wind between the stars, and about the
grandeur that was Greece, and about Hobson's choice,
and about Davey Jones's locker, and about the cause
of volcanoes, and about the curate's egg, and about
the best cures for baldness. For no information anywhere was hidden from the wisdom of Evaine, who
knew all things, and who served all gods.

" I perceive," said Gerald, " that you have knowledge, and I like your reflections extremely. So do you
speak yet further out of the stores of your omnis-
cience! "

He had been glancing all the while toward the
veiled Mirror of the Two Truths. But he of course
said never a word about this mirror. His present task
was simply to lure on this cultured and malefic creature to her complete ruin.

For the Fox-Spirit, as Gerald saw, was still about
the brutish magic of the wu, which drives men mad,
and she now spoke of more and yet more evil matters
such as were very well adapted to incite Gerald to
brutality. She spoke of the battle of life, and of the
feast of reason, and of the irony of fate, and of the
lap of luxury. She talked of the writing on the wall,
and of the scroll of fame, and of the lexicon of youth,
and of the cloud that had a silver lining. She touched
upon the two seas, of troubles and of upturned faces.
She discussed the durance that was vile, and the hours

that were wee and sma', and the consummation that was devoutly to be wished for, and the light that was dim and religious, and the heat which was not the humidity. She indicated the balm in Gilead, the place in the sun, and the safety in numbers. She afterward gave succinctly the recipes for making a mountain out of a molehill, a silk purse out of a sow's ear, and a virtue out of a necessity. For no evil phrase of any sort was hidden from the wisdom of Evaine, who knew all things, and who served all gods, and who was now intent to exercise upon Gerald the magic of the wu, which drives men mad.

But Gerald only smiled, almost approvingly. This woman was reminding him more and more of Evelyn Townsend, and his pulses had not ever been calmer.

" I perceive," said Gerald, " that you have a great deal of knowledge, with the vocabulary of a dear friend to back it devastatingly. Therefore, ma'am, to avail myself of your knowledge alone may serve my divine ends much better than your really most flattering proffers in other fields."

For it now was Gerald's turn to speak. So now he revealed to the baffled Fox-Spirit the fact that he was Fair-haired Hoo, the Helper and Preserver, the Lord of the Third Truth, the Well-beloved of Heavenly Ones, a very potent god who had temporarily mislaid his mythology. He told the omniscient Fox-Spirit, who knew all things excepting only how and at what time her knowledge would end, of Gerald's adventures during the rather crowded twenty-four hours since he had left Lichfield.

And now she was smiling over his obtuseness. For to all-wise Evaine it was at once apparent that Fair-

haired Hoo, the Helper and Preserver, the Lord of
the Third Truth, the Well-beloved of Heavenly
Ones, was a culture hero like Quat or Quetzalcoatl or
Cagn or Osiris or Dionysos. All these were former
acquaintances of hers: she knew, she said, every inch
of them, for each one of these had stopped to visit her
who served all gods, as each had passed downward
toward Antan. Evaine, if anybody, would thus know
a culture hero whenever she saw a culture hero.

Every mythology contained one of these glorious
philanthropists, born of a mysterious and superior
race, just as Gerald had been born in the United States
of America, a philanthropist, as the learned Fox-
Spirit said, very usually theriomorphic, who came in
the appearance of a jackass or of some other animal
among less favored peoples to teach them strange
new arts and mysteries, and to endow them with
every kind of cultural advantage and prosperity, just
as Gerald had benefited the people of Dersam and
of Lytreia, and was preparing to benefit Antan.

She pointed out, furthermore, that a culture hero
was in no way un-American. There had been, for example, Quetzalcoatl. She also remembered quite
clearly Yetl, — because a visitor in the form of a
bird was always, she said, rather difficult, — and Pos-
haiyankya, and Coyote, and Esaugetuh, and that
other waggish Indian deity — his name at present
evaded her, — who had traveled incognito in the
shape of a large spider. For all these aboriginal
American culture heroes had visited Evaine as they
passed downward toward Antan, and every one of
them had been in a somewhat earlier generation Gerald's fellow countryman.

" In the light of your forceful logic, ma'am, I concede that, over and above being a Savior and a sun God, it now seems probable I must be a culture hero too."

" But yet, in any case, — dear, unresponsive, frigid child," said the Fox-Spirit, speaking far more simply than she had done before, — " do you not know that all mythologies are controlled by the Master Philologist, so that he alone may say in which one of them and in what capacity you belong? "

" I find that saying obscure."

" It means only that sooner or later all gods save only Koleos Koleros and the upright spirit of the Holy Nose pass down into Antan."

" Yes, for, as they told me at Caer Omn, Antan is the heaven of all deserving gods, where they rest from their divine labors."

But the Fox-Spirit shook her head, rather forebodingly. " I, certainly, would not say that."

" Do you, then, but answer me this very simple question! What becomes of them there? what fate befalls in that place all which men have found most beautiful and most worshipful? "

" How can one say, when no god has ever returned? It is known only that, in one way or another way, the Master Philologist disposes of every deity that men have served, save only the two supreme gods of all mammals, — a class of vertebrates embracing bats, the warm-blooded quadrupeds, seals, cetaceans, man, and sirenians."

Gerald drew a long face. " Your account of the matter, ma'am, suggests that my predecessor upon the throne of Antan lacks piety. You imply that the creature is deficient in true religious feeling. That is a fault I would have to requite when I take from him his throne and all the great and best words of magic."

"To do that, child, needs power such as has not been shown by any god among the many millions of gods that men have worshipped since the first infancy of Chronos, — a Greek personification of Time, usually depicted as carrying a sickle and an hourglass."

"Ah, but, my dear lady, I, who am at once a culture hero and a sun deity and a Savior, must be a peculiarly powerful god. And, besides, ma'am, from what you tell me — Why, but, really now, it appears probable that the Master Philologist has damaged the Dirghic mythology to which I myself belong! No god can patiently endure such usage; and my divine wrath will, thus, redouble my power."

"But, still, — but, still, you dear, nice-looking and vainglorious baby — ! "

Evaine had paused. She was regarding him almost compassionately: and Gerald felt he could never get used to the flighty way in which people everywhere in the Marches of Antan seemed to pity the high gods. It was a quite friendly way they had of looking at you, but to extend commiseration where reverence was the proper thing savored almost of irreligion.

Gerald shrugged. He said:

" I shall therefore be resistless. I shall compel him to restore into general circulation the Dirghic mythology, after having amply repaired whatsoever damage he may have done to it, and then I shall assume, in addition to his throne, my proper station as a culture hero and a sun deity and a Savior in that mythology. So the affair is, virtually, settled: we may now turn to other matters: and in return for the gracious aid afforded by your large wisdom, I will make in your honor a sonnet."

"It is a very beautiful sonnet, — consisting of fourteen decasyllabic lines, expressing two phases of a single thought or sentiment," said Evaine the Fox-Spirit, — "and I am proud to have inspired it."

"You forget," said Gerald, "that I have not yet recited my sonnet. I will now do so."

And he did.

But his voice was so shaken with emotion that, when he had completed the octave, he paused, because it was never within Gerald's power to resist the beauty of a sublime thought when it was thus adequately expressed in flawless verse. So for an instant he stayed silent.

He caught up the lovely hands of Evaine the Fox-Spirit, and as he pressed them to his trembling lips he noted that these hands smelled like hops drying in the sun. It seemed to him exceedingly pitiful he had given that promise to Tenjo. It seemed to him there was a certain sameness in the dear women who made colorful the Marches of Antan, and, to some extent, a similarity in their more intimate love passages with Fair-haired Hoo, the Helper and Preserver. He found it depressing to reflect that destruction waited, so very near, for so much loveliness. He found it perfectly dreadful to foreknow that he would often regret this omniscient Evaine and her fine stores of useful information, once he had kept the divine word given to Tenjo, and had put an end to her living before she could do any further damage to the men of Lytreia.

Gods ought to abstain from all love-affairs: for through love alone might a god look to be wounded,

— upon rainy Sunday afternoons, perhaps, or after drinking a bit more than was good for one, — to be wounded, at such unavoidable seasons of low vitality, with recurrent, plaguing memories of his mortal playthings, so dear, so very dear, and so soon reft away from his immortal arms, irrevocably. . . .

After these cursory reflections, Gerald sighed, and — with the thoughtful commentary that, since this was a Miltonic sonnet, his poem here went on with the same sentence, — he continued his reciting.

And when he had ended, the Fox-Spirit sighed contentedly. She spoke with acumen and authority as to the main events of Milton's life and as to his principal works, and she added:

" That is a very beautiful sonnet, — a verse form of Italian origin, first used in English by Sir Thomas Wyatt in 1557, — and I am proud to have inspired it. That is the sort of poetry which would incline any living woman to trust you and to give you all the very moment you stopped reciting it. So now will you not come to bed? "

" No, Evelyn, not to-night — I beg your pardon, ma'am! My thoughts were wool-gathering. What I had meant to say was but that if you insist upon yet further displays of your great-hearted womanly confidence and generosity you shall be walloped with a broomstick — severely. No, do you retire now, my dear lady, by all means, and with my apologies for keeping you up so late because of the delight I have got from your instructive way of talking. But I shall pass the remainder of the night in the aloofness appropriate to a god, in this quite comfortable armchair."

And this he did.

[125]

WHEN Evaine was asleep, though, then Gerald rose softly from his chair. He approached the bed. Very carefully he inserted his hand between the young breasts of Evaine, and lightly he drew out the strange white gem. He waited now, looking down compassionately at this really very lovely girl. . . .

But at his touch the learned Fox-Spirit had moved, so that she now lay flat upon her back, with her mouth a little open. Evelyn slept thus. And that was why Evelyn snored. . . .

Gerald shrugged. He took up the sacrificial ax.

Now that dawn was at hand, he went out from the tomb, to the glorification tree, and he began to fell the tree with this ax. At the first stroke blood gushed out of the gray bark copiously, and Gerald heard a wailing noise. Gerald looked upward. The appearance of a young child dressed in blue garments was to be seen in a cleft in the side of the tree. It had the seeming of a boy child about seven or eight years old, a freckled boy, with tousled red hair, and with as yet only one upper front tooth.

This child wailed broken-heartedly: " A blasphemer is come up against the Two Truths; a vainglorious fool derides the pair that endure where all else perishes; and life is denied to me by his wrongheadedness."

Gerald had put down the ax. He was trembling. He did not like the love and the great yearning which had awakened in his heart. He folded his arms very tightly: he seemed tense and rather frightened looking as he waited there peering side-wise toward this boy.

" Child," Gerald said, " what is your will that you cry out for life from the glorification tree? "

" My father, I demand the life which you have not given me, that life which you owe to me, and that life which is denied me so long as you deny the Two Truths."

" I serve the demands of my appointed kingdom, child. I serve the needs of no other truth and the needs of no pawing women who would keep me out of that kingdom."

" My father, your kingdom is a doubtful dream, but the flesh of my mother is real."

" My dream is lovelier than any woman. Oh, and a doubtfulness also is more lovely than the body of a woman, for I know the shaping of that body over-well."

" My father, you refuse the pleasures which will not ever be returning."

" I am a god. I serve the needs of my own will."

" The gods also pass, my father, they also pass without any returning, upon the road which you now tread."

" Let us pass, then, unhindered! But no woman permits it."

" That is because these women, O my father, have a very rational wisdom."

" Such is, perhaps, the case. But a god has his irra-tional dream. And that is better."

" It is well enough, my father, for that dream to end contentedly in the arms of some woman."

" It is well enough. It is customary. But I am Fair-haired Hoo, the Helper and the Preserver. I go to my appointed kingdom: and I am Lord of a Third Truth, whose mightiness I must help and preserve."

Then Gerald hewed on: and as the tree fell, the child vanished.

Now Gerald set fire to the tree: and when a tidy blaze was crackling, he spoke the needed words, and into the heart of this fire he tossed the strange white gem which was the soul of Evaine. Straightway you heard a loud screeching. Out of the tomb of Peter the Builder came a vixen fox, screaming and shuddering quite horribly, but not ever ceasing to approach the fire. She entered the flames. Silence followed, and the dawn of a superb May morning which was marred only by an unpleasant odor of singed hair and burning flesh.

Gerald after that went back into the tomb from which the omniscient Fox-Spirit had been dispossessed. He looked rather sentimentally upon the empty disordered bed: then he passed beyond the brazier, in which the ruins of fig-leaves yet smouldered, toward the Mirror of the Two Truths.

The fact no longer mattered, perhaps, that any man who looked into this mirror straightway found himself transformed into two stones: but it very greatly mattered what effect this mirror would have upon a sun god and a Savior and a culture hero. So he removed the flesh-colored veil.

BUT he was not turned into two stones. Nor was there confronting him any mirror. Beyond the flesh-colored veil he found only an ancient painting very carefully done, but upon an unhuman scale which made this painting monstrous. The subject of the picture, however, is not known, because Gerald never told anybody.

But it is known that Gerald shook his head at this painting.

"Laborious daub of prevaricating pigment!" he remarked. "O futile painting, which so many foolish believers in Lytreia think to be the Mirror of the Two Truths! I question your arithmetic. For I myself am the Lord of a Third Truth, for all that I have just at present no precise idea as to its nature. In consequence, I know the two objects which you magnify are not all which exists. And I deny that their never-ending search of each other is the one gesture of life. No: I at least, I feel assured, am destined to take part in some quite other gesture, of a more graceful and more cleanly and more dignified nature, — a gesture of, it well may be, eternal importance. . . ."

Yet Gerald glanced about him a little forlornly. This place was now rather lonesome and ambiguous looking. In the crypt immediately beneath him, Gerald knew, lay all that remained of King Peter and the most of his numerous family; dozens upon dozens of peculiarly ugly objects were there, all that remained of a great conqueror and of the queens who had delighted him, all that attestedly remained now anywhere of a strong hero's pride and famous warfaring and of his many women's loveliness. . . .

"Oh, yes, it may be," Gerald conceded, half frettedly, because he did not like to be troubled with such reflections, "it may be that I am wrong in this belief. And that seems to me yet another reason for adhering to this belief. I, standing here alone upon the remnants of so many utter strangers, admit indeed to some depression of spirits. It seems to me, at this exact instant, that just conceivably I may be neither a Savior nor a sun god nor a culture hero, but merely another bull-headed Musgrave, for whom death waits, and after death, perhaps, oblivion. Nevertheless, I find it a more beautiful and a much more entertaining idea to believe in than to deny the immortality even of a mere Musgrave. There is to my mind nothing at all interesting in the idea of my own extinction. And it appears that my belief in this matter, with no assured knowledge anywhere to go on, must be simply a question of personal taste. Modesty even suggests that my belief is an affair of irrelevance."

And Gerald said also: "Therefore it furthermore appears to me, O peculiarly unimaginative painting, a sheer waste of opportunity to assume that anything is ever going to end even for a mere Musgrave all conscious experience. I had far rather play with a beautiful idea than with one utterly lacking in seductiveness. I very much prefer to believe that I at least am, in one way or another, reserved to take

part in some enduring and rather superb performance, — somewhere, by and by, — in a performance
concerned with some third truth, more august and
æsthetically more pleasing than are the only ever-
enduring truths apparent to us here. We copulate and
die, and that is all? — Well, perhaps! But, then
again, perhaps not! One must, you see, be broad-
minded about the matter."

He for a moment kept silence. That regrettably
candid painting and all the other adjuncts of this
place were certainly very depressing, now that the
learned diableries of the Fox-Spirit no longer en-
livened this tomb. Nevertheless, Gerald kept his long
chin well up.

" Yes, every man ought to be broad-minded about
this matter, and ought to cherish always, if only as a
diverting and inexpensive plaything, this pungent
notion of being immortal. It is really inexpensive,
because, should your notion prove ungrounded, you
run no risk, no tiniest risk, of being twitted, by and
by, for credulity, or even of ever discovering your
error. Meanwhile this faith in your own durability
and potential importance is in some sense a cordial;
and is in sundry ways a fine toy. It renders life, and
dying too, endurable: and it offers against all vacant
half-hours a variety of diverting speculations . . .
as to that possible third truth."

Again Gerald paused. For it seemed to him, as he
unwittingly repeated the age-old self-persuasions of
so many of his ancestors, that he had found now
another facet in this jewel of an idea that he was
playing with; and this fact considerably cheered
Gerald.

" Then, too," said he, " then, too, that rather widespread expectation of an oncoming triumph — somewhere, in some hazed roseate arena, beyond the discomforts of death and the incredible impudence of the mortician's titivating, — that triumph which is to be a perpetual triumphing of justice and of rationality and of kindliness and of all the other canonical virtues, this rumored triumph yet cows many persons, not infrequently, into one or another thrifty-minded practice of these generally beneficent virtues."

Gerald said then: " It thus makes for, at any rate, terrestrial ease and stability and repose: it gives people, as the phrase runs, something to go by, in that it supports the most of every nation's social and legal rules of thumb. And it tends appreciably to limit men's common greed and viciousness, and all the harsher lusts of human beings, to exercises through which there seems some quite tangible gain within tolerably safe reach."

And Gerald said also: " Yes: it is much better for men to believe in some third truth which will be revealed to them after the death of their bodies; and a general faith in the immortality even of mere Musgraves appears to me, thus, very plainly, because of its happy blending of the functions of a narcotic and of a policeman, a generally desirable assumption. It remains in all ways a desirable faith, no matter whether or not there be any grounds for it. And if this careful painting presents the entire truth, that fact is but another excellent reason for paying no attention to it."

Gerald now felt quite comfortable through having listened so respectfully to his own relentless logic.

" For these reasons, O foolish painting of the Two Truths, I deny your fleshly significance. Whether I happen to be a sun god or a Savior or a culture hero or just another bull-headed Musgrave, I deny that you present to me any truth whatever. I snap my fingers at your materialism; I turn up my nose at your indecorous anatomical studies; and I send the divine foot of the Lord of the Third Truth smashing through your ancient canvas. These things I do to proclaim the majesty of the Third Truth. And I depart from this Peter and this Peter's Tomb, to seek my appointed kingdom."

It was in this way that Gerald yet again put an affront upon Koleos Koleros and upon the Holy Nose of Lytreia.

PART SIX

THE BOOK OF TUROINE

"Weathercocks *Turn more Easily when Placed very High.*"

GERALD passed on, still riding upon the silver stallion, which Evaine the Fox-Spirit had not, after all, demanded of him that morning as her promised honorarium. And the next place he came to, and where he got his breakfast, was Turoine. This was a small free city given to sorceries of two colors.

To every side of him the inhabitants of Turoine were about their arts: and Gerald, as a former student of magic, quite naturally observed their various activities with interest.

Now the first sorcerer that he encountered was making a figure out of pink wax with which was mixed baptismal oil and the ashes of a consecrated wafer. The next sorcerer was murmuring charms over a very fat toad which was imprisoned in a net rudely woven out of the golden hairs from the head of some luckless, unresponsive woman, who was now about to meet a not wholly desirable doom after that toad had been buried at her threshold. And the third sorcerer huddled over a small fire wherein burned cypress branches and broken crucifixes and portions of a gibbet. In his hand was a skull filled with dark wine which had been seasoned with hemp and with the fat of a girl child and with poppy seed: and his familiar, in the shape of a large dun-colored cat, was lapping up that bitter drink.

[137]

SOMETHING ABOUT EVE

No sorcerer anywhere in Turoine was idle upon this fine May morning. And in this small, ever-busy city — where all the buildings were quaintly marked with stars and pentagrams and the signs of the zodiac and the two kinds of triangles, and were cozily overgrown with honeysuckle and arum lilies and black poppies and deadly nightshade, — everywhere in Turoine these sorcerers were about a bewildering variety of studies.

" I," one of them told Gerald, " am learning the secrets which proceed from Saturn, that cold and solitary master of the larger malevolence. I have especial power over all husbandmen and beggars, over grandfathers and monks of every order and ministers of the gospel, over all potters, and miners, and gardeners, and cow-tenders. I have learned how to make men envious, covetous, slow of thought, suspicious, and stubborn. And I am also able to afflict whatsoever person I elect with toothache and dropsy and black jaundice and leprosy and hemorrhoids, either severally or in unison."

Another said: " I study to divine and to make smooth the approach of every evil fortune, — with smoke and arrows and wax, with an egg, with mice, and with the simulacra of dead persons; — but, above all, as you may perceive, I have been most successful with the head of an ass in a brazier of live coals. And my guide is not any bow-legged, swarthy eunuch, but Leonard, the Grand Master of the Sabbat."

" I," said a third, " have found in Turoine the Great Juggle Bag, for my guide is Baalberith. So have I mastered all kinds of unheard-of, secret, merry feats and mysteries and inventions — "

[138]

"But what," asked Gerald, "what purpose does your knowledge serve?"

"By means of it, sir, those who are favored by my lord Baalberith, the Master of Alliances, may make real the sin performed in a dream; may open the locked door of any jail or bedchamber or counting house; may smite a husband with embarrassing weakness; may inspire strange maids and married women with flaming desires; may increase his natural height here by seven ells and here by three inches; may make himself invisible or invulnerable; may change his form into that of a cat or a hare or a wolf; may control thunder and lightning; may collect and talk with snakes; and " — here the sorcerer coughed, — " and may perform five other advantageous, extravagant and authentic devices."

But Gerald shrugged. " These sciences are well enough for a sorcerer; and I perceive that the industrious may pick up much useful information in Turoine. But I am a god who travels toward his appointed kingdom, and toward the mastery of secrets rather more vital than any of these. For your arts are of that black magic which hurts but cannot help; your guides are devils; and you deal only in misfortune and destructiveness."

" Then, perhaps, sir, you may be better pleased by the enchanters who live at the other end of this city. For these enchanters have no guides save restlessness and foiled desires and impotence; they get no direct aid from hell, but from somewhat less ancient intellectual centres; and they work all their magic, such as it is, with words."

" And what does the magic of these same enchanters create? "

" It creates, sir, a comfortable sense of equality with your betters wherever there is least reason for it."

" I find that saying obscure. Nevertheless, I will visit these enchanters," said Gerald.

And he rode on.

T HUS Gerald came to the enchanters who were accustomed to perform all their magic with words. And they greeted his coming with a very cordial enthusiasm for creatures so gray and vague and bedraggled looking as they sat huddled there, each one of them clothed in a blanket, and thoroughly drenched as though with sour smelling rain.

Now the first enchanter to speak wore a violet blanket. He arose; and dripping bilge-water everywhere about him, in the while that he smiled with wholly friendly condescension, he observed:

" Here is another rider on the silver stallion. Here is yet another figure of papier mâché which Horvendile has despatched upon a profitless journeying."

" But I — " said Gerald.

Without at all heeding Gerald, a second enchanter, in a well soaked green blanket, laid down his scissors; and he addressed the first enchanter with some fervor, saying:

" Let us not speak harshly of our good Horvendile's magic, for everybody ought to respect the impotence of the aging. We must concede, of course, that his magic is no longer fresh. It is not possible to deny that a woefully infirm magic has set this papier mâché figure on a hackneyed journeying. Candor compels us to grant that this journeying crosses once

[141]

sparkling rivers which have long ago run dry. We, as intelligent enchanters, must admit that a wearying fog lowers thickly about this journeying, that above it the sun of romance shines very pale and cold, and that this journeying is sterile and empty of gusto. Nevertheless, this journeying, as we ought not to ignore, is no doubt an afterthought, it is the belated invention of a tired mind, and a desperate and ill-advised proceeding. For these reasons, howsoever sorrowfully we, as Horvendile's fellow artists and well-wishers, must always deplore among ourselves the kindergarten notions of this poor Horvendile, and his ponderous playfulness, and the limitations of his few and unenterprising ideas, still we must be careful not to apply to his magic one single harsh word."

" Yet — " Gerald stated.

Nodding in profound and entire approbation, with which Gerald was not in any way connected, an enchanter in a sopping yellow blanket now remarked:

" I, too, am always ready to defend the magic of our fellow practitioner. My conscience forces me to grant that his magic is not faultless. In mere honesty I have to confess that his magic is stupid and stilted and silly; that it is sniggering and sly and nasty; that it wallows in a morass of self-satisfaction; and that it is steeped and soaked in ever-fretful egoism, in spite of our friendly candor in all dealings with him from the very first. Nor can I dispute that our con-frère behaves too much like a decadent small boy who is proud of having been haled into the police court for chalking dirty words on a wall. Apart, though, from his stinking filth and his vileness and

[142]

his tinsel cynicisms, and aside from his bestiality and his vulgar frippery and his dabblings in cesspools and his vapid sophistries, I stand always ready to defend the magic of Horvendile, because it is not, after all, as if he were a mage of any real importance, and one ought always to be indulgent to persons of third and fourth rate ability."

" Even so — " Gerald pointed out.

But now an enchanter in a thoroughly drenched scarlet blanket was saying, as he meditatively unclosed his pastepot:

" I quite agree with you. Nobody admires the merits of our esteemed confrère more whole-heartedly than I do. It would be merely silly to deny that he has weakened his always rather wishy-washy magic potions by too frequent blendings. It is impossible to ignore that his magic has become a cloying weariness and a mincing indecency. We are forced to acknowledge that Horvendile is insincere, that he very irritatingly poses as a superior person, that he is labored beyond endurance, that he smells of the lamp, that his art is dull and tarnished and trivial and intolerable, but, even so, we ought also to admit that he does as well as could be expected of anybody who combines a lack of any actual talent with ignorance of actual life."

" However — " Gerald explained.

The fifth enchanter to interrupt Gerald wore a black blanket; and he, too, appeared to drip with wisdom and bilge-water and judicious amiability, in the while that he said:

" It is, in fact, alike our duty and our privilege to be most lenient with this laborious bungler who, after all, is probably doing the best he can. So I, for one,

I never dwell even fleetingly upon the awkward fact that the banality of his magic is no excuse for the way he botches its execution. Indeed, I do not know but that a person of very lively imagination might conceive of our confrère's turning out worse work than he does. Nor do I think I am being over-charitable. For, upon my word, — while I can see that his magic is morbid, that it is sophomoric, that it is malignant, that it is plagiarized, that it is intolerably insipid, that it is sacrilegious, that it is naïve, that it is pseudo whatever or other may happen to sound best, that it is over brutal in cynicism, that it is incurably sentimental, and that it bores me beyond description, — yet otherwise I can, at just this moment, think of no especial other fault to find with his magic."

So it was that these dripping and affable enchanters went on defending Horvendile with such generous volubility that Gerald could get in no word.

Then each took off the single garment which he wore, and so vanished, because without their wet blankets these enchanters were in no way noticeable. And Gerald rode away from that place contentedly, because it was a natural comfort to know he traveled with a guide and a patron who was so well thought of by the best judges.

NOW upon the outskirts of Turoine, after Gerald had ridden through this city, Gerald paused to talk with the Sphinx who lay there writing with a black pen in a large black-covered book like a ledger. The monster had so long couched in this place as to be half-imbedded in the red earth.

"This partially buried condition, ma'am," Gerald began, — " or perhaps one ought to say ' sir ' — "

"Either form of address," replied the Sphinx, " may be applicable, according to which half of me you are considering."

" — This semi-interment, then, madam and sir, is untidy looking, and cannot be especially comfortable."

"Yet I may not move," replied the Sphinx, " in part because I have my writing to complete, in part because I know all movement and all action of every kind to be equally fruitless. So do I retain eternal bodily as well as mental poise."

"Such acumen borders upon paralysis," Gerald said: " and paralysis is ugly."

"Do you not despise ugliness! " the Sphinx exhorted, " who have traveled thus far upon the road of gods and myths. For what things have you found stable upon this road save only Koleos Koleros and the Holy Nose of Lytreia? and what is there more ugly than these two? "

Gerald replied: " That nose I found it my Christian duty to describe as a tongue; and the lady whom they call Koleos Koleros I have yet not seen. But, in any case, you, ma'am, — for, after all, it is not quite nice for me to have your loins upon my mind — No, really, it does seem more becoming for me to treat you as a lady — "

" So, and do you find me ugly? "

" You mistake my meaning. I was about to observe that you, ma'am, also appear tolerably stable. And the Mirror of Caer Omn, that likewise remains in worship."

" Dreams pass eternally varying through that golden mirror. Thoughts pass eternally varying through my wise head. But all these dreams and thoughts stay barren, as barren as they are irresolute. For we create nothing. We control no material thing. And we aspire toward no goal. That is why we are permitted to endure powerlessly in realms wherein two powers alone are never barren; wherein they control all; and wherein neither may ever be uncertain of its goal so long as the other survives."

Gerald found this wholly incomprehensible and of no striking interest. So he only shrugged.

" Nevertheless, in my worlds," Gerald said, " there shall not be any ugliness."

" Do you, then, possess many worlds? "

" Not as yet, ma'am. I allude to the worlds I shall create by and by, when I have come into my kingdom yonder, in the place beyond good and evil, and have

[146]

regained my proper station as the Lord of the Third Truth in the Dirghic mythology."

Now the Sphinx frowned. "I perceive you are only another downfallen god upon your journey to the Master Philologist. I might have guessed it, for Thor and Typhon and Rudra and the Maruts and all the other storm gods who have gone blustering downward into Antan, all had red hair."

Gerald slapped his thigh.

"Upon my word, ma'am, but that is a real clue! The storm gods did, in every mythology known to me, have red hair. I incline to believe that the wisdom of the Sphinx has solved the mystery of my being. I am no doubt a storm god also; I am rapidly becoming a complete pantheon upon two legs; and at this rate my waistcoat will end by embracing pure monotheism. Meanwhile I really do wonder, ma'am, at your offhand way of speaking about the gods, and I wonder, too, what grudge you can have against us gods?"

"For one thing, it is said that the gods created those men who interrupt me in my writing to plague me with just such silly questions."

"Men naturally seek wisdom from you, ma'am, to whom the whole story of human life is familiar."

"But the story of human life is not one story. There are three stories of human life."

"Ah, ah! And what are they?"

"Why, there was once a traveling man who came one night to an inn —"

"I believe I have heard of his indecorous adventures there. So do you spare my blushes, ma'am, and tell me the second story!"

"It seems, then, there were once two Irishmen —"

" That anecdote also, in all conceivable variants, I am quite certain I have heard. So what is the third story? "

" There was once a young married couple. And it seems that on the first night — "

" Yet that story, in a great number of versions, is equally familiar to me. And really, ma'am, I question if these intolerably hackneyed tales sum up all human wisdom."

" But the young married couple in the outcome got pleasure for their bodies in the service of those two powers about which I spoke just now. The Irishmen found an unlooked-for drollness in the mechanics of those two powers, which they preserved in a neat and nicely memorable phrase, getting pleasure for their minds. So, by the way, did the two Jews and the two Scotchmen. And the traveling man, upon the next morning, after those same two powers had obtained their will of him, went away from that inn, traveling nobody knows whither; and so got, through a darker night, an unbroken and an uncompanioned sleeping which was not bothered any longer by those powers. Thus these three stories really do sum up all the gains which it is possible for a man to acquire through human living and all the wisdom that it is salutary for any man to know about."

" Well, that is as it may be! I am persuaded that in the goal of all the gods there is a more august power than any which men know of hereabouts assuredly. For I note the sympathy and compassion and love and self-denial which human beings display toward one another, after all, rather copiously. I reflect that every art is a form of self-expression. And I deduce that the artist who created human beings was prompted in his embodiment of all these qualities by sheer egotism. He observed these qualities in his own nature: he approved of them: and so he embodied them. No actually reflective person, therefore, will ever imagine that human life does not go forward toward some kindly winding-up, since none who finds philanthropy in his own heart can doubt that philanthropy exists in the heart of his creator."

" And does that stuff which you are now talking really seem to you," the Sphinx asked, " sensible? "

" My dear lady, it seems to me something far better: it seems to me a rather beautiful idea. So I play with it sometimes. Now I dismiss that idea, out of deference to your proverbial wisdom: and I ask what far more gratifying and uplifting wisdom, ma'am, you may be writing in your black-covered book? "

" Oh, yes, my book! " said the Sphinx, with the livelier interest natural to an author. " You find me just now in some difficulty with my book. You conceive there has to be an opening paragraph. It would not be possible to leave out the first paragraph — "

" I can see that. I can recall no book in which there was not a first paragraph."

" — And this paragraph ought to sum up all things, so to speak — "

" That likewise is a familiar rhetorical principle — "

" — And it is with the composition of this paragraph that I am just now having trouble."

" Well, you could not possibly have consulted a more suitable person. I, too, used to dabble in the little art of letters before I became a god with four aspects. I am familiar with all rhetorical devices. I am

[149]

a past master of zeugma and syllepsis; at hypallage, and chiasmus also, I excel; and my handling of meiosis and persiflage and oxymoron has been quite generally admired. So do you read me your rough draft: and I have no doubt I can arrange all difficulties for you."

The Sphinx for a moment considered this suggestion, and, before the prospect of a connoisseur's efficient criticism, the monster seemed rather shy.

" Do not be vexed unduly," the Sphinx then said, " if you can find no meaning in this paragraph — "

" I shall not be excessively censorious, I assure you. No beginner is expected to excel in any art."

" — For this paragraph was placed here simply because there happened to be a vacancy which needed filling — "

" I quite understand that. So let us get on! "

But there was no hurrying the diffident Sphinx. " The foolish, therefore," the Sphinx continued in shy explanation, " will find in it foolishness, and will say ' Bother! ' The wise, as wisdom goes, will reflect that this paragraph was placed here without its consent being asked; that no wit nor large significance was loaned it by its creator; and that it will be forgotten with the turning of the one page wherein it figures unimportantly — "

" No doubt it will be! " said Gerald, now speaking a little impatiently, " but let us get on to this famous paragraph! "

" — So do you turn the page forthwith, in just the care-free fashion of old nodding Time as he skims over the long book of life: and do you say either ' Bother! ' or ' Brother! ' as your wits prompt."

" I will, I assure you, the moment your book is

[150]

published. But why do you keep talking about your paragraph? why do you not read me what you have written? "

" I have just done so," replied the Sphinx. " I have not been talking. I have been reading ever since I said, ' Do you not be vexed ' and now I have read you the whole paragraph."

Gerald said, " Oh! " He scratched his long chin a bit blankly. He approached the monster, and leaning over one forepaw, he read for himself in that black ledger the paragraph of the Sphinx.

Then Gerald said, " But what comes next? "

" Were I to answer that question you would be wiser than I. And of course nobody can ever be wiser than the Sphinx."

" But is that as far as you have yet written? "

" It is as far as anybody has written," said the Sphinx, " as yet."

" In all these centuries you have not got beyond that one paragraph? "

" Now, do you not see my difficulty? I needed an opening paragraph which would sum up all things, so to speak, and all the human living which men keep pestering me to explain. And when I had written it there was not anything left over to put in the second paragraph."

" But, oh, dear me! This is materialism! this is flat sacrilege committed in the actual presence of a god! I am embarrassed, ma'am. I hardly know which way to look before the spectacle of such conduct. For you fill your page, with your ambiguous para-graph — "

" Do you not be vexed unduly if you can find no meaning in this paragraph — "

" — Which has not anything to do with my exalted duties in this world — "

" This paragraph was placed here simply because there happened to be a vacancy which needed filling — "

" But I am not a paragraph, ma'am! I am no less a person, I may tell you in confidence, than Fair-haired Hoo, the Helper and Preserver, the Lord of the Third Truth, the Well-beloved of Heavenly Ones, upon a journey, — quite incognito, and therefore unattended by my customary retinue, — toward my appointed kingdom. And I confess that to my divine mind your writing has not any valid significance — "

" The foolish, therefore, will find in it foolishness, and will say ' Bother! ' — "

" — It conveys no valuable lesson — "

" The wise, as wisdom goes, will reflect that this paragraph was placed here without its consent being asked; that no wit nor large significance was loaned it by its creator; and that it will be forgotten with the turning of the one page wherein it figures unimportantly — "

" Quite honestly, ma'am, I am not a paragraph! No, I assure you that I really am the Lord of the Third Truth, upon my way to rule over Antan. I am the predestined conqueror who will force that irreligious Master Philologist to refrain from any further evil-doing, and to turn over a new leaf — "

" Do you turn the page forthwith, in just the carefree fashion of old nodding Time as he skims over the long book of life — "

" Yes, yes! " said Gerald, smiling, " I was thinking you could bring in that bit, neatly enough, if I gave you the simile to start on. And I know, of course, how all you authoresses love to quote your own works. So now, ma'am, if I were to remark, in a half puzzled way, that I hardly know what to say about your irrational paragraph — "

" Do you say either ' Bother! ' or ' Brother! ' as your wits prompt."

" Quite so! And that finishes it. You have now had the privilege of quoting in the course of one conversation your complete collected works, from cover to cover: and that ought to leave any authoress in a fairly amiable frame of mind. My complaint, then, ma'am, is that you have exhausted my time rather than your subject. There should be by all means a second paragraph. You see, dear lady, — and I am speaking now from the professional knowledge of a god, — it is the gist of every religion that — still to pursue your bibliomaniacal metaphor, — one has but to turn over that page in order to begin upon the most splendid of romances."

" What kind of romance can any dead man be getting pleasure out of in his dark grave? " the Sphinx asked, in frank surprise.

" Well, I must not speak over-hastily. I cannot supply offhand your second paragraph until I have learned what the Dirghic religion states to be the nature of this second paragraph. . . . For, you conceive, ma'am, in the opinion of many wise and virtuous persons that paragraph deals with a voyaging in the great sun boat, to a hidden land very far down in the west, after the heart of each passenger has been weighed against a feather, and forty-two judges have passed favorably upon his claims to free transportation. But dissenters, just as wise and virtuous,

[153]

and just as numerous, declare the subject of that paragraph to be a pleasure garden in which properly behaved persons will recline in continuous tipsiness upon golden couches covered with green cushions, cosily shaded by lotus- and banana-trees, and will have no other occupation than perpetually to remove the virginity of large-eyed celestial ladies. Yet, other sages declare that paragraph to deal with the crossing of a bridge — in which transit a peculiarly obliging dog will serve as the guide, — into the presence of the bright Amshaspands. Whereas, still other estimable people contend that your second paragraph should treat of a four-square city builded of gold and jasper, upon a twelve-fold foundation of various precious stones, and irrigated by its own private crystal sea. . . . For, I repeat, ma'am, the best-thought-of religions vary quite noticeably as to the nature of this second paragraph: and it would be wholly a sad thing if by speaking over-hastily I were to run counter to my own mythology. But, in any case, I have no sympathy whatever with the mental morbidity of such materialism as would deny the existence of any kind of second paragraph."

Then Gerald frowned, and he rode on.

GERALD now passed beyond Turoine, and, crossing Mispec Moor, he came thus to the tumbled-down hut of a decrepit old woman. "And how are you called, ma'am?"

"What is that to you?" she answered, peevishly.

And this wrinkled creature seemed to Gerald remarkably red and inflamed and regrettably hideous among her tousled tresses. About her head was wrapped a dirty white towel.

"Well, ma'am," replied Gerald, pleasantly, "a name is a word: and words are my peculiar concern."

"If it matters to you, young Carrot-top, I have had many names. And under one name or another I was used to deal with every man. Now my powers fall into decay, and one month is like another month, with never any changing in it. All about me is bleached, dearie, all is colorless. There is no more employment for me: and I am an old worthless flabby white-haired creature, still palely quivering with desire for the good ever-busy days — oh, and for the nights too, dearie, — that are overpast. Eh, dearie, though you would not ever think it, once I was Æsred, a mother of the Little Gods and of much else. And I fared handsomely then, taking liveliness and color out of all things, and turning men into useful domestic animals. But now the world is old, and I

[155]

am the world's twin: and all vigorousness has gone from me, and one month is like another month, with never any changing in it."

" I am a god who brings with him all vigor and all youth," said Gerald: for he remembered what the Sphinx had said about not despising ugliness.

Gerald spoke the appointed words: and he baptized the old whining trot after the rite of the Lady of the First Water-Gap. He straightway saw the dingy towel about her shaking head transformed. This towel had now become a crown composed, a bit surprisingly, of the four suits from a pack of playing cards. There were four clubs set upright, like the strawberry leaves in a duke's coronet, and alternated with four spades: and the band of this crown was moulded in bas-relief with eight hearts and with sixteen diamonds.

In fact, everything near Gerald was changed. To Gerald's right hand and to his left were seen neat fields of green things growing pleasantly, and the tumbled-down hovel was now a spruce new cottage. But what seemed even more interesting to Gerald was the circumstance that the wrinkled angry looking old woman had become a quite personable creature, not young and callow, but in the very prime of life: and the name of Æsred now, as she told him, and as he noted at least two other reasons for believing, was Maya of the Fair Breasts.

But she said also, forthwith: " Now that I am young, and have not any chaperon in the house, it would look better for you to be getting on with your journey, because you know how people talk. Yes, and how quick they are to be talking about all widow women anyhow — "

[156]

TRANSFORMATION OF A TOWEL

"Oh! oh!" said Gerald: "are you not, then, prepared to trust me?"

"— With or without," continued Maya, "the least provocation. As for trusting you or any other young fellow living, I never heard before of such nonsense. It is only the elderly men that any woman can depend on, just as far as she can see them, in broad daylight, a good while after they can be depended on at night."

"You are not even ready to give me all?"

Maya was reasonable. "I will give you your dinner, and on top of that your hat. For I can have no vagabond god hanging around my neat cottage when I am trying to get the dishes washed, and have the name of a widow to keep respectable."

"Here," Gerald stated, with conviction, "is an unusual woman. I search the pages of history in vain to find any parallel to the strange behavior of this woman."

And Gerald reflected. Very certainly this Maya of the Fair Breasts did not excel all the other women his gaze had ever beheld. Yet the colors of her two eyes were nicely matched, and a fairish nose stood about equidistant between them. Beneath this was a tolerably good mouth, for all that the lips were sullen: and the indefinitely brownish hair, which was queerly arranged in nineteen formal braids, no doubt concealed a pair of well-enough ears. This rather heavy-visaged woman was reasonably young, she seemed hardly more than thirty-seven or thereabouts: she exhibited no deformity anywhere: her figure was acceptably preserved, her breasts were positively alluring. . . . In fine, the appraising glance of the young man could with the kindly eyes of twenty-eight perceive in this Maya no really grave fault.

Moreover, she reminded him of no woman that he had ever seen anywhere before this morning.

So Gerald said: " I am satisfied. I shall stay for dinner. I shall thankfully accept all the refreshments you proffer, of every kind."

Then Maya answered: " But, indeed, you sauce-box, you quite misunderstand me. So do you keep your proper distance! For I am not the sort of woman that you seem only too well acquainted with."

Gerald said, with a caressing thrill in his voice, " Yet, do you but answer me this very simple question — "

Maya replied, " Oh, get away with you! "

Thus speaking, she boxed the jaws of the predestined ruler over all the gods of men; and with a few well-chosen words she placed their relationship upon a more decorous basis.

PART SEVEN

THE BOOK OF POETS

" He *Goes Farthest That Knows Not Where He is Going.*"

GERALD, after they had dined, persuaded
Maya of the Fair Breasts to permit him to
rest over for supper also, now that his journeying was virtually complete. For beyond the home
of the wise woman upon Mispec Moor the way lay
unimpeded to the ambiguous lowlands of Antan,
where Queen Freydis and her consort the Master
Philologist ruled in, it was said, a very old, red-
pillared palace which had once belonged to still another queen, named Suskind.

But, as to this Antan, Gerald could not, even now,
learn anything quite definite, because of all the gods
and myths who had passed down into Antan none
ever returned. It thus stayed, as yet, regrettably dubious whether these glorious beings now all lived
together in unimaginable splendor, as Gerald had
gathered at Caer Omn; or whether, as ran the
gloomier report which prevailed in Lytreia, they had
each been destroyed by the Master Philologist.

In any case, from Mispec Moor you clearly saw
Antan. Thus, there remained for Gerald hardly more
than an hour's ride, and perhaps a morning's spirited
work, in order to complete his predestined conquest
of his appointed kingdom. Gerald therefore rested
until to-morrow, with this not over-hospitable host-
ess, — who viewed him with such uncalled-for suspicion that (as he found toward midnight) the

woman had actually bolted the door to her room, out of a foolish notion that he might be trying to enter this immovable door, from which he was, instead, with entire dignity tiptoeing away. He rested so as to be in his very best fettle when he approached, to-morrow, the climax of his superb achievements.

Meanwhile he questioned Maya of the Fair Breasts as to his future kingdom; and she told him it was a poorly thought-of place. Nobody ever went there, Maya said, except such trash as poets and threadbare myths and over-inquisitive persons and such celestial riffraff as had lost their station in human esteem and their priests and their temples, said Maya, nodding her head rather gravely. That curious crown of hers sparkled cheerily with every movement of her head, for she sat at the window in a patch of sunlight, about her darning. And as to what became of such worthless people, Maya continued, after they reached Antan, that, certainly, was a question of no importance —

" Yes, but what is the general opinion hereabouts, among the sorcerers and enchanters of Turoine? "

" Our opinion is that the matter is not worth bothering about."

" Yes, but what do you think — ? "

Maya looked up from her darning, in mild but candid surprise. " You really do ask the silliest questions! For one, I do not think at all about those out-cast tramps and vagabonds except to see that they steal nothing as they go by."

So then Gerald questioned her about Freydis.

" I have heard of the woman," said Maya, rather absent-mindedly, as she went on with the darning upon which stayed fixed her actual attention, — " of

[162]

course: but nothing to her credit. They report, for example, that she has a mirror — "

" I, too, have heard continually of that mirror, but never of exactly what she does with it."

" For that matter, Gerald, I also have a mirror, if that is all which is needed. Everybody has a mirror. In fact, I have a number of mirrors."

" I know. I have noticed them everywhere about the cottage. But all your mirrors, dear lady, are rose-colored."

— To which Maya replied irrelevantly, and without looking up from her darning: " But did you not know from the first that I was a wise woman? In any case, it is said that Queen Freydis holds her mirror up to nature, and that she does not scruple to hold this mirror up to her disreputable visitors, too. For they really are, you know. It is all very well being a god while it lasts. Only, it never does. And then where are you? Why, exactly! That is why the overlords of Turoine have always seemed to me more business-like. And there is no flaw in it, people say," — now, though, as Gerald deduced, Maya was talking about the Mirror of the Hidden Children, — " no distortion of any kind, no flattering in it, and no kindly exaggeration. It is not in anything like my more sensible rose-colored mirrors. And nobody could of course be expected to approve of such a mirror."

" Nevertheless, if there indeed be any such mirror, I mean to face it, when to-morrow I enter into my kingdom, and liberate the great words of the Master Philologist, and restore the Dirghic mythology, for in that mythology, I must tell you, I am a god with four aspects."

" What nonsense you do talk! " said Maya, comfortably, as she slipped the darning-egg into another stocking.

Then Gerald confided in her. Then Gerald told Maya how he, howsoever unmeritorious, was heir to all the unimaginable wonders which harbored yonder. He told her that he and none other was Fairhaired Hoo, the Helper and Preserver, the Lord of the Third Truth, the Well-beloved of Heavenly Ones. He told her of everything that had happened in his triumphant expedition, thus far. He told her of somewhat more than had happened, for under Gerald's expansive handling of the rather beautiful idea of his own invincibility the tale became an epic. And Gerald told her, too, of how he intended to rule in the goal of all the gods. He briefly indicated his summer and winter palaces, the probable personnel of his harem, the deities who would serve in his immediate household, and, in a general way, the worlds which he would create: and he promised to remember Maya, liberally, after he had come into his kingdom.

And Maya all this while went on darning placidly. She admitted that men —

" But, as I was telling you, I am a god, — a god with no less than four aspects."

This did not really matter, Maya considered. The gods, as near as she had been able to judge those scatter-brained ne'er-do-wells that went tramping by, were just the same, and, if anything, more so. It was simply incredible, she continued, how little wear there was in a stocking nowadays. She then admitted that male persons did have these notions, even about such unlikely places as Antan. And Gerald would,

in any event, be finding out for himself all about
Antan to-morrow, because if he for one solitary instant thought she was going to have him hanging
about her cottage forever — !

"Come now, my dear, but hospitality is a very
famous virtue: and, besides, you owe it to me that you
are now the handsomest woman in these parts."

"But that, Gerald, — even if it were the truth,
of course, for you need not think you are fooling me,
you scamp, — that is just why people will be imagining things if you continue to stay here."

"Then let us take good care not to be suspected
unjustly, because that would be unfair to everybody — "

"Oh, get along with you! and do you pick up
every one of those stockings, too, now you have scattered them all over the floor. And really, you red-
headed pest, I am not joking, either. That horse
of yours — "

"Ah, yes, that horse of mine! I admit that to the
discerning eyes of a woman it is not the handsomest
beast in the world. And I suppose you are about to
point out that this horse is unworthy of me, and that
I ought to dispose of it, in one way or another — "

"But whatever nonsense are you talking, now!
It is an extremely handsome horse. There is some
sort of prophecy about it, too, is there not? So you
would be even more foolish than you seem to be, to
part with that horse."

"Well, to be sure, there may be something in what
you say."

" — And what I was attempting to tell you is that,
if you will simply permit me to talk for one minute
without interrupting — "

" Hereafter I remain as quiet, my dear, as a belch in polite society; and you may go on."

" Why, then, I was trying to say that your horse can get you to Antan within an hour. You can find out for yourself all about the place. And I daresay this Queen Freydis, from all I have heard of her, will not have the least objection to your rude way of grabbing and pawing at people and interfering with my housework and generally misconducting yourself. It is the sort of thing she is quite used to. But I do not like it: I feel you would not do it if you really respected me. And I am sorry if anything I have said or done has given you any such wrong notions about me. And if you stuck yourself with that needle it was simply your own fault. And that is all there is to it."

Gerald replied: " You are regrettably lacking, my dear, in the confidence and the generosity peculiar to your sex. It is impossible for the mind to conceive of anything more dreadful than your conduct. Nevertheless, I must stay until Wednesday, for otherwise I cannot possibly judge of your magics."

" Oh, very well, then! " Maya answered, with unconcealed regretfulness over the fact that she would have to put up with Gerald for yet another day.

xxv. The God Conforms

F OR Gerald, upon reflection, had decided it
would be really amusing to remain upon Mispec Moor until Wednesday, since only upon
Wednesday could Maya show the perfection of her
thaumaturgy. Thursday, though, as the wise woman
forewarned him candidly, was her cleaning day; and
she simply could not be bothering over company with
the house all topsy-turvy.

"And I also warn you well in advance, my darling," said Gerald, "that the performance musṭ be
gratis, since I have no material possessions, save possibly my riding-horse, to barter for the privilege of
witnessing your parlor magic."

"Why, but what in the world would I be needing
with another horse, who already have dozens of them
eating their heads off all over the moor? and when in
the world, you pest, I became 'your darling' I would
really like to know!"

"Now, but have you, indeed? The very first moment I saw you, my dear."

"I do wish you would sometimes, just for a
change, talk half rationally. And of course it has
always been my custom to further the true happiness
of the men with whom I was particularly intimate by
turning them into domestic animals of one kind or another. Quite a number of them came out horses —"

[167]

" I do not altogether approve of such a custom. Still, women have incalculable fancies: and all men find out sooner or later that it is less trouble to indulge these fancies than to thwart them. At any rate, a god has no concern with these minor sorceries."

" Of course not! " Maya agreed. " A scatter-brained, talk-you-to-death, carrot-topped, and generally good-for-nothing god is not concerned with anything except with getting on to that minx Freydis."

Gerald waved aside the insinuation. He continued to talk about more immediate matters, and he said:

" Nevertheless, your story interests me. It would be droll to have a horse like that. So suppose, now, my dear, suppose I trade my divine steed for one of those unusual horses of yours? "

" No, Gerald, really I would rather not. For the men that I put my magic upon used once to be fine knights or barons or even kings, — and, for that matter, there were a couple of emperors, though only in a small way, — and I confess to a certain sentiment about them still."

Then in a clay chafing-dish Maya of the Fair Breasts burned fig-leaves with benzoin and macis and storax. And she showed Gerald how one might master mercurial things. She displayed to him the small magics which are Wednesday's. She revealed to him — cursorily, since they had only a morning at their disposal, — the secrets of remunerative mediocrity in the learned professions, in truth-telling, in upholstering, in the removal of mountains into the sea, in the erection of bridges over any unpassable place, in the preparation of rose-colored mirrors, in criticism, in oratory, in jurisprudence, and in the safe interpretation of Holy Writ. As himself a former

[168]

student of magic, Gerald found these formulæ of interest: but, as a god, he regarded Maya with profound respect, as one who, with no native divine advantages, had yet mastered this quite reputable stock of knowledge and ability.

Yet the workings of these magics were not apparent until Gerald had put on the spectacles which Maya gave him. He found these glasses so soothing to the eyes that he retained them, just for the remainder of his visit to her cottage.

For, after all, Gerald decided to stay over the week-end, since Maya was so unflatteringly eager to be rid of him. It was an eagerness troubling to his self-respect. Here was he, a god whom women had always run after, and had pestered beyond reasonable endurance, here was he, of all persons, being treated with unconcealed indifference by a mere hedge-sorceress, by a creature who had not even any remarkable good looks or wit to justify her impudence. This Maya of the Fair Breasts needed taking down quite a large number of pegs. So Gerald fell to wooing her with an ardor that somewhat surprised him. For it was eminently necessary, it was, indeed, a rather beautiful idea, to win the woman, and then to jilt her, so as to teach her, once for all, not ever again to make free and easy with the will of a god.

Meanwhile, Maya had suggested that he conceal the fact he was a god; and that she should introduce him to the local gentry of Turoine as a visiting sorcerer.

"For I must tell you, Gerald," Maya said, "all the best-thought-of people hereabouts are in one or another branch of sorcery. We have, thus, never had

[169]

any relations with Heaven. All our connections have been with another quarter. And it is not that we are unduly conceited and exclusive, it is simply that it has just happened so. Nevertheless, so many gods have straggled by, on their way to an ambiguous end, as they went down to encounter the Master Philologist, and whatever it is that he does to them, that there is a tendency among the best people hereabouts, as I will not conceal from you, to regard them as not quite the sort that one meets socially."

" But I — " said Gerald, in uncontrolled indignation.

" I know, my poor boy, you are entirely different. And I am perfectly broad-minded about it, myself. But other people are not. And it would sound much better."

Then Gerald spoke with dignity and firmness. Gerald said that not for one moment would he stoop to such a subterfuge. Not for an instant would he who was a lord of all exalted white magics pretend to be a sorcerer soiled with infernal traffics and patronized by mere devils. After that, Gerald passed as a visiting sorcerer.

AND Gerald used to amuse himself by talking with the travelers who passed by the
neat log and plaster cottage of Maya the
wise woman, upon their way to the court of Queen
Freydis and her consort the Master Philologist. For
it was a good and shrewd policy, Gerald felt, for a
monarch to familiarize himself with his future subjects: so he would sit by the wayside, in the shade of
a conveniently placed chestnut-tree, — incognito, as
it were, — and would artfully allure them into conversation.

" Hail, friends! And what business draws you to
the city of all marvels? " said Gerald, on the first
morning that he fell into this long-sighted course.

He was told — by the big-bellied, yellow-haired
man, whose skin was so curiously spotted, — that
they were two poets upon their way to Antan, the
goal of all the gods, and the friendly haven of true
poets, where poets might hope to find at last that
loveliness which they desired and could nowhere discover in their everyday life upon earth. To Gerald
this was excellent news, since it increased the number
of his future subjects very gratifyingly.

But he said nothing, while the big-bellied, spotted,
thin-legged gentleman, in the purple robe adorned
with golden stars, went on in his answer to Gerald's
first question, by explaining that the speaker was

Nero Claudius Cæsar, the king of all poets, and that his scrawny companion, in a brown doublet of which both elbows needed patching, was an artist of considerable talent from out of the Gallic provinces, who was called François Villon.

Gerald found this also of some interest, in view of what he remembered about the Mirror of Caer Omn. Not often did you thus come face to face with two discarded personalities. But Gerald said nothing about this either. Instead, he questioned Nero yet further, and he thus learned that these two poets were on their way to the court of Freydis, because there alone in the universe was art properly regarded: for there, indeed, true artists were manufactured out of common clay, and were informed with the fire of Audela.

It was one or another old hero from out of Poictesme, Nero had heard, who had first modeled these earthen images; and Freydis, as occasion served, gave life to these images and set them to live upon earth, as changelings. But, above all, said Nero, in Antan the true poets of this world fared happily among the myths and the gods who once had afforded to these poets such fine themes, so that to-day of course these poets wrote even more splendid poems now that they composed with the eye upon the object.

Yet, Nero thought, playing idly with the emerald monocle which hung upon a green cord about his scrawny neck, this Queen would not be very likely ever to create in clay, or to find coming to her court, such another artist as Nero himself had been in the days of his Roman pre-eminence. No other person known to him had ever excelled in all the polite arts.

[172]

" QUALIS ARTIFEX! "

For in dancing and in oratory, in wrestling (even with such dreadful adversaries as lions) and in music both vocal and instrumental, — alike as a charioteer and as a tragic actor, — but, above all, as a poet, and equally as a dramatic, a lyric and an epic poet, — Nero had been unanimously awarded the first prize in every contest. He did not care to appear boastful: yet, by all canons of criticism, one had to consider the list of his overwhelming triumphs, in Rome, in Naples, in Antium, in Alba, — at the Parthian games, at the Isthmian games, at the Olympic games, — and, in fine, in each contest which Nero had ever entered anywhere in all the kingdoms of which he was Emperor. No other artist had a record to compare with that: no other of the world's great geniuses had ever been confessedly supreme in every polite form of æsthetic endeavor.

Of course, as a student of history, Nero conceded that the elect artist was not to be placed, not permanently, by his ranking in the eyes of his contemporaries, who might often be swayed by such matters, really extraneous to enduring art, as the artist's ingratiating manners and his personal beauty. As a man of the world, he even conceded the judges of the sacred games in awarding all the first prizes to Nero might furthermore have been influenced by the large sums of money which the Emperor always conferred upon his acclaiming judges after such occasions, as well as by the dexterity of the tortures which would have followed any decision less just.

But the indisputable fact, the fact of superb importance, was that Nero had made of his life a poem which was wholly a unique masterpiece in the way of self-expression. He, above all other men, had served the one end of every poet's art, by revealing the true nature of man's being; for Nero had embodied, with loving carefulness, each trait which he found in himself, through some really memorable action, — rearing, as it were, among marshes and quicksands, and in yet other places which other persons feared to visit, those strange and passionately colored orchid growths which alone could express the highly complex nature of every man's desires —

" That jargon becomes somewhat senescent," said Gerald. " Still, as a museum piece, — yes, even now, sophistication does display something of the quaint beauty of thorough obsoleteness. It has acquired the charm, and, as it were, the patina, of sedan chairs and of full-bottomed wigs and of girdles of chastity and of suits of armor, and of all other things, once useful enough, which are nowadays endeared to every poet's heart by the fact that they are forever outmoded. So let us grant it, O Cæsar, in the days that are gone you were a devil of a fellow and a sad rip among the ladies — "

" Why, but, for that matter — " Nero began.

" I know. You broad-mindedly despised neither sex. You were in amour a Greek scholar. You were something of a surgeon also. I concede it, I blush, and I urge you to omit all embarrassingly personal details."

So Nero went on, saying that other emperors, with very much his chances, had lacked the genius necessary to develop these chances. There had, of course, been minor artists. Caligula, for example, among so much hackwork in the way of throat-cutting, had shown at least one jet of rather lovely inspiration when he attempted a criminal assault upon the moon; that was a really finely imagined bit of work. Then, also, Domitian and Commodus and Tiberius had displayed praiseworthy ambitions; quite neat little things had been done by Tiberius, in an amateur way, at Capri; Caracalla too had been so-so: but they had all tended to wallow unimaginatively in cut and dried executions; merely to chop off anybody's head was not art, no matter how often you did it. Besides, work done upon a public scaffold inevitably coarsened one's touch. And Heliogabalus, whatsoever the lad's thin vein of undeniable talent in the way of lyric lechery, had lacked the stamina and gusto for any sustained masterpiece in Nero's copious epic style.

For Nero alone had been, in every branch of self-expression, the sincere, skilled artist, enriching his handiwork always with that continual slight novelty which art demands. He had builded his appropriate stage, in the Golden House —

" A house entirely overlaid with gold," said Gerald, reminiscently, " and adorned everywhere with jewels and mother of pearl, a house so rich and ample that it had three-storied porticos a mile long, and huge revolving banqueting halls, and ivory ceilings which perpetually scattered perfumes and red rose-petals — "

Nero, at that, had out his emerald monocle; and through it he now regarded Gerald with the childlike amiability of a sincere artist whensoever his vanity is flattered.

Yes, Nero admitted, he had endeavored to express himself in that house also. The Golden House had been (to play with metaphor) the handsome binding of that poem which was his life, when, in a setting such as the world had never known before or since, he had given to his every human trait its full color value. In the Golden House he had reared his orchids, he had labored to open many frank and incisive and utterly unstinted avenues of self-expression to that somewhat complex thing called human nature. . . .

But here he entered rather explicitly into details. Gerald felt the style of this emperor to be growing woefully un-American; and Gerald fidgeted.

" Let us, I again urge you," said Gerald, " speak of less personal matters, and diversify the vividness of these orchids with a few fig-leaves! "

Perhaps, of course, the Emperor continued, he, like every other really great artist, had been somewhat the anthologist, in that he had invented outright none of the art forms among the many in which he had distinguished himself. He had taken over from his predecessors a number of inspirations and a formula or two, as he would be the very last to deny: but the fine craftsmanship was all his, as well as that distinguishing, that peculiarly Neronic, touch of romantic irony, by virtue of which this artist had slain with suavity, had destroyed with a caress, and had ennobled all that was most dear to his human nature by killing it. He spoke now of the deaths of his wives, of Octavia and Poppæa, and of others who had been his wives just for the evening; he spoke of Sporus, of Aiëtes, of Narcissus, and of that other exceedingly beautiful boy, Aulus Plautinus. . . .

And again Gerald raised a protesting hand. " Let us still," said Gerald, " avoid these quite un-

" QUALIS ARTIFEX! "

American personalities! Meanwhile, you do not
speak of your mother Agrippina."

He surprised in the spotted face of Nero something very like terror. But Nero said only, " No."

And besides, the Emperor continued, with rising
animation, that happy chronological accident, the
fact that in the days of Nero Christianity began its
advance toward world supremacy, had enabled him,
by pure luck, to lend to the great poem of his life
just the needful felicitous touch of working in a new
medium. To burn well-thought-of taxpayers and
putative virgins as the torches at your supper parties
was a device which, out of a natural desire to surprise
and to amuse one's guests, might have occurred to
almost any host in quest of that continual slight
novelty which the art of hospitality also demands.
But that these flambeaux should later become the
brightest glories of a triumphant church had made
these supper parties, which were really quite modest
affairs, unforgettable. Nero had expressed himself
— not merely, as he thought at the time, through
persons supposed to be deficient in patriotism and
more or less suspected of being (here again, to play
with metaphor) not one hundred per cent Roman, —
but, as it had turned out, through saints and apostles,
and through consecrated religious martyrs, such as
not every artist could get for his themes and raw
material. So, the succeeding discouragements of
Christians had, æsthetically, fallen flat, in their im-
pression upon posterity: their authors had come into
this field too late, to find that tragic vein worked out,
and all its most striking possibilities exhausted, by the
great artist that was Nero. It was hardly remembered that Marcus Aurelius and Diocletian and many

[177]

others had broken and flayed and mutilated and burned to the very best of their ability: these plodders were but the epigoni and the unimaginative plagiarists of Nero.

So had it come about that of all the emperors Rome had known, and of all the tyrants and despots in every land and era, who had followed the fine art of self-expression, and who had shown what human nature really is — in, as it were, the nude, when any man is released from time-serving and is made omnipotent, — of all these, there had remained just one whose name was remembered everywhere; just one whose fame was imperishable; just one who had become a never-dying myth: and that one was Nero. The legend of Nero was, in a world wherein every other man stayed more or less unwillingly an unfulfilled Nero, the supreme type of the literature of escape. The legend of Nero was a poem which men would not ever forget: it was a poem familiar in all languages: and it was a poem which, now, everybody could cordially admire and delight in, because time had removed the need of considering any current moral standards or one's own physical safety in judging this poem, now that Nero was only a character in a book, like — as the Emperor said, with a quaint revealment of his retained interest in literature, — like Iago or Volpone or Tartuffe. For whether you called any particular book a history or a poem or a drama did not, of course, affect the inpressiveness and vigor and complexity of the character drawing in it, nor the value of the author's apt and edifying revelations as to any eternal verities of man's being.

" For, certainly," said Nero, " my life presented, as

no other artist has ever done, the gist of all human nature as that nature actually is, when freed of such inhibitions as constrain it in but too many baffled lives. My life was, thus, a connoisseur's production, and a work of art which escaped even the grave risk of anti-climax. For there was not anything lacking in the ending of it, either. My fall and the circumstances of my death were so æsthetically right that, as an artist, I never in my life enjoyed anything quite so much. Nothing could conceivably have been in better taste. For, overnight, as you may remember, I passed from the throne of the world, to hide in a tumble-down out-house, under a ragged, very faded blue coverlet, and to perish thus by my own hand, — with an appropriate tragic verse upon my lips, — and without any friend remaining anywhere. No tragedy could have been more boldly proportioned, with all the Aristotelian unities so exactly preserved. And it was most gratifyingly led up to, too. For just as I was about to approach the dénouement of my poem, the statues of my Lares toppled down miraculously, the hind quarters of my favorite riding-horse were transformed into the hind quarters of an ape, and the doors of the mausoleum of Augustus having unclosed of their own accord, there issued from the tomb a divine voice which summoned me to destruction. These incidents, I repeat, were gratifying, for they showed that the exercise of my art had been viewed by Heaven appreciatively. Ah, yes, in all I was peculiarly favored."

VILLON spat meditatively between his yellow front teeth. He fingered, in the while that he continued his reflections, his scarred and puckered lower lip. Then he confessed that he dissented from a great many of his predecessor's remarks.

• " You were impressive. Your life was a competent job, boldly executed, and nobody denies its merits on their own melodramatic plane. Yet it lacked the indispensable touch of tenderness, without which no work of art is of the first class. No: it was I who was truly favored; and I made of my life a flawless poem without dragging in such gaudy accessories as thrones and burning cities and the wasting of a lovely, mother-naked virgin on a mere lion."

And this François Villon went on to speak of the great blessings which had been accorded him. He had been granted irresolution, and lewdness, and poverty, and cowardice, and a large weakness for drink, and an ingrained dishonesty, and a disease-wrecked body, and everything else which was needed to make him a knave as contemptible as any man could hope to be.

" I was, in brief, gentlemen, as I have elsewhere remarked, a hog with a voice. And there was no voice like my voice."

[180]

For out of the mire that wallowing, lustful and cowardly beast had sung. Now he sang jeeringly, and made fun of the whole world with satire and mockery and invective, and with plain filth-flinging, — which was all quite good art, because it pleases people to see a man superior to his fate. Now he sang piercingly of the great platitude that death conquers and ruins everything: and to that sentiment nobody can ever turn a deaf ear, because it is the only sentiment with a universal personal application. But, above all, he sang of his regret for his past indiscretions, and of his yearning for spiritual cleanliness, and — " soaring," as Villon now quoted, with admirable complacency, " to the very gates of Heaven upon the star-sown wings of faith and song," — he had proclaimed his trust in that divine love which, ultimately, would redeem all properly repentant persons from the logical outcome of their doings in this world, and would give to the marred life of every properly repentant person a happy ending in a fair-colored paradise agreeably full of harps and lutes. And people liked that, too, of course, because such a philosophy made everybody feel muggily consoled and, for no especial reason, magnanimous.

So had Villon become a very great poet whose art was a fine blending of mirth and of pathos and of faith, and so might he hope to win to high honors in Antan, where, if anywhere, poets were properly rewarded. And the squalor and degradation of his terrestrial living were, now, but so many picturesque ingredients in the superb poem of his life, now that Villon too was — just as his Roman confrère had pointed out, — to be regarded as a character in a book. The difference was that Villon had become a

never-dying myth of vagabondage with its heart in
the right place, and a parable which revealed how
much of good always survived in the most vile and
abandoned of criminals and even in persons unsuc-
cessful in business life. The legend of Villon thus
proved exactly the contrary to that which was proved
by the legend of Nero: as the one demonstrated the
real nature of man to aspire only to lust and cruelty
the moment that inhibitions were removed, so did
the other legend show the real fundamental nature
of every man to be incurably good and lovable under
all possible surface stains. And the legend of Villon,
Villon repeated, had in it tenderness, — that indispensable flavor of tenderness and of a sentimentality
as wholesomely nourishing as molasses, without
which no work of art can ever really be of the first
class so far as goes its popular appeal.

" For my life, gentlemen, was truly a superb parable. And it has been properly appreciated, it has
even been paid the fine compliment of being plagiarized by Holy Writ. Why, what the devil! if the parable of the Prodigal Son be good art in the New
Testament, is it the less good art for being acted out
with the vigor and the brio I brought to that task?
For I too wasted all my substance, with some feminine assistance, and went down among the swine and
the husks, without ever forgetting that by and by I
was to be comforted with never-failing love and
veal cutlets. In brief, although I lived perforce in
the gutter, yet my eyes were upon the stars."

Then Gerald remarked, to this one of his discarded
personalities: " You move me, Messire François.
You sound upon my heart-strings a resounding chord,
through your employment of a figure of speech which

is always effective. I do not know why, but any imaginable observations conveying a statement manifestly untrue can be made edifying and sublime through ending with the word ' stars '. We poets have convinced everybody, including ourselves, that there is some occult virtue in the act of looking at the stars. So, when you said just now, ' Although I lived perforce in the gutter, yet my eyes were upon the stars,' I was moved very mightily. I seemed to hear the yearning cry of all human aspirations, foiled but superb. Yet, if you had asserted your eyes to have been habitually, or at least every clear night, upon the planets — or, for that matter, upon the comets or the asteroids, — I would not have been moved in the least."

" It is sufficient that you were moved without knowing why," observed Nero. " That is the magic of poetry. Very often when I recited some of my best poems, to commemorate the sorrows of Orestes or Canace or Œdipus, I myself could not quite understand the springs of that terrible misery which convulsed my hearers. They wept; they fainted; a number of the women entered prematurely into the labors of childbirth; and I was compelled to have the doors and windows guarded by my Praetorian soldiers because so many of the audience invariably attempted to escape from the well-nigh intolerable ecstasies which my art provoked. Such is the magic of great poetry, a thing not ever wholly to be explained even by the poet."

Then Gerald said: " Yet, you two poets who have traveled through the Marches of Antan, wherein only two truths endure, and the one teaching is that we copulate and die, — do you not look to find when you have reached Antan, which is the goal of all the gods, some third truth? "

It seemed to him that the faces of the two myths had now become evasive and more wary.

Nero replied, " For a poet, there exist always just as many truths as he cares to imagine."

And Villon remarked: " I would phrase it somewhat differently. I would say there exist more truths than any poet cares to imagine. But it comes to the same thing."

" Yes," Gerald assented, — " for it comes to an evasion. Yet I, who also am a poet, I retain my faith in the rather beautiful idea of that third truth."

And then Gerald told them that he himself had long dabbled in the art of poetry. " Indeed," he added, generously, " I will now recite to you one of my sonnets which appears appropriate to the occasion."

" Dog," Villon replied, taking up his hat, " does not eat dog."

And Nero very hastily stated that, howsoever unbounded their regret, they really must be hurrying on to the city of marvels.

So these myths departed, traveling together, with an intimacy somewhat remarkable in the light of their flatly diverse teachings. And Gerald warned them to make the most of the present state of affairs in Antan, because the day after to-morrow the Lord of the Third Truth, a deity with several not uninteresting aspects, would be descending upon Antan, to take over all the powers of the Master Philologist, and to deal with Queen Freydis afterward as his divine inclinations might prompt.

Thereafter Gerald went back to Maya and to his

dinner quite jauntily, now that he knew in his appointed kingdom the true poets of this world were assembling to purvey his amusement: and he felt himself to be afire with impatience to reach that city of all marvels, yonder behind him, as he walked away from Antan, leisurely ascending to the trim cottage of Maya the wise woman, who went as a crowned queen, and would have none of his love-making, and yet was such an excellent cook, in her plain way.

PART EIGHT

THE BOOK OF MAGES

"Not *Every Good Scholar
is a Good Schoolmaster.*"

XXVIII. Fond Magics of Maya

GERALD delayed his departure until Friday,
because Gerald was cordially amused by the
fond magics of Maya of the Fair Breasts.
He regarded them, as he did her, through those
roseate spectacles which the wise woman had loaned
him to be an unfailing comfort to his eyes: and he
found all very good.

He had known many lovelier and more brilliant
women, alike in the relinquished world of Lichfield
and in his journeying through the Marches of Antan.
But Maya contented him: he had really not the heart
to disappoint his Maya by not forcing upon her —
after four prolonged and tender arguments, — those
physical attentions which all women seemed to expect.

After that, she put aside her crown; and Gerald
never saw it any more.

After that, also, the date of his departure from
her neat cottage was postponed until after Sunday,
though it was quite understood that, the very first
thing after a particularly early breakfast on Monday,
he would pass on to enter into his appointed kingdom,
and to possess himself of the Master Philologist's
great words, and to reanimate the Dirghic mythology
in which he was a god, and would come to know the
third truth over which he exercised celestial authority.

Meanwhile he stayed upon Mispec Moor, to regard with indulgence, and even with some pity, his predecessors in Maya's affection, those beguiled men whom she had converted into domestic animals. His divine steed was for the while turned out to graze with those docile geldings that had once been knights and barons and reigning kings: all wandered contentedly enough about the neat cottage, along with a number of steers and sheep and three mules, who, also, had once been noblemen and well-thought-of monarchs.

Gerald saw that these animals seemed not dissatisfied with their transfiguring doom. Yet it appeared a bit wanton — even to him, who had once been a tortoise and a lion and a fish and a boar-pig, — that these gentlemen should have been snatched from positions of responsibility and worldly honor, from thrones and tournaments and large bank accounts, and set to eating grass in a field. And Gerald sincerely pitied them for their ignorance as to the correct way in which to deal with the small magics of Maya.

The dear woman herself you could not blame. She could not help trying, out of pure kindliness and affection, to hold men back from daring and splendid exploits, because she really thought they would be much safer, and more happy, as domestic animals.

And, in fact, she justified her charitableness with a logic which was plausible. She argued that all men were better content after they had become domestic animals. She pointed out that her lovers, in particular — Why, but Gerald could see for himself how little vexed were her steers and geldings, now, by affairs of the heart. Upon every imaginable moral ground they had been made better by their double transformation. They did not run after lewd females, they were not bloodthirstily jealous of one another, and they were asleep every night at a respectable hour. If Gerald had only known them, as she had known them, when they were gentlemen of high distinction and reigning monarchs, he would never argue about an improvement so obvious.

Besides, domestic animals were spurred by magnanimity and altruism into no devastating wars, thrift did not often make them covetous of money, neither did self-respect induce them to spend money foolishly: religion did not lead mules to bray in any pulpit, nor did the conscientiousness of a sheep ever make of him an ever-meddling and pernicious pest. In fine, the domestic animals were undisfigured by any human virtues, and were quite easy to get along with. Whereas, if any woman attempted to have that number of men about the house — ! Maya, who had lost so many husbands (at least partially) did not complete the statement. But her expression made the aposiopesis eloquent.

Gerald had no smallest doubt but that, if he himself had not been divine and beyond her arts, Maya of the Fair Breasts would long ago, out of pure kindliness and affection, have transformed him too into a sheep or an ox or some other useful quadruped, and would thus have held him back from his appointed inheritance in Antan. And he did not blame her. The placid, stupid, rather lovable woman simply did not understand that to be contented was not all: she did not comprehend the obligations which were upon a god to live with generous splendor and to perform very tremendous feats in the way of heroism and of philanthropy.

[191]

Of course, just as she said, the exploits of a champion who came to enlighten and improve any place — even to redeem it from what, by the standards of the United States of America, was iniquitous and backward and probably undemocratic, — did of necessity upset the routine to which the inhabitants had grown accustomed. Antan, as Gerald looked down upon it from the porch of Maya's cottage, seemed a contented and tranquil realm. No matter by howsoever un-American standards people might be living there, to redeem the place from those standards would bring upsetment and confusion. And it did seem almost a pity — just as Maya said, — to be bothering people who were contented enough, when you too were contented. . . . Even so, there was an obligation upon a god. To be contented, to have no cares to worry you by day, to lack for nothing by day, and every night to induce decorously through connubial affection a profound and refreshing slumber, that was not everything a god desired. Yonder there was a third truth. Yonder was Gerald's appointed kingdom, and not here upon Mispec Moor. Yonder the gods and the dreams of men attained to a noble and worthy goal. Yonder was Freydis. . . .

For Gerald had now begun to wonder more and more about Freydis. By all reports, it was she who really ruled those hills and lowlands yonder, which to-morrow — or at least, next week, — would be Gerald's hills and lowlands; and it was she who controlled in everything the Master Philologist, whom Gerald was appointed to overthrow. It had not been prophesied, however, so far as Gerald knew, how he would deal with Freydis. That, to every appearance, was a matter left to his divine election. Well, one would not be over-harsh with any woman whom rumor declared so beautiful, Gerald decided, half drowsily, as he sat there so utterly comfortable in the spectacles and the dressing-gown and the brown carpet slippers which Maya had provided, and so pleasantly replete with Maya's excellent cooking.

AND upon another day, as Gerald sat by the
roadside beneath his chestnut-tree, and
waited for supper to be ready, three persons
passed toward Antan, traveling together. They were
all notable looking men; and Gerald greeted them
with the sign which is known only to supreme mages.
They returned his greeting, but they shaped signs
that were of an older magic than any which was familiar to Gerald.

And then the first of these men said, " I was Odysseus, Laertes' son."

Gerald thus knew that before him stood yet another of his discarded personalities. But Gerald made
no comment.

And Odysseus continued: " I had wisdom. My
prudent wisdom was to men of every calling an object of considerable attention, and the fame of it
reached Heaven. I ruled in Ithaca, an island kingdom, well situated toward the west. I went unwillingly with the other well-greaved Greeks to besiege
Ilion: the enterprise to me seemed rash, and unlikely
to be remunerative: yet, being engaged, I dealt prudently, and in the end, where so many merely brave
persons had failed, it was through my prudence that
the enterprise succeeded. For ten years Ilion defied
the strength of Achilles and of Ajax; Ilion derided
all the endeavors of auburn-haired Menelaus and of

godlike Agamemnon: but the cunning of Odysseus felled Ilion in one night. I took my share of the spoils; I left the glory to them that wanted it. I returned across the world to that which I more prudently desired, toward the quiet comforts of my home in craggy Ithaca. The prayer of the blinded Cyclops, the wrath of earth-shaking Poseidon, the white thunder of offended Zeus, and the twelve winds of Æolus, all fought against me. I prevailed. The seawitch Scylla, an exorbitant lady with twelve arms, a ravening monster whom none might pass and live, I passed. Charybdis, which devoured all, did not devour me, for I clung prudently to a fig-tree."

" Indeed," said Gerald, " the leaves of that tree are very often a great protection, — O much-enduring and crafty Odysseus," Gerald added hastily, as became a Greek scholar.

" Moreover, the sun's daughter, fair-haired Circe, and bright Queen Calypso, the divine one of goddesses, these also detained me rather more amiably. I embraced them; they did not find me slothful in their beds. For they were goddesses, as quick in anger as they were in lust. It is not prudent to deny a goddess. From the fond arms of these immortals I passed on toward my desired goal. Yet nobody is always prudent. When my ship approached the island of the man-devouring Sirens I caused the ears of my sailors to be stopped with wax; but I caused myself to be bound to the mast, so that I might hear the song which Leucosia sang in the while that Parthenopê and Ligeia made a sweet music. I desired to hear without any hurt that song which was so lovely that it drew less prudent men to the arms of its singer, wherein, as they well knew, dark death

awaited them. I heard that song. It did not matter
to me that I saw how the low beach about those
music-makers gleamed, like silver, where a thin sun-
light fell upon the scattered bones of many men
whom they had slain. I struggled to cast myself into
the gray sea-water, so that I might go to Leucosia.
But my bonds held me. I was bound, both my hands
and feet were bound, with very strong cables. The
black ship passed onward, whitening the water with
its polished blades of fir-wood; and I wept as I too
passed onward, away from my own ruin, and drawing nearer to the goal which my prudent wisdom had
desired."

" Truly, the enchantment of her singing must have
maddened you. Yet such is the magic of great poetry," Gerald remarked, " a thing not ever wholly
to be explained even by the poet. . . . Yet your
goal, nevertheless, was reached, they tell me, O
much-contriving Odysseus. Your goal was reached,
as I remember it, in the many-pillared hall of your
home in Ithaca, and in a fine slaughter of those suitors
who were pestering your wife because they believed
that she was your widow."

" Very naturally my goal was reached. I was Odysseus. Very naturally I made an end of those wasters
of my substance who had been eating and drinking
for nine years at my expense. There arose, as one
by one their heads were smitten off, a hideous moan-
ing. The floors ran with blood. It was wholly plain
that Odysseus faced those imprudent persons who had
made over-free with his flocks and his wine jars and
his wife and the other goods of his household. Yet
I knew, by and by, that what I now desired was not
to be found in craggy Ithaca nor in the calm em-

[196]

braces of Penelope nor in the tranquillity of my well-ordered home. I gave laws. I heard cases. I decided squabbles between one shepherd and another shepherd. I who had contrived the burning of Ilion now oversaw the branding of my cattle. War did not trouble Ithaca, of whose king all other kings were afraid. For I was very famous. I lacked for nothing in wealth. I lived at ease. But no man hears the singing of Leucosia except at a great price. I heard Leucosia no more. I heard, instead, the voices of fools praising my strength and my prudent wisdom, and the voice of my wife talking sensibly about I never noticed exactly what. I lacked for nothing which prudent men desire, in my snug, sleek, well-ordered Ithaca. But I had seen too much in my voyaging about a world which was more lewd and riotous than I permitted anybody to be in my Ithaca. I remembered too many things. No, I did not regret Calypso nor Circe nor that fine girl Nausicaä. I could at will have returned to them. But I remembered the singing of Leucosia, to whom I dared not return. For no man hears the singing of Leucosia except at a great price."

" But of what did she sing, O much-planning Odysseus? "

" She sang of that which haunted me, and which derided the rewards of my prudent wisdom. She sang of the one way to that which I truly desired."

" That, O noble son of Laertes, is not a remarkably explicit reply."

Now the wise Greek regarded Gerald somberly. Odysseus said, by and by:

" She sang of that which troubles a prudent person's soul and despoils his rational living of all fat contentment. Let it suffice that she sang, I think, of Antan. That is why I must travel to Antan, wherein — it may be, — is my desire."

— It was only then that Gerald recollected something. He recollected that Evadne of the Dusk, that feathery-legged Evadne, who, Horvendile had said, was called Leucosia in the days of her sea-faring. But Gerald said nothing about what, after all, was none of his affair. . . .

AND then the second traveler spoke. He spoke of that which had been his in the days when all riches and all pleasures and all power had been accorded to Solomon because of his sixfold wisdom. To no other being that ever lived among mankind was given such mightiness as was granted to King Solomon in the time that he reigned over Israel and ruled this world.

For Solomon had sexanary wisdom. Solomon knew the six words which were not known to any other man. He understood the speaking of these words.

The word of the beasts. It was spoken, and there assembled in the sight of Solomon a pair of every creature that walks or creeps upon earth, from the elephant to the smallest worm. Upon the neck of each was pressed the seal of Solomon, so that the race of each must henceforth be subject to him. They revealed to him the wisdom of the beasts that perish and do not bother about it. He feasted them at a table of silver and iron which covered four square miles; and at that banqueting Solomon the King served as the pantler, bringing with his hands to every beast and reptile its food according to its kind, from the elephant to the smallest worm.

The word of Morskoï. It was spoken, and all manner of fishes rose to the surface of the sea's water near Ascalon. Upon the neck of each was pressed the seal of Solomon. Then came a hundred thousand camels and a hundred thousand mules laden with new corn, and all the creatures of the water were fed, and after that they served King Solomon, and they revealed to him the wisdom of the Sea Market.

The word of the fowls. It was spoken, and the sky was hidden by the birds who came to render fealty and to instruct King Solomon in the wisdom of the Apsarasas. The peewit alone did not come. But he came afterward, crying, " He that hath no mercy for others, shall find none for himself." And it was the peewit who fetched to Solomon wise Balkis, and who taught Solomon to look through the surface of this earth as a man peers through a sheet of glass.

The word of the Adversary. It was spoken, and the entire citizenry of hell kneeled before King Solomon, saving only Sachr and Eblis. The female Djinns were shaped like dromedaries with the wings of a bat; the male Djinns were like peacocks with the horns of a gazelle. The Mazikeen and the Shedeem came also. To the neck of each was pressed the seal of Solomon: and they revealed to him both the black and the gray wisdom.

The word of Arathron. It was spoken, and there came to King Solomon the Seven Stewards of Heaven. The eyes of Solomon were closed, and his hand had shaken a little, as he pressed to the neck of each kneeling Steward the seal of Solomon, for he was troubled by the exceeding glory of the supreme Princes of Heaven. Of these the most terrible were Ophiel and Phul, whose reign is not yet. But these seven Stewards also served King Solomon; and they revealed to him the white wisdom.

The word of the mirror. It was spoken, and

before him stood a wicker cage containing three pigeons. Beside this cage lay a small mirror three inches square.

All these six words were known to the wise King. It was the power of these six words which made him lord over the wild beasts and the birds of heaven, and over the devils and the elemental spirits and the ghosts of the dead, and over the sea-depths, and over the cherubim. All creatures upon earth trembled before King Solomon because of these six words: no other king withstood Solomon, nor sent forth his chariots against the army of Solomon. For the soldiers of Solomon were the beasts of the field and of the wild wood; the birds of prey were his horsemen; the little birds were his very cunning spies. His admirals were the huge whales and sea serpents, and Leviathan also served in the navy of King Solomon. His lieutenants were the overseers of hell; the supreme angels were his counsellors. He had likewise his mirror. The power of these six words was exceedingly great.

Yet there remained one other word, that word which was in the beginning, and which will be when all else has perished. There stayed yet unrevealed that word which is spoken by the Master Philologist to all the gods of men. That word alone was not known to King Solomon. His little mirror showed him that word, as it showed every other thing; but the word was written in a language which he could not read.

" What need is there for you to be bothering about that word? " said all the women who loved and cherished him. He answered, " I do not know." The wives and concubines then stated, speaking with nine hundred voices in unanimity, that no one of them had ever before heard of such nonsense. And he answered them again, " I do not know. . . . "

For this reason King Solomon must pass down into Antan, to hear the speaking of the last great word of power.

THEN said the third of these wise men: " I was Merlin Ambrosius. The wisdom that I had was more than human, for it came to me from my father. But I served Heaven with it. The land was starved and sick and frightened. Many little chieftains fought in its wild naked fields, and murderously waylaid one another in its old forests, causelessly. I made the land an ordered realm. I gave the land one king, a king whose sword was as bright as thirty torches. That sword flashed everywhither about the land to enforce justice and every other virtue commendable to Heaven. So powerful was Caliburn, that sword which Jurgen had flung away. It served Heaven, now that Arthur Pendragon and those who served him all served my whims. They were my toys. . . . I in my playing gave to the gaping, smooth-chinned boy, and to his shaggy followers, a notion to play with in their turn. This notion was that each one of them, and that every other man, was the child of God and his Father's vicar upon earth; and that each human life was all a journeying home, toward a not ever ending happiness, and that it was a journeying which should be performed in a style appropriate to Heaven's heir apparent. Those savages believed me. They were joyous both night and day. They learned to be envious of no one, to love God, and to support no unjust cause.

[203]

They learned to speak seasonably and graciously, to be generous in giving, to clothe themselves neatly, and to sing and dance, and to war fearlessly against evil. It all quite upset my father. . . . Yet my notion was, I still believe, a very beautiful notion. It created beauty everywhere, because, as I have said, the heir apparent of Heaven must journey homeward in an appropriate style. Yes, the results were eminently picturesque. Caerleon arose; there was no city more delectable upon earth than was the pleasant town of Caerleon, builded upon Usk between the forest and the clear river. Arthur sat there upon a daïs over which was spread a covering of flame-colored satin. Under his elbow was a cushion of red satin. The lords and princes and the knights sat about King Arthur Pendragon, each in his order and degree. The oppressed and the unhappy came to Arthur. He was to the young a father, to the old a comforter. Wrong was loathsome to him, the right was very dear to Arthur, and he knew not what it was to fear. My father did not think at all well of him. . . . But I was pleased with my toys, for now I found in every part of the land a romantic strange beauty. The knights rode at adventure upon enormous stallions. They clanked as they rode. They went masked in blue armor and in crimson armor and in silver-speckled green armor. Upon their heads were brightly colored lions and leopards and griffins and sea horses, and very often their helmets were wrapped about with a woman's sleeve. The giants that these knights fought against were mighty giants who ate at one meal six swine: the dragons that they fought against were marvelous huge worms with shining scales and wattles and magnificent whiskers. The

[204]

maidens whom they rescued were each more lovely than the day. These maidens had blond curling hair and frontlets of red gold upon their heads. About each tender and rose-tinted body was a gown of yellow satin. Upon the feet of these maidens were shoes of variegated leather fastened with gilt clasps. . . . In fine, the heirs of Heaven discharged their moral and constabulary duties quite picturesquely as they rode homeward. It was in this way I who was Merlin Ambrosius played with heroic virtues: it was thus that I who was the son of my father made, for my amusement, men that were more virtuous and colorful than Heaven had ever been able to make them. Still, still, it really was a rather plainly outrageous notion upon which all this was founded: and by and by the dear and droll and heart-breakingly beautiful antics of my flesh and blood toys did not content my desire."

Gerald remarked, now that the old gentleman had paused in his meditative speaking, " Your desire, Messire Merlin, as I remember it, was for an enchantress who outwitted and betrayed you."

" Men," Merlin answered, with a grave smile, " have made a mistake in that report. Is it likely that I could be outwitted? No: I was Merlin Ambrosius."

And then Merlin told Gerald about the child Nimuë, who was the daughter of the goddess Diana, and of how old, wearied, over-learned Merlin had come to her in the likeness of a young squire. He told of how they played for a long while with ancient magics, there in the spring woods, beside a very clear fountain in which the gravel shone like powdered silver. To make this twelve-year-old child laugh, as

[205]

she did so adorably, the mage had turned into prettiness and drollery every infernal device. He created for the child Nimuë, there in the April woods, an orchard full of all those fruits and flowers, howsoever unseasonably mingled, which have the liveliest sweetness and flavor. Phantoms danced for her wide-eyed amusement, in the shaping of armed knights and archbishops and crowned ladies and goat-legged fauns: and it was all quite excellent fun. . . . Then Merlin told to Nimuë, because she pouted so adorably, the secret of building a tower which is not made of stone or timber or iron, and is so strong that it may never be felled while this world endures. And Nimuë, the moment that he had fallen asleep with his head in her lap, spoke very softly the old runes. In the while that she continued to caress her lover, she imprisoned Merlin in an enchanted tower which she had builded out of the magic air of April above a flowering white hawthorn-bush, so that Nimuë might keep her wonderful, so wise, dear lover utterly to herself.

"And I was happy there for a long while," said Merlin. "My toys, now that I played no more with them, began to break one another. Dissension and lust and hatred woke among them. They forgot the very pretty notion which I had given them in their turn to play with. The land was no longer an ordered realm. My toys now fought in the land's naked fields, and they murderously waylaid one another in its old forests. Arthur was dead, at the hands of his own bastard son begotten in incest. It was an awkward ending for the heir apparent of Heaven. The Round Table was dissolved. The land was starved and sick and frightened."

THE CHIVALRY OF MERLIN

Now Merlin, the old poet who did not any longer delight to shape and to play with puppets, had paused: and he sat gazing thoughtfully, with wholly patient, tired eyes, at nothing in particular. Then Merlin said:

" I heard of all these things. They did not matter. I was happy. Yes, I suppose that I was happy. My ways were utterly domestic. They stayed thus for a long while. . . . There was no variety. In that small heaven which a child had builded out of the magic air of April there was no variety whatever. There was no enemy, no adversary for me to get the better of through some cunning device. There was only happiness. . . . Nimuë stayed always young and kind and beautiful and contented just because I was there. The child loved me. But there was no variety. No son of my father stays forever a domestic animal. So in the end I who was Merlin Ambrosius found my desire was not in that tower of April air. There was only heaven. There was only just such a never-changing happiness as I had once talked about to the gaping, smooth-chinned boy and to his shaggy followers."

" Yet how could you escape from the blessings of a happy home life, Messire Merlin, if that tower was truly enchanted? "

" It does not seem reasonable that I should tell you all my secrets," Merlin replied, drily, " any more than it seemed reasonable that the son of my father should share every secret with Nimuë. The child loved me utterly. And I loved her. Yes, I loved Nimuë as I have loved no other creature fluttering about earth. She did not seem to walk. . . . Even so, I was Merlin Ambrosius. So in the end I left my child mistress. I quitted the small heaven which a child's pure-mindedness had contrived. And I go now into Antan to get, it may be, my desire."

Then there was silence, now that the three mages had all spoken.

And Gerald shook his head. " You gentlemen have talked with gratifying candor. You have expressed yourself, with chaste simplicity, in very plain short sentences. You have reasoned powerfully. You imply that neither a wife nor a mistress, or even a harem, is able to dissuade a wise man from this journeying toward the goal of all the gods. I infer that, to the contrary, the domestic circumstances of no one of you were wholly satisfactory in the old time. Well, that is a situation still to be encountered more frequently than is desirable, even in Lichfield, and it is the reason that I too am on my way to Antan. I am stopping here just for the week-end. Yet I still do not know what in the world you gentlemen really desire."

" For one, I desire nothing that is in this world," replied Odysseus.

" Yet, do you but answer me this very simple question! What do you three expect to find in Antan? Because I can assure you that, after the impending changes to be made in the government and other civic affairs of Antan by the Lord of the Third Truth, — a deity, gentlemen, with several not uninteresting aspects, a deity with which I may without boasting say that I have considerable influence, — why, then, the moment everything is in tolerable working order, it will be a real pleasure to afford you three gentlemen all possible courtesies."

But the three mages did not seem impressed.

" I was wise," said Solomon. " I knew all things

save one thing. I did not know that word which was in the beginning, and which will be when all else has perished. And that word no god knows until he has heard it spoken by the Master Philologist."

"My desire," said Merlin, "was for the maid Nimuë and for the love of my child mistress. When I had my desire it did not content me. So I now go into Antan to find, it may be, something which I can desire. But my father's son does not go asking favors of any god."

Then Gerald said: "Yet, you three mages who have traveled through the Marches of Antan wherein only two truths endure, and the one teaching is that we copulate and die, — do you not look to find in the goal of all the gods some third truth?"

It seemed to him that the faces of these myths had now become somewhat evasive and more wary.

But they said only, speaking severally: "A wise man knows that no truth is affected either by his beliefs or by his hopes." — "A wise man accepts each truth as it is revealed to him." — "A wise man will risk nothing upon the existence of any truth."

"Still, gentlemen, these are enigmas! These sayings are not a plain answer to a plain question: and I do not quite understand these sayings."

They answered him, "There is no need that you should understand."

Then these three passed down toward the sunset statelily. And Gerald, gazing after them, once more shook his red head. These wise myths seemed to him in a bad way: it would not be easy to content the more eminent sages among his future subjects, because these three at least, for all their wisdom, appeared never to have found out what they wanted.

[209]

Gerald shrugged. He, in any event, perfectly well knew what in this bracing country air he wanted at once. So Gerald went in at once to supper with his Maya who was such an excellent cook in her plain way.

WHAT more is needed," Maya had asked, "to make this last day with me pass pleasantly?"

— For this, again, was the very last day which Gerald could possibly spend in the trim log and plaster cottage. Maya had decided, without any reticence, that it was high time he attended to whatsoever foolishness he seemed to think himself committed to, in that disreputable low place down yonder, and that to keep putting it off in this way looked like shirking, and that, for her part, she simply could not understand why he did not get his nonsense over with. . . .

And Gerald said, " It would be nice if we had a son."

But Maya at once dissented, as, it seemed to Gerald, she nowadays dissented, at least in part, from everything that Gerald proposed.

" No, Gerald," said Maya. " For you would grow far too fond of him. You would be foolish about him. You would be unwilling to leave him, you probably never would leave him. And it would end in your being in my way, and bothering me in the night season, and being under my feet all day, for the rest of your life — "

" But I am a god — "

" Yes, Gerald, to be sure, you are. I had forgotten. I apologize. Now, do not be upset about it! Stop pouting! You are a god, that is quite understood. You are immortal, you are going to outlive me indefinitely, and you are going to perform wonders in Antan, and it is all going to be very nice. I hope so, anyhow. I was only saying it would be much better for us to have no son."

But Gerald answered: " Do not keep contradicting me in that maddening way! If you again fly out at me like that, Maya, you will rouse my temper. Then I shall rage and roar and, quite possibly, ramp. I will bluster and speak harshly. I will huff, I will puff, I will blow the house down. For I insist it would be uncommonly nice if we had a son."

" Oh, very well, then! " said Maya; and she turned, with that sulkiness which she ever and again displayed — nowadays, — toward a large basket of magics.

" — I mean, though, once he were old enough. Babies are too limited in conversation, they are too vocal, and they are too leaky."

Maya had lifted from an amber basin a small shining lizard. She held it toward her mouth, breathing softly upon the creature, in the while that she answered Gerald.

" I think, myself," said Maya, " that, since you insist upon having a son, he might as well be seven or eight years old to begin with."

Then Maya took off the top of the basket, she reached far into the blue basket with the hand in which she held the shining lizard, and out of this basket, clinging to Maya's hand for support, climbed a freckled red-haired boy, about eight years old, in blue garments, and having as yet only one upper front tooth.

[212]

A BOY THAT MIGHT BE

" We have now got a splendid son," said Gerald, contentedly. " But who is to christen our son? For I shall of course call him Theodorick Quentin, just as my father and my oldest brother were called."

The boy was, thus, named Theodorick Quentin Musgrave. Gerald delighted in the child, now that the Lord of the Third Truth put off once more his entry into his kingdom. . . .

" I told you so! " said Maya.

" But, really now, my darling, would you have me lacking in all proper paternal feeling! It is necessary I give the child a fair start in life; and I ask you, candidly, could any parent discharge that duty, with any real thoroughness, in less than a week? "

" That, though, is not at all what I said. And for any full-grown man to be talking such nonsense — "

" So now you see for yourself! Therefore I shall be leaving you both next Tuesday, and it is quite useless for you to implore me to stay a half-second longer than that. Besides, I rather like him."

Yet the child showed peculiarities. For one thing, his tongue had no red in it, but was formed of perfectly white flesh. When Gerald noticed this odd fact he said nothing about it, though, because Gerald comprehended the limitations of gray magic. And for another thing, on the third day of Theodorick's existence, Gerald happened to lay aside his rose-colored spectacles while he was playing with his son. Then the boy was not there. Gerald shrugged, just in time to avoid shuddering. He replaced his spectacles, and all was as before, to every freckle and each red hair.

After that Gerald wore his spectacles always.

For Theodorick Quentin Musgrave had become

[213]

very dear to him. No more than any other father could Gerald rationally explain this dearness or justify it by any common-sense logic. He only knew that the brat aroused in him a tenderness which came appreciably near to being unselfish; that it worried him to have the brat go unchristened in this neighborhood so full of sorcerers and wizards; that when he touched the brat it pleased him, for no assignable reason; and that when the brat displayed the mildest gleam of intelligence, it at once seemed quite brilliant and profound, and inexpressibly beyond all other people's children.

For Theodorick noticed everything. And Gerald delighted particularly in the child's intelligence and powers of observation, because, since no sort of cleverness could possibly be inherited from poor dear stupid Maya, all the boy's more excellent mental traits were obviously paternal.

For example, " There is a lady," Theodorick had stated, pointing toward Antan.

" Oh, any number of ladies, my son," Gerald assented, as he thought of the many beautiful goddesses and feminine myths who (for all that, he reflected, he had never seen any female creature pass toward Antan) must be aiding to make yet more glorious that kingdom over which Gerald would by this time next week be ruling.

And Gerald's hand went to the shoulder of the freckled brat whom, after next week, he would not ever be seeing any more: and Gerald wondered at the wholly illogical pleasure he derived just from touching this child.

" Oh, yes, there are no doubt a great many ladies in Antan," said Gerald, " and the coincidence is truly quaint that I have not yet seen any woman traveling in that direction."

But the boy explained he meant the very large lady lying down over yonder as if she were dead, but not dead, because her heart was breathing.

Then Gerald saw that, in point of fact, the hills toward the southwest had, from this station, the shaping of a woman's body. She seemed to lie flat on her back, with her long hair outspread every-whither about her head, of which the profile, now that you looked for it, was clear and quite definitely formed. Also you saw her throat and her high breasts, whence the hills sloped downward into the contour of a relatively smallish, flat belly. Just here the out-line of the vast violet-tinted figure was broken by the nearer green hill immediately across the road which led to Antan, but all that you could see of this womanlike figure was complete and perfectly moulded. Moreover, Gerald noted that, near where the heart would have been, a forest fire was sending up its languid smoke, which was, of course, what Theodorick Quentin Musgrave had meant by say-ing that the lady's heart was breathing.

Gerald was very proud of Theodorick's clever-ness in noticing the shaping of these hills, which Ger-ald himself had not ever observed, in the entire three weeks he had spent upon Mispec Moor. But when this odd accident of nature was pointed out to Maya, she only said that she saw what you meant of course, but that, after all, it was only two hills, and that hills looked much more like hills than they looked like anything else.

PART NINE

THE BOOK OF MISPEC MOOR

"To Tame the Wolf You Must Marry Him."

IT WAS at this time, toward the middle of June, that Gaston Bulmer came from Lichfield. Gerald was sitting, as was his daily custom now, under the chestnut-tree beside the road which led to Antan. He waited there to engage in conversation the next of his future subjects who might pass by in that perpetual journeying toward Antan. Gerald, under this same chestnut-tree, had by this time talked with many such unearthly wayfarers: and if the rather interesting things they had told him were all written down, it would make a book unutterably enormous and utterly incredible.

In such circumstances it was, just after two not unfamiliar mountebanks had gone by carrying with them the paraphernalia of their Punch and Judas show, that Gerald noticed a small sulphur-colored cloud sweeping rapidly from the east. It descended: and when it was near to Gerald, it unclosed. Gaston Bulmer then stepped, a bit rheumatically, from its glowing depths, and he laid down a rod of cedar wood tipped with an apple carved in blue-stone.

There was not in all this anything in itself astonishing, since Gaston Bulmer was an adept in the arts of which Gerald, in the strange days before he knew that he was a god, had been a student. But to note how Gaston had aged in the last week or so was astounding. Yet Gerald, in any case, was wholly de-

[219]

lighted to see again his old friend and preceptor, and a person who had for so long been virtually his father-in-law.

Gaston would not come up to the cottage, though, for dinner, because, as he confessed, he preferred not to encounter Maya. Rather, it was his wish, and it seemed, indeed, to be his errand, to free Gerald from what Gaston Bulmer, surprisingly enough, described as the wise woman's pernicious magic.

Gerald said: "Oh, bosh! For really now, Gaston, if such nonsense were not heart-breaking it would be side-splitting. I am inexpressibly shocked by your hallucination, which is, I trust, of a most transitory nature. However, let us not discuss my wife, if you please. Instead, do you tell me how my body is faring."

So they sat down together under the chestnut-tree. And Gaston Bulmer answered, —

"That body, Gerald, since you quitted it, has become a noted scholar and a man of letters."

"Ah! ah!" said Gerald, greatly pleased, "so my romance about Dom Manuel of Poictesme has been completed, and is now being admired everywhere!"

"No, for your body has become, just as I said, a scholar. Scholars do not write romances."

"Yet you referred to a man of letters — ?"

"Your body is now a rather famous ethnologist. Your body deals with historical and scientific truths. Your body thus writes large quartos upon topics to which no romance, howsoever indelicate, could afford to devote a sentence."

Gerald fell to stroking that long chin of his. "Still, I recall that the present informant of my

[220]

body once informed me there were only two truths of which any science could be certain."

" And what were these two truths? "

Gerald named them.

Gaston said then: " The demon is consistent. For these two are precisely your body's scientific specialty. To-day your body writes invaluable books in which the quaint and interesting customs that accompany an interplay of these two truths, and the various substitutes for that interplay, are catalogued and explained, as these customs have existed in all lands and times. Lichfield to-day is wholly proud of the scholarship and the growing fame of Gerald Musgrave."

" I am glad that my body has turned out so splendidly. And I trust that all goes equally well with your daughter Evelyn? "

" Gerald," the older man replied, looking more seriously troubled than Gerald ever liked to have anybody seeming in his company, " Gerald, it is an unfair thing that your Cousin Evelyn, without knowing it, should be living upon terms of such close friendship with a demon-haunted body."

" Ah, so that friendship continues! "

" It continues," said Gaston, " unaltered. It may interest you, Gerald, by the way, to hear that your Cousin Evelyn has now a son, quite a fine red-headed boy, born just a year after you relinquished your body to that treacherous Sylan."

Gerald answered affably: " Why, that is perfectly splendid! Frank always wanted a boy."

" My son-in-law, in fact, is much pleased. It is about my daughter I was thinking. It seems to me the situation is hardly fair to her, Gerald."

Gerald replied: " My body is all of me that she was ever acquainted with, Gaston. So I fail to perceive that anything is altered."

" Yet, when I reflect that a beautiful and accomplished and chaste gentlewoman, Gerald — "

" Ah, ah! But, yes, to be sure! you speak in the time-hallowed terms of Lichfield. And I really do not know why I interrupted you."

" — When I reflect that, without knowing it, a gentlewoman is living upon terms of such close friendship with a mere demon-haunted body — "

" And is, in fact, trusting and giving all? "

" All her friendship and the natural affection of a kinswoman. Yes, that is a sad spectacle. It is an unsuitable spectacle. So it seems to me your duty as a Musgrave, and as a Southern gentleman, to return forthwith to mortal living and to your mortal obligations, and in particular to the obligations of your life-long friendship with your Cousin Evelyn."

Gerald said, for the second time, " Oh, bosh! "

For the notions and the chivalrous assumptions of Gaston Bulmer all now appeared to Gerald out of reason, in view of the divine predestination which was upon him. A god had no concern with such slight imbroglios as the code of a merely terrestrial gentleman and the proper maintenance upon Earth of polite adultery. It would, indeed, be positively ill-bred for a Dirghic god to meddle with any of the affairs of a planet which, according to Gerald's Protestant Episcopal faith, had been created and was controlled by an Episcopalian deity; for Gerald had of course retained, provisionally, that religion in which he was a communicant until he could find out something rather more definite about the religion in which he was a god.

Gerald therefore said: " My good Gaston, that your meaning is excellent, I do not doubt. And it is not your fault of course that, in your merely human condition, you do not quite understand these matters, and certainly cannot view them with an omniscient eye."

The older man said: " I understand, in any event, that through all these years you have stayed here bewitched with terrible half-magics, and that your own eyes are blinded with the woman's rose-colored spectacles. And I seek to preserve you."

" You would preserve me for the provincial life of your little Lichfield! You would make me just another chivalrous, bull-headed, rather nice-looking and wholly stupid Musgrave! In fine, you would urge me to become genteel and to deny my glorious destiny. Yet to do that would be cowardly, Gaston: for, whether I like it or not, there is upon me the divine obligation to fulfil some very ancient prophecies."

" What sort of prophecies are these? "

" They are Dirghic prophecies. But, then, it is not the language in which a prophecy is uttered that matters, rather it is — Well, it is the spirit of the thing! For you must know — although, in view of my wife's social position, I have compelled her, after some little argument, to introduce me hereabouts as a visiting sorcerer, — yet I may tell you, in strict confidence, Gaston, it is decreed that, as the Lord of the Third Truth, I am to reign in Antan."

" And who told you any such unlikely nonsense? "

[223]

"Some people that I met upon the road. Oh, quite honest looking people, Gaston! "

"And who told you that you were the Lord of any Third Truth? "

"There my authority is unimpeachable. For I had it from the lips of a beautiful and accomplished and chaste gentlewoman, Gaston, who was speaking with all the frankness begotten by our being in bed together at the time."

"And how can you reign in Antan, or anywhere else, when you do not ever go there? Through all these years, I gather, you have loitered here within a man's arm's reach of Antan! "

Gerald said, with the slight frown of one who finds trouble uncongenial: "I am puzzled, my dear friend, by your continued references to all these years. And I admit that various matters have a bit hindered my technical and merely formal entry into my kingdom. Yet I shall be leaving Mispec Moor the instant that this week's washing is in, on Thursday afternoon — "

"But, my poor Gerald! you will not go, either forward to Antan or back to Lichfield, on what you think to be next Thursday. You have lost here all sense of time, you do not even know that the days you have spent in this place have counted as four years in Lichfield. I tell you that the wise woman, with her half-magics and her accursed spectacles, holds you here bewitched. And I now perceive that nothing whatever can be done for you, who are ensnared by the most fatal of all the magics of the wrinkled goddess."

— To which Gerald, for the third time, replied: "Oh, bosh! No sorceress has any power over a god.

And so completely do you misunderstand my wife, Gaston, that I must tell you hardly a day passes without her urging me to hurry on to Antan."

Gaston Bulmer was still regarding him with that extraordinary and wholly uncalled-for look of compassion.

" How completely," Gaston said, " she understands you Musgraves! Yes, you are lost, my poor Gerald."

" — It follows that your notions are preposterous. Oh, that is not your fault, my dear fellow, and not for an instant am I blaming you. Your conduct, from your human point of view, is very right, very friendly, very proper. So your rather laughable blunder does not offend me in the least. And if, as you declare, I have lingered here for some four years as you human beings estimate time, what do four years amount to with an immortal who has at his disposal all eternity? Come now, Gaston, do you but answer me that very simple question! "

But Gaston answered only: " You are content. You are lost."

AND Gaston said no more about the matter, because just here their talking was interrupted. For now, as these two still sat at the roadside, they were joined by a brown man, dressed completely in neat brown, who was journeying toward Antan.

" Hail, friend! " said Gerald, " and what business draws you to the city of all marvels? "

And the brown man, pausing, said that, in point of fact, it was upon a slight matter of business routine that he desired to consult with Queen Freydis. All gods, he said, had rather speedily passed downward to encounter the word which was in the beginning, — for it was thus that the brown man spoke, very much as King Solomon had spoken, — all gods, that is, save only one, who so bewilderingly altered his tenets that there was no telling where to have him.

The brown man thought that, nowadays, in a comparatively enlightened nineteenth century, was perhaps the appropriate time for something to be done about this celestial chameleon. And in any case, the brown man said yet further, he always enjoyed his little conferences with Freydis, who was rather a dear —

" So, so! " said Gerald, " you, sir, have previously visited Antan? "

" Oh, very often. For I am the adversary of all the gods of men."

And Gerald viewed with natural interest the one person who pretended to know at first hand anything about Gerald's appointed kingdom: yet, even so, if this brown gentleman, as Gerald had begun to suspect, happened to be the Father of All Lies, there was no real point to questioning him, inasmuch as you could believe none of his answers.

" —For, I infer," said Gerald, " that you who travel on the road of gods and myths are that myth not unfamiliar to my Protestant Episcopal rearing; and that I have now the privilege, so frequently anticipated for me by my nearer relatives, of addressing the Devil? "

" I retain of course in every mythology, including the Semitic, my niche," replied the brown man, " from which to speak to intelligent persons in somewhat varying voices."

Then Gaston Bulmer arose, and the aging adept shaped a sign which to Gerald was unfamiliar.

" I suspect, sir," said Gaston Bulmer, " that my mother's father, who was called Florian de Puysange, once heard the speaking of that voice."

" It is a tenable hypothesis. I in my day have spoken much."

" — As did, I believe, yet another forebear of mine, the great Jurgen, from whom descends the race of Puysange, and who once encountered someone rather like you in a Druid wood — "

" I cannot deny it. The Druids also knew me. I, who am the Prince of this world, meet however, as you will readily understand, so many millions of people during the course of my efforts to keep them

[227]

contented with my kingdom that it is not always possible for me to recollect every one of my beneficiaries."

"Still," Gerald said, "you have played in large historical events a strange high part; you have known all the very best people: and you must have much of interest to tell me about. You, sir, at least shall dine with me, since my friend here is obdurate. My wife avoids the usual run of gods, but to devils I have never heard her voice the slightest objection. So, if you will do me the honor to accompany me to my temporary home, in that cottage — "

But the brown man smiled. And he excused himself.

"For your wife and I are not wholly strangers. And the circumstances in which we last parted were, I confess, a bit awkward. So I really believe it would be more pleasant, for everyone concerned, for me not to meet your wife just now. Do you present, none the less, my compliments."

"And whose compliments shall I tell her that they are?"

"Do you say a friend of her earliest youth passed by, one somewhat intimately known to her before she first became a mother; and I make no doubt that Havvah will understand."

"But my wife's married name is Maya, and before our marriage it was Æsred — "

"Ah, yes!" the brown man said, precisely as Glaum had done, "women do vary in their given names. Do you present my compliments, then, to your wife: for that word, by and by, means the same thing to every husband."

"I will convey the message," Gerald promised:

[228]

" but the aphorism I would prefer to have delivered by somebody else."

And he so parted from both his guests.

For Gaston Bulmer embraced Gerald and then went sorrowfully back to Lichfield, in a cloud which the aging adept's despondency made quite black: and the brown man leisurely strolled on toward Antan, with the ease of one who was well used to walking to and fro about the earth.

He did not hurry, nor did he look inquisitively about him, Gerald noticed, as had done the other travelers toward the city of all marvels. The brown man, alone of the many that had passed toward Antan, appeared to travel upon a road with which he was thoroughly acquainted, toward a familiar goal.

XXXV. OF KALKI AND A DÖPPELGANGER

SO IT was that Gerald stayed yet a while longer
upon Mispec Moor. July passed uneventfully.
Each pleasant summer day found Gerald sitting beneath his chestnut-tree at the roadside. This
tree had flowered now, with a very glorious white
blooming, cloyingly sweet in smell, and then this
blooming had become cream-colored, and after that,
brown; but now the tree was all green again, with a
subdued sprinkling of darkly golden yellow burrs.
And Gerald, as he idled there, day after day, in the
shadow of this ever constant changing, was well
content.

He had talked with many wayfarers who have no
part in this tale. For almost all these travelers told
the same story. Nine out of every ten of them had
yesterday been a god whom human beings served;
each had been worshipped by mankind in one or
another quarter of the world: to-day their human
concerns were over, and they journeyed toward the
goal of all the gods. What did they look to find
there? Gerald would ask: and — to this very simple
question, — every one of them replied evasively.
They went to hear that word which was in the beginning, and which would be after everything else
had perished, that word which was unknown to all
the gods of men. They would say no more: and
Gerald did not deeply bother about the matter, be-

cause he was nowadays quite well contented, and when he went to Antan would soon be clearing up every mystery for himself.

And the divine steed Kalki also appeared content enough, nor was his aspect altered by inaction. The horse retained that uniform strange shining and that metallic glitter which made him seem actually to be made of untarnished silver. Of course when you saw him grazing upon Mispec Moor just after a rain-shower his back would be dark and sleek, and his broad sides would be streaked with wavering, oily-looking bands. But at all other times he kept his glowing silver color, which was unlike that of any other horse Gerald had ever seen.

Meanwhile the divine steed grazed with the geldings who once had been the human lovers of Maya. He went as they did, lifting each hoof with somewhat droll carefulness as he grazed forward on the sloping ground about the cottage. For Gerald would often watch this grazing. And to him these horses as they moved slowly and irregularly windward seemed continually to pick up and to replace their hoofs upon the ground as though they believed each hoof to be a rather fragile parcel. The pendulous, stretched, heavy necks of these horses, each neck staying always monotonously parallel to all the other necks, appeared to him too heavy ever again to be lifted erect. To wonder in the drowsy summer afternoon how this lifting could possibly be achieved aroused an unpleasant sensation in Gerald's collarbone.

So Kalki fed all day among the geldings, and on windy nights he huddled with them in the lee of the cottage. Each day Kalki went looking downward, grazing interminably, and without ever ceasing to

[231]

move those wobbling, dark, prehensile, rotatory, snuffling lips as the divine steed fed upon the sparse grass of Mispec Moor. He, just as greedily as the geldings, would contort his lips and twist his head when he attempted to get at the longer and more luscious grass which grew almost inaccessibly about the fence posts. And to reflection there was something of the incongruous in the spectacle of a divine steed engrossed by this problem.

Now and again, as Gerald noted also, the stallion would raise his superb head, and Kalki would look almost wistfully toward Antan. But soon he would be back at his grazing: and, upon the whole, he seemed content enough with the pleasures appropriate to ordinary horses. And Gerald thought too that, nowadays, Kalki looked less often toward the goal of all the gods.

Yet Kalki turned out to be not wholly unique. For, one morning, as Gerald went toward his chestnut-tree, he noted the approach from afar of a traveler who rode upon a horse that had very much the appearance of Kalki. And when Gerald had reached the roadway he saw that the newcomer was in fact mounted upon a steed which might well have been Kalki's twin.

" Hail, friend! " said Gerald, " And what business draws you to the city of all marvels? "

Then a regrettable thing happened; for the young horseman pretended not to have heard Gerald, and as the boy passed he looked investigatively about Mispec Moor, and he pretended not to have seen Gerald, who stood within a few feet of him.

He was a notably handsome boy, too, in a blue coat and a golden yellow waistcoat, colored just as

[232]

were the burrs above them, and with a tall white stock and ruffles about his throat. His hair seemed red. Gerald noted, moreover, the lazy and mildly humorous, half-mocking gaze with which this boy regarded Mispec Moor, as he rode by unhurriedly toward Antan, without any pausing, and Gerald noted in particular the very lovely smiling of this boy's so amply curved and rather womanish mouth, as the boy went by upon the horse which was astonishingly like Kalki.

Yes, he had quite the air of a gentleman. It was a great pity that this young whippersnapper had not the manners of a gentleman also, Gerald reflected, as Gerald stood there, feeling unwarrantably snubbed, and blinking behind his rose-colored spectacles.

AND upon yet another day Gerald talked with
the comely but now aged knight Tannhäuser, as this famous myth passed by, in
full armor, upon his journey into Antan.

" There," said Tannhäuser, "there I may find
again, it may be, the fair Dame Venus and all the
brave and high-hearted sinners who would not compromise with the narrow and cruel ways of respectable persons."

" My friend," said Gerald, mildly, " there is considerable virtue to be found, here and there, among
respectable persons. There is even a virtue in compromise."

And Tannhäuser shouted: " That I deny! All my
life denies that, and so long as my name lives I am
that lie's denial! For it was the good and the respectable who betrayed me. I found pride and world-
liness and a lack of cordiality to exist among the
bourgeoisie and even among those professional
churchmen who should have been the first to sustain
and guide a repentant sinner. And so I turned again
to that frankly pagan beauty which is hateful to pious
and small-minded persons."

Then this resplendent gray-haired myth spoke
heatedly of his own life history and of how his love
for this frankly pagan beauty had led him into the
hollow mountain called the Hörselberg, to live there

as the lover of Dame Venus in all manner of frankly pagan pleasure-seeking; and of how, after seven years of frankly pagan recreations, when repentance smote him, abetted by the frailties of middle age, it was among the leading church members, and in the heart of the very head of the church, that he had found no sympathy. Therefore Tannhäuser was returning to those frankly pagan recreations, so far at least as they were consistent with late middle life, because he was disgusted by those whining and hypocritical, cruel church members.

And Gerald listened. He remembered how in the Mirror of Caer Omn he for a while had been Tannhäuser. Yet it was a queer thing, and a circumstance which made Gerald suspect time to be changing him, somehow, who used to be such a tremendous iconoclast, that now this old rebellious myth — which represented yet another of Gerald's discarded personalities, — appeared to Gerald remarkably over-colored and rather pitiably foolish. For here was a story which led to wrong conclusions. It ended by depicting a god at loggerheads with the head of his own church: and it begot, somewhat inevitably, those loud sneers at the bourgeois virtues, and those denunciations of people who, after all, had done nothing worse than to live quiet and common-sense lives which Tannhäuser was now declaiming, and which to Gerald appeared unutterably childish. There was no conceivable reason why a well-thought-of pope should be hobnobbing with and coddling a broken-down old lecher just come out of a superior brothel. In fact, in reproving Pope Urban so publicly, Heaven had been, to Gerald's finding, rather tactless, and had violated the *esprit de corps* which ought to be preserved among the fellow workers in every church. And in any case, Tannhäuser's present reflections upon religion were not such as Gerald, now that he had become a god, could listen to with approval.

Still, Gerald did listen: and Gerald smiled, friend-lily enough.

" I know, I know! " said Gerald. " I know, Messire Tannhäuser, all about you. When you repented of evil-doing, — and really, you did take your time about that, — then you turned hopefully to religion, but, alas! you were repelled by its ministers. You found them to be human beings subject to human frailties. You found that — in Heaven's eyes, any-how, — even a pope might make a mistake. And so, quite naturally, you proceeded to drown the surprise and horror awakened by this discovery, in out-and-out debauchery and in cutting reflections upon all pew-renters. For your discovery was revolutionary; no doubt the stars were shaken in their courses, to observe a human being making a mistake; and you also must have found the spectacle extremely trying. Still, you in this way became useful to romantic art."

Then Gerald said: " Lord, man, but what a fol-lowing you have had! and what a number of people have got harmless pleasure out of developing the discovery which Tannhäuser first made, that incon-sistency and mean-spiritedness may be found among the clergy and the churchgoers! You will thus con-tinue to be a benefactor of your kind for centuries, I have not a doubt. Yet I sometimes fancy that in-consistency and mean-spiritedness may be found even among recognizedly depraved persons who do not go to any church at all. I find that every religion cows

[236]

a number of its devotees into a thrifty-minded practice of generally beneficent virtues. The average of
desirable qualities in the congregation of every church
appears to me, after all, quite perceptibly higher than
is that average among the regular customers of any
brothel or the clients of the public hangman. I do not
deny that my discovery also is, from any æsthetic
standpoint, revolutionary. I confess that it is nowhere
represented in romance, as yet, and that no conceivable realist can ever regard such a remarkable fancy
with anything save loathing. But I believe that some
day an intrepid handling of this daring theme will
prodigally repay some very great innovator, and will
become useful to romantic art."

And Gerald said also: " Moreover, you remain
quite invaluable as a pretext and a palliation whenever youth hungers for its fling. Only, I must dare
point out, my dear sir, that your second, century-long
fling was, by the best people, unavoidably, felt to be
excessive. All of us, more or less, have had our flings:
even so, a fling needs to be conducted, and above all
to be wound up, with some discretion. It ought to be
high-hearted and lyrical in every feature: it ought
especially to have the briefness of the lyric. And it
ought not, no, it really ought not, to wind up in the
Hörselberg. Now I, too, my friend, for example,
have had my fling. But I have had it in a quiet, self-
controlled and gentlemanly way, without overdoing
the thing. Thereafter I settled down, — just temporarily, to be sure, but still I have settled down, —
in no lewd and feverish Hörselberg, but here, where
a contented husband risks no further chance of becoming useful to romantic art."

" It is possible for one to exist, but not for anybody to live, here! " replied Tannhäuser, scornfully, as his wild gaze swept over the still stretches of Mispec Moor.

"Allow me! " said Gerald, with the tiniest of smiles; and he perched his rose-colored spectacles upon the beaked high nose of Tannhäuser.

There was a pause. And Tannhäuser sighed.

"I see," said the knight then, — "a quiet little home of your own, in the country, with your wife and with the kiddies, too, I daresay. And with fresh vegetables, of course, right out of your own garden."

"In just such a home, Messire Tannhäuser, as is the cornerstone of every nation, the cradle of all the virtues, and the guiding-star of I forget precisely what. It is also the brightest jewel in the crown of something or other, and it aids some yet further fine abstractions in the capacity of a bulwark, a spur, and an anchor. It is, you may depend upon it, the proper place in which to end one's fling."

"And I! I might, if only I had married that dear fine sweet girl Elizabeth, I, too, might have had such a home! For, after all, there is nothing like marriage and the love of a good woman. An endless round of perpetual pleasure-seeking rings hollow by and by, and one hungers for the simple sacred joys of home life. I must, oh, very decidedly, I must settle down. I, too, must have just such a home as this."

But the thought of all which he had been missing so affected Tannhäuser that he took off the spectacles and unaffectedly wiped his eyes. After that the aging, comely knight sat for a while silent and rather frightened looking. He stared again at the cottage and at the moor, and then he stared at Gerald.

"And you live in this hole, with a muddy brat and a dull-witted, middle-aged, not at all good-looking woman for your only companion! I marvel at the enchantment which controls you. At least Dame Venus held me with an intelligible sort of sorcery."

"That," Gerald replied, as he contentedly put on his rose-colored spectacles again, "is nonsense."

"Instead, the life which you lead here, messire, is nonsense. It is a soul-destroying and besotting non-sense, from which I flee to look for the less terrible enchantments of the Hörselberg."

Then Gerald put his question. "You, who have traveled through the Marches of Antan, wherein only two truths endure, and the one teaching is that we copulate and die, — do you not look to find in the goal of all the gods some third truth?"

But the comely knight seemed not to have heard this question, in his frank terror of domesticity. Tannhäuser had mounted his horse, and he now rode galloping like a madman toward Antan.

NOW life contented Gerald as he lived it through this recognized parenthesis in his divine career. Very soon this little episode of his stay upon Mispec Moor would be ended: it would even be forgotten, perhaps, in the press of regal and superhuman affairs. Meanwhile he lived in quite tolerable ease. He had nothing to trouble him. Hardly a morning passed without his finding some more or less interesting celestial outcast to talk to under his chestnut-tree. Maya continued to be an excellent cook, in her plain, unpretentious way: and she saw to it that the cottage was kept comfortable and efficient in all appointments.

And Maya was dear to him. She nowadays found fault with virtually everything that Gerald did. And whenever he ventured any suggestion, as to Theodorick or the economics of the cottage or their social engagements in Turoine, — or even if Gerald as much as suggested opening or closing a window, — Maya at once produced at least nine grounds upon which the suggestion was plainly very foolish and would never have occurred to anyone of real intelligence. And she cherished the most imaginative views as to the extent of Gerald's selfishness and lack of consideration for other people, and of his habit of never doing anything whatever for her pleasure.

Sometimes, though, she would go for as much as an hour without dwelling, at especial length, upon what a trial Gerald was to her in one way or another. And in all respects she was a capable woman who made him an excellent wife, and treated him far better than she could have found any excuse for doing in what she said about him.

And Gerald loved Theodorick Quentin Musgrave, also, with an affection which rather troubled Gerald. The child, he knew, displayed no extraordinary charm nor talent: no course of reasoning could justify any extreme fondness for Theodorick upon the ground of his physical or mental gifts. Theodorick Quentin Musgrave was not brilliant, he was not lovely, he was not especially amiable: he was, indeed, by way of being a particularly selfish small tyrant, continually adding to the disorder of the cottage, to the dismay of Gerald's finicky liking for neatness, and continually devising unneeded trouble and commandeering manual tasks from his parents because of the droll pleasure which Theodorick appeared to derive from seeing his parents fetch and carry in his service.

Yet, whensoever Gerald put his arm about the small, warm, yielding, sturdy, but so helpless body, it was as though Gerald's own body were melting in a grateful glow of what was — bewilderingly — a sort of panic terror. He loved this freckled, fragile creature with an unwisdom which was, as Gerald knew, an assuredness of more or less future discomfort and, it well might be, of anguish, for him who quite honestly disliked trouble of any kind. Since this child had been created, Gerald's well-being was not any longer a matter which Gerald could hope to

[241]

control or even to protect: his happiness was now risked upon what might befall this imp. It was the helplessness of the child which frightened Gerald with a sense of his own helplessness. Life was so cruel to children. Life damaged and hurt children in so many ways inevitably. And every hurt to this child, now, would be an anguish to Gerald, who could avoid none of them. He could not even manage to get the child properly christened, in this neighborhood so profuse in sorcerers and wizards, who used, as everybody knew, unchristened children in horrible ways which it was not comfortable to think about. . . .

Then, too, Gerald was not certain Theodorick Quentin Musgrave was real. Gerald remembered always, at the back of his mind, that frightful instant when he had removed his spectacles, to find the child had vanished. Gerald assured himself that the cause was a slight indigestion, and that the moment's blur of vision came from a disordered stomach. But he was wholly careful not ever again to look at Theodorick except through the rose-colored spectacles which made visible the magics of Maya. He kept resolutely out of his full attention the fact that Theodorick might be an illusion which Maya had created. And he grew accustomed to that unusual milk-colored tongue, which showed like a white snake within the red moist little mouth whenever the child laughed.

And Gerald sometimes wondered if Maya had over-ambitiously designed to make permanent this mere parenthesis in his career. She had attempted, to be sure, no magic such as that with which she had transformed his predecessors. No sorceress would dare, for that matter, thus to presume against a god.

[242]

CONTENTMENT OF THE MISLAID GOD

. . . Gerald knew that, instead, it was his Maya's wholesome simplicity and the prosaic human comfort which he did get, after all, from living with this middle-aged and fault-finding and not in the least beautiful woman that had detained him, just for the while of this parenthesis in his career. He of course would pass on, to enter into his kingdom, by and by. And there was no conceivable hurry about it, now that his journeying to Antan was for every practical purpose finished, and now that whensoever he elected he might within the next half-hour or so be taking over the realm and all the powers of the Master Philologist.

Meanwhile, though, Gerald would now and then wonder amusedly if his dear, stupid Maya could perhaps have struck upon the device of detaining him by not using any magic whatever: if she in secret flattered herself that this device was succeeding: and if she actually cherished the delusion that she was hoodwinking omniscient Fair-haired Hoo, the Helper and Preserver, the Lord of the Third Truth, the Well-beloved of Heavenly Ones?

Anyhow, his life here very amiably contented him for the while. The local circles of sorcerers and wizards were pleasant enough, barring only that haunting memory as to how they used unchristened children. Gerald and Maya did not go out a great deal; but they were on friendly terms with the neighbors; they attended an occasional Sabbat; and they kept in touch generally with the affairs of Turoine. And for the rest, the little happenings of his home life temporarily contented the Lord of the Third Truth.

And he began to reflect that, just possibly, Antan might be to him, after he had entered into his kingdom, a disappointment. From here Antan seemed uniformly wonderful. It was astonishingly pleasant to sit upon the western porch of the small cottage, especially toward evening, when your shoes propped up before you on the porch railing reflected a pinkish glow from the sunset, and to imagine what was going on in that broad expanse of yet unvisited fields and hills which now were turning into gray and purple mists directly beneath the gold and crimson of the sunset. The trouble was that you, who were gifted with the imagination of a god, were very certainly imagining more wonderful happenings for that mysterious theatre than could by any chance be enacted there.

For one matter, after dark, Antan always displayed eight lights, six of them grouped together in the middle of the vista with the general effect of a cross, and the other two showing much farther off to the northwest. About those never-varying huge lights Gerald had formed at least twenty delightful theories, all plausible as long as you remained upon Mispec Moor, whereas if you went to Antan, only one of these theories could prove true.

To go to Antan thus meant the destruction of no less than nineteen rather beautiful ideas as to those lights alone. However, Gerald felt, there was no help for this: and he whole-heartedly meant to take over his appointed kingdom without any unpleasant criticizing, no matter what might be the deficiencies of the place, by and by. Meanwhile, there was no great hurry: and it was, indeed, a prudent and long-sighted course for him to be pausing here to enjoy these fine scenic effects, because by and by he would not ever again be seeing Antan from this distance.

CONTENTMENT OF THE MISLAID GOD

After nightfall those eight lights never varied. But by day there was always a different and, as it seemed, a more lovely display of rounded, parti-colored, cleared hills, which here and there were darklier streaked, no doubt with orchards. Beyond them many flat-topped mountains showed, yet farther to the west, like a sleeping herd of gigantic blue crocodiles all couched across the west and facing north. And above so much terrestrial graciousness moved an incessant pageant of clouds, not a bit like the flat clouds which you looked up at from Lichfield, because the clouds which brooded over Antan were seen, from Gerald's station upon Mispec Moor, as on a level with you: and, when they were thus con-sidered sidewise, they resembled moving walls and crags and drifting curtains through which the sun-light smote in slanting and huge and pallid and quite tangible looking shafts.

Always, too, you noticed, nowadays, that vast and violet-shrouded, high-breasted woman's figure lying yonder, motionless, with that ever-burning heart; and you were visited by an odd fancy. You fancied that Queen Freydis, the as yet unwon-to queen of your appointed kingdom, was like that woman. And this fancy came to you none the less often because of your plain perception of its illogic.

" Come, now! " said Gerald, " a mistress of that size would be unsuitable. Charms of so diffuse an acreage would create, even in a god, a sense of in-adequacy. Nevertheless, I am falling rather ardently in love with those two hills. I begin to adore the cas-ual play of lights and shadows upon yonder piled-up dirt, which when seen from any other station than this would not in the least resemble a woman. And

[245]

such amorous notions, apart from their insanity, are not befitting in a contentedly, if temporarily, married person."

The transience of his comforts made them very dear. It was well worth the inconvenience of sleeping in his spectacles (as Gerald, for his own reasons, did) so that in the night season he could awaken, to see Maya's tranquil brown head yonder beside the smaller and tousled and livelily red head of Theodorick Quentin Musgrave, — both visible yonder because of the lamp which the child demanded at night, and because of his insistence that Mother was to sleep with him instead of with Father.

Outside, Gerald would hear those of his transformed predecessors who now were horses, shuffling and restively stamping, and at times snorting and whinnying, in the chill outer darkness; or a misguided gentleman who lived nowadays as a steer would low, much farther off; or Gerald would hear yet another one of Maya's former husbands coughing, with the far-reaching and morose scornfulness peculiar to a sheep. And then the difference between the estate of Gerald's predecessors and the snug warmth of his so comfortable soft bed, and his knowledge of that unmarred bodily ease which, just now, was his through every hour of the day, would trouble Gerald, because he knew it all to be so satisfying and so transient.

PART TEN

THE BOOK OF ENDINGS

" Trust *Nobody but Thyself, and
None Other will Betray Thee.*"

S O GERALD stayed content enough, all through those pleasant summer days. It was odd to reflect that these days were counting as he did not know how many years in Lichfield. He would now and then contrast himself with his great ancestor Dom Manuel, the same about whom, in that quaint far-off time when Gerald had believed himself merely human, and was interested in such human nonsense, Gerald had intended to write a romance, — because the Redeemer of Poictesme, as Gerald remembered it, had passed a month with the wood demon Béda, in the forest of Dun Vlechlan, where the company consisted entirely of evil principles, and where the passing of each day left Manuel a year older.

Gerald would reflect how much more sensible and pleasant was the course which he was following, surrounded with every domestic virtue, where the days did not count at all. For Gerald was content, and certainly he had grown no older in body. He had become used to living upon Mispec Moor: he wondered sometimes if Antan could afford any splendor which he personally would find more to his taste; and he felt that he would honestly miss the simple wholesome ways of Maya's log and plaster cottage after he had entered forever into the red-pillared palace

[249]

of his kingdom beyond good and evil, — next week, perhaps, or at all events not later than September.

And it stayed diverting to observe those persons who almost every day passed beyond Mispec Moor in their journeying toward the goal of all the gods of men. Then by and by one of these wayfarers turned out to be a stalwart, white-bearded old gentleman dressed as a bishop. And the sight of him delighted Gerald: for here at last was somebody who could perhaps christen Theodorick Quentin Musgrave.

Meanwhile this traveler was asking hospitality of Maya. She, who disliked travelers, prepared the white and tender flesh of a calf, she kneaded cakes of fine meal and baked them upon the hearth, she fetched milk and butter. All these she set before the seeming bishop upon the front porch of her cottage quite affably. For this old gentleman, it appeared, had known Maya of the Fair Breasts a great while ago, at the very beginning of a career confessedly so populous in husbands that Gerald always felt a certain delicacy in asking questions about it.

" But there was never any reasoning with you, my dear," said the old gentleman, as they all ate amicably together upon the porch. " So you eluded my purpose, and you preferred to content that first man of yours for his loss of the over-wilful beauty and the rebellious wisdom of your predecessor — "

Maya replied: " I do wish you would try just one more of those cakes, for I made them myself, exactly as you used to like them in the plains of Mamrê, when you were up to your nonsense with Sarah. Yes, I believe that a girl, a really nice girl, that is, should keep her caresses for her husband. Oh, I am casting no reflections upon either of your sweethearts. It is a matter every woman must decide for herself. I merely say that, for my part, I think a love-affair with a god while he is still in power is ostentatious and can only end in unhappiness — "

" But — ! " Gerald had begun indignantly.

She patted his hand. " No, Gerald, I did not mean you. Your power is limitless, and you are quite different from all other gods, and nobody knows that better than I do. So please do not start any pouting while we have company! He thinks that he is a god, too," Maya then stated, casually, to her visitor. " That is why his feelings are upset. He believes he is the Fair-haired Hoodoo, the Yelper and the Pretender, or something of that sort. As for that woman, Adam was very lucky to get rid of her."

" I wonder," said the white-bearded gentleman, smiling reminiscently, " I wonder if he always thought so? "

" My dear old friend! but you and I know quite well what the creatures are! Of course he cherished the memory of her for the rest of his life, long after the worthless piece had gone, just literally, to the devil. She was not bad looking: that much, anyhow, one can say in her favor: and so the poor fellow had always his memories of that beauty which he had known, once. He used to say it was too lovely to be retained by any man. And I agreed with him. No man had the least chance, with infernal connoisseurs about. . . . And his sons," said Maya, as she reflectively scratched at her nose, " have, somehow, all preserved that memory. There is no one of them but now and then finds my daughters rather inadequate, and half remembers that woman and gets lackadaisical over her. It is just another thing about the creatures which my daughters have to put up with."

" She too is yonder, they tell me," — and the old gentleman nodded toward Antan. Then he continued: " And I suspect there is no one of your daughters but is jealous of this ever-living memory of that Lilith who stays always the first, never quite forgotten love of every son of Adam; and who prevents more of them than you would care to acknowledge, my dear, from ever utterly giving over their hearts to any of your daughters."

" We are jealous, within limits," Maya replied, in the while that she hospitably refilled his glass with fresh milk. " No woman likes playing second fiddle, even in the moonstruck brain of a poet. Yet my daughters know it does no real harm. And if men were not up to something, they would be up to something else. Besides, it gives them their nonsense to be romantic over in private, without pestering their poor sweethearts, and their wives too at first, to be romantic along with them, which is a thing no nice woman really feels comfortable about — "

But the old gentleman had sighed. " You touch upon a somewhat harrowing subject. For I fancy that no other luckless being has ever had to cater to the shifting needs of popular romance so arduously or so variously as I."

And Maya now was beaming upon him quite fondly. " Yes, but how clever you have been about it! In fact, I suppose that nobody anywhere has ever had a more wonderful career than yours. And it seems only yesterday — does it not? — that we were all young together in the Garden, and your reputation was merely local. But you Jews are so adaptable! ”

“ I was not even a Jew, my dear, to begin with. Perhaps that is why I never quite got on with them. I was a storm deity of the Midianites. But the Jews kidnapped me, in some way or another, when I was just a godling playing happily with my thunderbolts about the crags of Sinai.”

“ Even so, when I think of what a position you have attained in the best Christian circles, and of the perfect respectability of the church to which you now belong, and of all the splendid poetry you have inspired, and of how generally famous you have become everywhere, I am wholly proud that you once, when we were both younger ” — and Gerald saw that Maya had colored up rather prettily, — “ had other plans for me.”

“ You,” said the old gentleman, — who, as Gerald now observed, was really quite Jewish looking, — “ were the first of my disappointments. Yes, I suppose that in many respects my career has been unusual. Yet it has ended by placing me in a most awkward position: and nothing ever turned out in accordance with my plans, somehow.”

Then the stalwart, white-bearded old gentleman who was dressed as a bishop spoke of his first family, and of how his descendants through a son named Isaac went astray. He spoke of his efforts to retain the affection of his family, through the vigorous methods appropriate to a storm god. But nothing had seemed to avail. There had been fine plagues and deluges and captivities and decimations and devastating miracles by the score. He had sent the swords of Babylon and of Philistia and of dozens of

[253]

other kingdoms to slay them, and huge dogs to tear their corpses, and many birds of prey and all the wild beasts of earth to devour and to destroy them, without arousing one ray of real affection. He had laid waste their cities; he had made their widows as the sands of the sea; he had starved them, and had smitten them with leprosy, and had burned them with lightnings; he had afflicted them with the most voluble and pessimistic prophets: he had, in a word, done absolutely everything he could think of as likely to requicken their waning affection. But the more he annoyed his descendants, the less they had seemed really to love him. Upon the heels of every warning, and immediately after each paternal correction, the survivors of it seemed only the more inclined to prefer some other patron: and it was all exceedingly discouraging.

And of his second son he spoke also. Here he became remarkably vague, and he talked as if muddled by the whole affair. There had been a great sacrifice and an atonement, the workings of which the old gentleman could not pretend to understand. He could not yet say just who had been put in a more amiable frame of mind by that atonement, since personally he imagined any father would have found it most distasteful and upsetting. Anyhow, the affair had resulted in a church with which he had felt it rather his duty to associate himself. And, awkwardly enough, after he had thus been persuaded by them formally to commit himself to a policy of peace and forgiveness and general loving-kindness, his incomprehensible servants had gone on squabbling and murdering, only much more often than before, because now they did it on high moral grounds. They had fought over transubstantiation, and over Greek diphthongs, and over the respective merits of complete and frontal baptism, and over infant damnation, and over redemption through faith alone, and over a number of other recondite matters which no Arabian storm god, very simply reared in the country during the really formative years of his life, and with no regular academic training, could well be expected to understand: and it was all exceedingly discouraging.

Nor to-day was his position much happier. He found himself ranked rather high in the church with which he was associated professionally. Yes, the old gentleman admitted, with plain bewilderment, his name was honored. But all his actions — even such quite notable actions as holding a conference with his disciples in a fiery furnace, and affording his messengers inter-urban transportation by means of a whale, and causing the sun itself to stand still, — all these fine exploits, along with his every natural exhibition of the irascibility and truculence appropriate to a storm god, had been reduced to poetic inventions. His very existence had been complicated with a triplicity which, since the mind could not grasp it, prevented his existence from being, actually, believed in by anybody. That had seemed, from the first moment he heard of it, a doctrine a bit difficult for him personally to accept, after having been an undivided deity in regular practice for so many thousands of years. And eighteen centuries of pondering upon that doctrine of his triune nature, to which he was through his official position committed, had showed a matter so abstruse and puzzling to be far beyond the comprehension of any country-bred Arabian storm god, howsoever faithfully he had broadened his mind, at the courts of various Christian monarchs and in the larger nunneries, since the commencement of his religious training among the farming element of Seir and Sinai. Nor could he honestly say that he had ever been able to take quite kindly to the notion that his being was confessedly a mystery not to be understood by prelates graduated from the best seminaries, and that his actions were all poetic inventions. For that left of him, so far as could be seen by a plain-thinking Arabian storm god, nothing which the human mind could grasp as an actuality; it made every one of his really thorough-going servants who accepted utterly the teachings of his church, so far as he could infer, a devotee of vacuousness: and it was all exceedingly discouraging.

" Altogether," said the old gentleman who was dressed as a bishop, " I feel that my present ranking in the Christian church is a perplexing and, in some sense, a false position for an Arabian storm god. I have aged under it. Oh, I have tried to be quite fair about the matter. Sometimes I even go so far as to concede that people who have never met a particular person might, just possibly, believe that person to be three persons whose actions were all poetic inventions. The human imagination is vigorous. I must point out to you, though, my friends, that nobody could conceivably believe that about himself. These very curious theories about me thus postulate the existence of at least one sceptic, and they hinge indeed upon the existence of that sceptic, in me. Now, I feel instinctively there must be an error in any such logic. I feel it unfair that I alone of all the persons connected with my church should be inevitably doomed

[256]

to remain an atheist. And I have aged steadily under the injustice and unreason of it all. Otherwise, if I yet retained the vigor of my youth, I might yet, in my frank way, attempt to clean the slate, as it were, with whirlwinds and thunderbolts and another deluge or so, and to make a fresh start all around. But, alas, I have aged, my dear Havvah, since the days of our first acquaintance. The inexplicable theology and the rationalization, as they call it, to which I have been subjected by my incomprehensible servants, now for some eighteen centuries with ever increasing rigor, have brought me to the point that I cannot logically believe in my own existence. The things they tell me simply do not hold together. And so — "

He comprehensively waved his hand toward Antan.

But Gerald rose, and Gerald put aside his glass of milk and his veal sandwich.

And Gerald said, beamingly: " You who have traveled through the Marches of Antan, wherein only two truths endure, and the one teaching is that we copulate and die, — you at least, I know, must, as a leading official of the Protestant Episcopal Church, look confidently forward to finding in the goal of all the gods a third truth. The fact emboldens me to ask that you do but answer me this very simple question — "

" Alas, my friend," the badgered looking old gentleman broke in, " professionally, of course, my faith is all that it should be. But in my private capacity, as a plain-thinking Arabian storm god, now that I am retiring from active churchwork, I suspect that when anybody anywhere once understands the nature of any two truths, that will be quite time enough for

[257]

him to be requiring a third truth to exercise his wits upon."

" That truism, sir, is not to be denied," said Gerald, rather crestfallen. " Yet that is likewise an evasion."

" In fact," said the bewildered old gentleman, shaking sadly his white head, " in fact, ever since I acquired triplicity, I have been accused of duplicity also. The Gnostics, I remember, said very unkind things about that: the Valentinians were no more charitable: whereas I would really hesitate to repeat, my friends, the remarks of the Priscillianists."

" — And in any case," Gerald said, emphatically, " howsoever you may evade me, it would not do for you to evade your duties to the Protestant Episcopal Church. The world as yet has need of bishops and of all that they signify. I must point out to you, sir, that the wild talking of bishops yet frightens many persons into a thrifty-minded practice of generally beneficent virtues. Indeed, sir, bishops remind me rather of calomel in the effect which they have upon the run of men, because I find their effect too to be, ultimately, beneficial. There are also other points of resemblance. And if the strange ways of episcopal action now and then upset you, sir, you ought to remember that it is, after all, for the general good. I, moreover, must point out that it absolutely would not do for you to go into Antan and be one of my subjects — "

" He thinks," Maya once more explained, parenthetically, to her guest, " that he is a god, you understand."

" But I am! " said Gerald. " These continual interruptions are really very awkward, my dear. And the present situation also is awkward, in view of my Protestant Episcopal upbringing. It is a situation which must at any cost be avoided. This gentleman simply must not go into Antan."

"But what is to be done about it?"

"Oh, do you not be uneasy! Your age, sir, and its attendant delusions, such as wanting to go into Antan, are matters quite easily remedied by any competent Dirghic deity. You could not possibly have pursued a wiser course than to come to me for assistance. So, if you will permit me, sir — "

Thereafter Gerald, still in something of a flutter, baptized the old gentleman who was dressed as a bishop with the last remaining drop of water from the Churning of the Ocean.

FORTHWITH the old white-bearded gentle-man became a most personable looking young-ish Oriental, who shone with a fiery radiance, and about whose head played a continual flashing like small lightnings. And he said, approvingly:

"That is a fine magic which has restored to me my youth and the vigorousness I had in Midian before I was kidnapped by those stiff-necked and unaffec-tionate Jews."

"And will you now be going into Antan?" asked Gerald, rather anxiously.

"Not yet, my friend," replied the merry, strong, young Arabian storm god. "Oh, very certainly, not yet! No, I have had quite enough of my illogical position as a Christian and of the worries of being rationalized by incomprehensible foreigners. I shall thankfully return to my Midianites and to my little shrines upon Seir and Sinai and Horeb, and to the quiet living of a local godling. I shall be hearing again my own people's sane and intelligible prayers for rain, and I shall be snuffing up the smoke of such rational offerings as kids and goats and an occasional prisoner of war, just as I used to do, where I was given due credit for my actions, and where you heard no unpleasant personal scandal circulated about my being triplets. In the mean while, my benefactor, is there not any favor which, in my turn, I can do you?"

BAPTISM OF A MUSGRAVE

" Indeed, my dear sir," Gerald answered, harking back to that worriment which in a neighborhood so full of sorcerers and wizards stayed always in the rear of Gerald's mind, " there is a small one, now you mention it. For we have a boy, as you perceive. And it occurs to me that this is the first chance to have Theodorick Quentin Musgrave properly christened according to the rites of the Protestant Episcopal Church — "

The storm god asked of Gerald, in good-humored surprise, " But do I now look to you much like an Episcopalian clergyman? "

" Well, sir, I admit the situation is perplexing. Nevertheless, you remain, so far as I can see, one of the three official heads of the Christian church, in every denomination. And as such, you must be wholly competent to administer the sacred rites of that baptism to which we Musgraves are accustomed."

He who had been a bishop laughed again. For an instant he glanced sidewise at Maya, rather impishly. Then the god called to him Theodorick Quentin Musgrave.

The boy came forward without speaking. There had never been any dearer brat since time began, Gerald reflected, than was this sturdy droll redheaded jackanapes who waited there holding his small chin well up in order to look with politely puzzled interest at the storm god's glittering face and the tiny lightnings which played about it. Gerald was abeam with the most fatuous sort of pride in Theodorick's perfect behavior. Gerald glowed all over, now that awkward matter of the boy's christening was being at last attended to, by the very highest authority. And Gerald nodded smilingly and with some inconsequence at his dear stupid Maya, so that she too might note how splendidly Theodorick was behaving. The boy was displaying the composure and the excellent manners of a true Musgrave.

Then the storm god dipped his fingers in his unfinished glass of milk, and upon Theodorick's lifted forehead he drew a sign. Gerald was not wholly certain, afterward, that it was the sign of a cross.

" This is another sort of baptism than that which restored my youth. For youth this child already has, — to every seeming," the god said, a bit unaccountably. " Therefore I now release this child whom I did not create, I release him from the bondage of the woman and of the Adversary who caused him to live upon this earth. I decree a forgiveness for the seven crimes. I cry a remission of the seven punishments."

" I must say, though, you have been long enough about it," Maya placidly observed. . . .

As for Gerald, now that the ceremony was over, he was unaffectedly hugging Theodorick, and telling him that he was far too big a boy to be kissing people, and the vaguely puzzled, clinging child was asking, But who started it, Father? . . .

And the storm god was saying to Maya, " Do you forget, my dear Havvah, that it is from your service I am releasing him? "

She answered, still quite placidly: " So far as that goes, the imp has well earned a holiday; and it is not as if I were dependent upon him. No, but I confess to wondering — and not for the first time, either, — just what you may be up to."

S O THE Oriental storm god went back into the world of everyday, to look for his old shrines upon Sinai and Horeb: and Gerald was happily rid of a future subject whom, he could not but feel, it would have been a bit awkward to have as a subject. And the evening passed tranquilly, although it seemed to Gerald that Theodorick was rather moody and quiet after his christening.

But it was not until the next day that Theodorick, just after breakfast, spoke with a voice which seemed to Gerald not quite the voice of a child: and Theodorick told his parents he wanted to go down into Antan.

Gerald was troubled. Yet he suggested, with very careful levity, " If — ? "

" If you please," the but half-smiling, ugly, so dear brat now added, docilely.

" Why, it must be as your father says," Maya replied. She had paused in her sweeping off of the porch, and for a moment she held the broom slantwise as she meditated over the boy's notion. " But for one, I see no great harm in your having a little outing, for I will put a protection on you. Only, you must promise to be back in good time to have your face and hands washed for supper."

Gerald said forlornly, " But what are those small yellow things you are sweeping from the porch, my dear? "

" They are fallen leaves from a sycamore-tree, left here last night by that wind, Gerald: and I really do wish you would not ask such silly questions, when I was talking about something quite different."

" But that means summer is ending, Maya. It means an end of all growing. It means that not anything now will become any larger or more lovely."

" Upon my word, but I never did hear of any such nonsense as you do talk sometimes, for a grown man, Gerald, as if summer did not always end! "

" That is it, precisely. It always ends: and the warmth and comfort of it perish. Yes, there is death in the air. I do not find that cheering. And that is all, my darling."

" Why, then, Gerald, if you are quite through with that up-in-the-air sort of talking — which may be very deep and clever indeed, only I happen not to understand it, and certainly have no wish to, — why, then, I was asking you about something entirely different. But that is the way it is. For all the attention you ever pay to me, I might as well not be living, much less trying to get this porch clean, with your clumsy feet everywhere I turn, instead of your showing the least natural interest in your own child."

" Oh, yes, you were speaking of Theodorick! Well, boys do get restless without any playmates, I suppose. I will talk to him about his notion while you are making up the beds."

Nothing could have been more prosaic. Yet Gerald was troubled. He could hear Maya inside the cottage, already thumping at the pillows. All about him seemed matter of fact, and comfortable, and familiar, and stable. And yet everything, as he somehow knew, was about to change. There awoke in him as yet no real sorrow, but a faint uneasiness mixed with resentment, now that he noted the fall of the first leaf in autumn, and knew he was powerless to stay the beginning change in everything about his small, snug home.

THEN Gerald followed the child down to the roadside. And they talked together under the chestnut-tree, just where Gerald had talked with so many strange beings who had passed beyond Mispec Moor in that continuous journeying toward Antan.

First Gerald performed that needful rite which would reveal the truth. The child watched quietly. By and by Theodorick began to smile. But he said never a word until his father was through with these droll doings.

Then Gerald questioned his small son. Theodorick replied. The appearance of a little child still sat there, and the soft red lips of a child were moving, but that curious tongue which was like a small white serpent was speaking about matters never known to any child.

No one of Gerald's excursions into the darker magics had prepared him for what was now in part revealed. About the spaces which are outside the world apparent to human senses Gerald knew; and of the realms beyond Earth's orbit he, as a former student of magic, was not ignorant. But now he understood from what remote abyss his wife had drawn the being which seemed his child: a bit unwillingly, he could even surmise with what kind of enchantments Maya had fetched this seeming into

[266]

the happier superficial world which is apparent to human senses.

And Gerald was moved: he was, as so many husbands have been, before and since, now almost frightened by this glimpse of the unswerving and whole-hearted and unscrupulous love which women nourish for that man whom marriage has given them to look after. He was not worthy, he contritely felt, of being thus idolized and of being coddled at the fearful price of such unearthly indiscretions. And Gerald was sincerely touched, now that he comprehended to what lengths Maya had gone to gratify his whim of wanting a son, out of hand. She had warned him, too, that he was contriving for himself grief. Yes, her womanly intuition had, somehow, foreseen that to which all his cleverness had been blind. And yet, even so, Maya had not denied him his desire, because poor Maya pampered him in everything, to the accompaniment of a commentary howsoever tart.

Gerald thought also of how, a moment since, his worst dread had been that the boy was an illusion. He looked at his beloved son, knowing now what inhabited that freckled and droll, sturdy little body. The boy had of a sudden become strange; he was now a threat of unimaginable danger, and a creature worse than evil: yet Gerald knew, with a dull wonder, that he loved Theodorick Quentin Musgrave even now. . . .

Gerald by and by put yet another question to this dreadful parody of a child's innocence and helplessness, to the being whom Gerald invoked as Abdel-Hareth.

" But I have served her purpose, — my father," the child replied, with a rather perturbing smile.

[267]

SOMETHING ABOUT EVE

" Oh, but I know! She has had many husbands. Most of them desired a son. I have always been that son."

Then, after an instant of silence, the being who was speaking through the child's dear lips told of the bonds from which the Midianite storm god's touch and absolution had released him. Gerald found this part of the story particularly unpleasant. And Theodorick Quentin Musgrave, whom Gerald still addressed as Abdel-Hareth, went on to tell why he must now go downward into Antan, to encounter, not the Master Philologist, but Queen Freydis.

Gerald asked, What was needed of Queen Freydis? The child told him. Gerald shivered. He felt, if only for the instant, physically cold and nauseated. Still, that this creature should desire to return to its unearthly home was natural enough.

" I comprehend," said Gerald. " I comprehend a great deal which was unknown to me ten minutes ago. I confess to being surprised by much that I have learned from you. Nevertheless, my son, — if you will pardon the force of habit, sir, and the love I had for my own little, so dear son — ! But I drift into emotional remarks which would be wholly out of place. My voice, as I note with sincere regret, evinces a distressing tendency — "

Gerald paused. He gulped. The seeming of a child regarded Gerald with cool and over-intelligent eyes; but the tongue which was like a small white serpent did not utter any word. Then Gerald spoke again, in a voice that was light and high-pitched and rather hysterical.

" In fine, my dear Abdel-Hareth, as you see, I incline somewhat to blubber like a badly whipped baby. I can but ask you to respect the emotions of a sud-

denly bereaved parent, without bothering to understand his confused utterances. No: you have given
me my desire, and my great happiness. A part of that
dies now. But I have had it, utterly. I am content.
I will see to it that you, in your turn, sir, get what
you desire."

IT WAS after using his handkerchief a bit that Gerald returned to Maya. Nor did it surprise him she had already prepared a neatly wrapped up lunch for Theodorick Quentin Musgrave to be eating that day in Antan.

Gerald said, with painstaking carelessness, " Well, my dear, after talking the matter over, I have decided we may as well let the boy go."

" Why, to be sure! " said Maya. " And a great deal of bother, too, there has been made this morning over nothing, as if I did not already have quite enough to bother me! "

And with that, she summoned from among her enchanted geldings the handsomer of the pair who formerly had been emperors.

" For a child of mine must go in proper state," said Maya.

Then Gerald said: " No. An imperial steed is well enough, but a divine steed is better. Let him take Kalki! "

" Now, really, Gerald, your unreasonableness sometimes surprises even me! For you know perfectly well that Kalki is your own horse, and that you will be needing him yourself when you ride down to the appointed kingdom you are always talking your stuff and nonsense about."

[270]

Gerald looked at her for some while. . . . He was conscious of a hushed great exultation that in a world wherein all else seemed doubtful and unstable he had, somehow, through blind luck, won to his Maya and her snappishness and her unswerving and whole-hearted and quite unscrupulous love for him. She was not pretty, she was not brilliant, she was not even easy to live with. But Gerald knew now that he and this woman were one person; and that there could be nothing in Antan to repay him for the loss of this dear and ever-wrangling, dull-witted Maya. His dependency upon her almost frightened him. . . .

Gerald said: " But it is prophesied that the power of Antan shall pass to the rider upon Kalki. No harm can befall the rider upon Kalki. So we will let — we will let our son take Kalki. For in this way we will secure his protection, and we will remove the one chance of my ever leaving you, who are worth all the kingdoms that have ever been."

Maya said, " But — "

Gerald, smiling, replied, " Nevertheless! "

Then the illusion called Theodorick Quentin Musgrave was lifted up by Gerald to the back of Kalki, and it was Gerald who adjusted the stirrups for his successor upon the divine steed. And the seeming of a child rode down toward the goal of all the gods, a rather quaintly pathetic little figure perched up there so high upon the back of the huge shining stallion.

Gerald watched the two pass out of his sight. His arms lifted after them ever so slightly. His arms seemed to ache as he recalled the feel of that small body and the warmth and yieldingness of it, which

were now lost forever. Theodorick Quentin Musgrave was only an illusion contrived by forces which
it was not comfortable to think about. Gerald knew
that now with certainty. And it did not matter. Nor
did it cheer him to reflect — as he did, — that he was
in no worse case than all other fathers, no one of
whom might ever retain the child that was little and
helpless, and was loved for no reason at all, as nobody could quite love the hobbledehoy thumping
schoolboy or even the estimable young man into
whom that warm and yielding, sturdy, so small body
might develop. . . .

Then Gerald turned to Maya. " I have only you.
But that which I have suffices me. I have been lucky,
O my dearest, very far beyond my merits."

She was regarding him with a sort of troubled
fondness; and her speech now was hardly snappish at
all. " You really are, my poor Gerald, quite too
ridiculous about the child! You talk, you actually do
talk, as though he were not ever coming back, —
and in good time for supper, too, unless he wants a
spanking."

At that, Gerald raised a protesting hand. " Do you
not trick me into optimism, also! Too much ambition,
and high dreams, and that which was perhaps divine,
have now departed forever. The illusion which you
created to be our son has departed, forever. But use
and wont and a great deal of honest love remain. I
do not say these things are heroic. I do say that these
suffice. So do you let the strong bonds which are
about me content you, my darling, without wreath-
ing them in the paper flowers of optimism."

" But are you, also," Maya said, " content? "

Gerald answered: " I am well content. Day in,

day out, let there be between us faith, and aid, and a
great fondness, O my dear, and no parting! I am
well content and very contrite. I know that any life
without you would be a maimed business. I know that
I desire only to continue in our quiet way of living
upon Mispec Moor. For the middle way of life is
best. What need have I to be a god or to be seeking
unfamiliar places so that I may rule over them?
That way is troubled, and too full of noise and striv-
ing. It is better to be content. It is better to be content with the dear, common happenings of human
life, shared loyally with the one woman whose love
for you is limitless and does not change, for all that
it is blind to none of your failings. It is the part of
wisdom to know that these things are enough and
very far beyond your deserts. It is the duty of an
honest husband not ever to be insanely hankering
after any more high-hearted manner of living which
is out of your reach or, at any rate, is attained through
more trouble than it is probably worth. And in the
cordial glow of his own hearth fire each one of us discovers by and by that the middle way of life is best."

"At least it is some comfort," Maya answered,
"to hear you talking almost sensibly."

Then she reached up, still with a grave and rather
tender smiling upon her beloved, homely face; and
she took away from Gerald's eyes the rose-colored
spectacles.

"In fact," said a male voice, "the woman's task
is ended."

FOR now had come to them, traveling back from Antan, the brown man. This brown man came, he said, to summon Maya to her appointed task of transforming yet other men into domestic animals.

" — For women," he said, also, " have always their fond task and their beneficent labor. Here, I repeat, the woman's task is ended. But yonder many men go untamed and unbroken to the sane ways of compromise."

Then Maya a bit absent-mindedly assented, as she put away those spectacles of hers for future use, that, in point of fact, she supposed she had done everything that was actually necessary in Gerald's case, although nobody ever would really know what a trial he had been to her.

And Gerald for one instant looked at his wife. He found in his wife's face that which it is the doom of most husbands to find there at one time or another. And it caused Gerald to laugh a little.

" Nevertheless," Gerald said, quietly, " I am Fair-haired Hoo, the Helper and the Preserver, the Well-beloved of Heavenly Ones. I am Lord of the Third Truth, in this world which knows of only two truths and of the compromises which they beget."

The brown man greeted that with a thin smile. " You have been long expected. Oh, very long have

[274]

scepticism and despair, with somewhat varying voices, invoked your name, saying, ' Who will over-throw the Master Philologist! ' "

" Well, and now," said Gerald, with the outline of a swagger, for he was getting himself more in hand, " now that prophecy is about to be fulfilled, for I am Hoo, and none other."

" But, really, friend, I do not see how you can be an interrogative pronoun."

" To a god, and more particularly to a Dirghic god, all incarnations are possible. There is no reason whatever why I should not be an interrogative pronoun. It is merely a matter of divine election."

And the brown man civilly inclined his grave brown head, as he remarked:

" Do you have it your own way! Indeed, my people have very often derived their deities from less promising locations than the pages of a grammar. And upon the whole, your epiphany is most gratifying. For I try to keep my people content: yet it has been lamented, from the beginning, that no mythology revealed a god who might answer that word which the Master Philologist speaks to all the gods of men. And so, between despair and scepticism, those of my people who were so unwise as to exercise their minds in fields wherein thinking does not make for happiness, have very long been saying, ' Who will redeem the goal of all the gods of men from the Master Philologist? ' Now it appears that this word also has become flesh; and that this interrogative pronoun Who? stands here before us. Yes, I consider that quite gratifying; for it is desirable that the sceptical and the despairing also should be contented, by being justified in their faith."

[275]

"You quibble," Gerald replied, "you quibble very tediously and frivolously, in the divine presence of a god who is about to take over his appointed kingdom, and to make known that Third Truth which is not known upon Mispec Moor, where the one teaching is that we copulate and die."

"But uncelestial common-sense has always been my failing. So I must tell you, friend, that it seems to me, now that you have abandoned the Redeemer's steed to a small freckled illusion, Antan has nothing to expect even from the mysterious awfulness of an interrogative pronoun. And yet, for one, I abandoned the place when your dwarfed deputy approached it —"

"And you acted wisely, sir," Gerald replied, with simple dignity. "No matter how potent may be the impious sorceries of the Master Philologist, a child has entered into his domain, fearing nothing and loving all. The fact that the powers of evil cannot prevail against this conjunction is well known to every citizen of the United States of America."

But the brown man still seemed rather moody. "I cannot say. . . . No, you and my friend Jahveh have, between you, loosed against Antan a power which is not of my kingdom. I therefore do not pretend to say what may come of the experiment. I merely await with lively interest, and at a reassuring distance, the upshot of this experiment, now that — of all the beings from beyond Earth's orbit, — Abdel-Hareth has been deputed to ride upon the Redeemer's steed."

"And, in any case, it is always very certain, dearie," Maya said, "that no real comfort can ever come of such foolish notions as I have ridded you of

[276]

a little by a little. And in exchange for those toplofty dreams, I have trusted you as far as seemed expedient, and I have given you all that was really good for you. I have given you a season of content and every wholesome joy of domesticity now for some thirty years of mortal time. No man gets more from life, my poor dearie. None attempts to get more without ending in disappointment and discontent: and so no sane man tries to get any more than you have had. And the end finds even the most wise and reasonable son of Adam — though, to be sure, that is not saying much, — if he but lives rationally enough to survive all thirty of those quiet happy years, with a wife who is just as I am, whatever she may have seemed to begin with."

Gerald saw, without any grief or horror, that he had now lost both his child and his wife. For Maya had become old. She was again the shrivelled and wrinkled creature, red and inflamed and hideous among her tousled tresses, that he had first found upon Mispec Moor. And fleetingly he reflected that she spoke the truth: all women, howsoever dear and beautiful, did become like that, provided they did not first die and become even more repulsive carrion. . . . But Gerald lacked time to discuss these generalities just now: for he had been looking toward Antan. . . .

" To this chatter about domesticity and pessimism and content," Gerald replied sternly, " I answer that the Well-beloved of Heavenly Ones is above all aphorisms. I answer that I am Hoo, the Lord of that Third Truth whose nature is unknown to you. Now that Third Truth is loosed. Do you look now upon Antan! "

The woman and the Adversary had turned when Gerald pointed, quite as majestically as though he knew just what he was talking about. In the midst of Antan they could see, as Gerald had already seen, a flaring green flame. Now this great flaming sunk earthward, much as the waters of a fountain descend; the flame spread evenly to every side, sweeping outward in an ever-widening circle; and now this flaming was no longer green, but red and glowing. You saw this flood of fire pass equally and swiftly, surging outward toward the horizon, where at once the mountains collapsed and disappeared. All that remained was flat and black and bare. Antan no longer existed.

It was after witnessing such an unanswerable performance by the Lord of the Third Truth that the woman and the Adversary looked back toward Gerald, with every sign of sincere respect.

And Gerald's bewilderment was rather more profound than theirs. He could surmise only that the dreadful being to whom he had given Kalki had held to its plan, as voiced by the lips of a child, and had loosed elemental fires of a nature incomprehensible to Gerald, since they were drawn from beyond Earth's orbit. Yet that seemed to Gerald no real reason for marring a fine attitude or for failing to preserve his self-respect before the woman and the Adversary. Tricked he might have been: that was a wholly different thing from ever admitting that he had been tricked. Gerald knew at least that the illusion which had appeared to be his son had entered the perhaps equally illusory place where Gerald now might never enter; and that, whatever had befallen the best loved but one of his illusions, the rider upon the silver stallion had destroyed Antan. And it seemed obvious, too, that Abdel-Hareth had returned homeward. . . .

Therefore Gerald claimed with a clear conscience the miracle which Gerald had, in fact, actually performed, at one remove. And Gerald kept his long chin, resolutely, well up. . . .

" So that," observed the brown man, quietly, " that is the end of Antan. I do not complain."

" I had forgotten," then said the wrinkled old woman who had been Maya of the Fair Breasts, " I had forgotten how wilful is that Abdel-Hareth who got his being upon Earth from me. Something of this sort was to be looked for, the first moment that the headstrong wretch was freed from my control. Still, Jahveh has gained less than we have gained through Jahveh's meddling. Abdel-Hareth has served me even at the last by removing Antan from the horizon. Earth will be quieter now; and my daughters will not be so hard put to it to keep men in reasonable order."

" I forget nothing," the brown man remarked, drily. " And so I did not await the coming of your first-born in the likeness of a child whose fearless innocence surmounts all evil. For it was the seeming of a little child who rode up against Antan, you conceive, with every appearance of that faith against which the snares of no sorcerer and of hardly nine woman in ten can prevail. Such innocence is a quite dangerous counterfeit. For one, I do not meddle with it nor with any other unearthly phenomenon. I have my realm. It suffices me."

The woman asked, " But what, what, Janicot, do you suppose has happened? "

" How shall we ever know, dear Havvah, when

[279]

SOMETHING ABOUT EVE

manifestly there are no survivors of that happening?
Antan, in any case, is no loss to us."

Here Gerald broke in upon their talking; and Gerald shook at them his red head lordlily.

" You little creatures guess in vain at the means which I have employed. And equally in vain will you supplicate me to reveal those means. For I shall tell you nothing. It is sufficient that the Well-beloved of Heavenly Ones has accomplished the mission of his tenth incarnation with a thoroughness not customary in interrogative pronouns. I came to redeem my appointed kingdom from the rule of usurpers. I came as the Lord of that Third Truth which is unknown to those who teach only that we copulate and die. That Third Truth has been loosed. No, I shall tell you nothing of its nature, for you are not fit to comprehend the Third Truth. But the mightiness of it your own eyes have witnessed. So Antan is now redeemed — "

His voice broke here. But Gerald presently continued:

" Antan is now redeemed at a great price. That woman and that child to whom my heart was given have perished. I remain. I know that these two were illusions. Nevertheless, I remain. There is no bond upon the Lord of the Third Truth to be happy: there is a strong bond upon every Helper and Preserver not to evade the full discharge of his mission. What, you may ask of me, is the mission of the Lord of the Third Truth? And I will reply to you out of my divine wisdom. It is the mission of the Lord of the Third Truth, howsoever he may palter or struggle against his doom, to destroy that which he most loves."

NOW Gerald sat with his head bowed. He heard a talking between the old woman who had been his Maya and the brown man who was the Adversary of all the gods of men.

"What is it men desire?" said the woman. "My daughters prepare for them fine food and drink, my daughters see to it that their homes are snug, and at the end of each day my daughters love them dutifully. All things that men can ask for, my daughters furnish them. Why need men cherish strange desires which do not know their aim? for how can any of my daughters content such desires?"

"I also marvel at the desires of men," replied the Adversary. "I, too, am ready to accord whatsoever a man can ask for sensibly and in plain words. I, who am the Prince of this world, remain a generous and ever-indulgent monarch. I will to make my people happy. My curious opulence awaits at every hand to afford my subjects whatsoever they can ask. But men want more. They desire that which was never in my kingdom. They have followed after impalpable gods: they have been enamored of phantoms. They have believed that their desire was in Antan, in part because they did not know what was their desire, and in part because they did not know what was Antan. Yes, it is a large blessing to my people that Antan has perished."

SOMETHING ABOUT EVE

" This world is well enough," the woman said. " It is well to be born into this world of an ever-loving mother. It is well to be a young man in this world wherein one may follow after young women and be cherished by them. There is soft living in this world when you have come as near discretion as men ever get and have had the wit to find a wife to take care of you. And at the end it is well to fare out of this world quietly and incuriously, with a deft-handed woman to nurse you and to wash your body afterward. But men want more."

" This world is very good. My kingdom is a wholly sufficing kingdom," agreed the Adversary. " The wise man, as goes human wisdom, will be content with the inexhaustible goodness of those material things which all are mine. For the five senses are an endless comfort; the five senses are an endless store of anodynes. A man may purchase bodily ease and a drugged brain with his five senses. But men want more."

" So they have passed beyond my daughters," the woman said. " One by one, a many have passed, perversely and so lonelily, from all my daughters could contrive to content them: and one by one a host of demented romantic men have struggled toward Antan, and toward what befalls all mortals and immortals there. Yes, it is very well that Antan has perished."

" One by one," said the Adversary, " they have derided my kingdom. They have followed after impalpable gods. These gods passed futilely. But they drew many of my subjects from me, all to be lost forever in that beguiling Antan."

" Men are great fools, " the woman said, " and

my daughters may not control the folly of all men. That which my daughters can do, they perform willingly. But not all men could my daughters preserve from the madness which drew men toward Antan and into ruinous desires to judge the goal of every god. At last, Antan has fallen: it is very well."

The Adversary said, more leniently: "Men are, beyond doubt, great fools. But they are my people; and those that I can save I save. Yet many evade me. And their dreaming troubles all my kingdom, and me, too, they trouble now and then. But Antan has fallen: and after that foolishness at least my people will not be following any more."

The woman answered him: "The daughters of Eve are not troubled now and then, they are troubled at every moment, by the dreams of men. Such of these blundering men as fond and eternal laboring may save, my daughters win away from their toplofty dreams. But the work is hard; the work is endless; and our losses are many."

And then the Adversary said: "We two who began in the Garden to contrive for the happiness of men, and to be speaking always for the real good of men, — yes, certainly, our work is hard and endless. For men stay romantically minded creatures who aspire beyond my kingdom. Yet we do not despair."

WHEN Gerald raised his head he was alone on the naked moor, for the brown man had departed, and Maya had gone away with the first of all her lovers, and her illusions had vanished, including the neat log and plaster cottage. And mists were creeping up from the ruined kingdom of Antan, in billows of ever-thickening gray which seemed to be the smoke from that great burning.

Then Gerald said:

" I have come out of my native home on a gainless journeying with no profit in it: yet there has been pleasure in that journeying. I do not complain. Let every man that must journey, without ever knowing why, from the dark womb of his mother to the dark womb of his grave, take pattern by me!

" For all that every pleasure is departed from me, I have had pleasure. I do not grieve because I have gained nothing in my journeying. The great and best words of the Master Philologist stay unrevealed; that supreme word which was in the beginning, and which will be when all else has perished, I may not surmise: but I have played with many words which were rather pretty. In the art of magic, which I chose to be my art, I have performed no earth-shaking wonders, yet in small thaumaturgies I have had some hand. I did not ride the divine steed to my journey's end: but a part of the way I rode quite royally.

" That which I heard of from afar I have not won to in my foiled journeying. So I now cry farewell to that Queen Freydis whom, I suspect, I might have loved with a great love if lesser women had not solicited me. I cry farewell to the Mirror of the Hidden Children in which, I believe, I might have found myself as I am, and might have come to knowledge of the Third Truth. And I cry farewell to Antan, to that never-won-to goal of all the gods which was, I think, my appointed kingdom. I have surmised high things. I have gained none of them. My doom has been a little doom. It contents me.

" I may well be content, because all that a man may hope for I have had, who have learned at least that the lot of a man is more sure than the lot of any god. For the deceit which you put upon me, O venerable and subtle Æsred, I cry out my gratitude. There was the seeming of a home and of a woman who loved and tended me and of a child. I may not speak of my love for these illusions. Now they have perished. But my memories remain: and they are more dear to me than is any real thing.

" All, all, is perished! It may be that I have offended the two truths which I did not esteem sufficiently august. And I who willed to be Lord of the Third Truth have found no third truth anywhere. I have found only comfortably colored illusions. But I am content with that which I have found here upon Mispec Moor."

In the while that Gerald had been speaking, the mists rose thicker and thicker from destroyed Antan. He had noted in the while that he spoke how the first wavering thin billows crept tentatively up the hills and along the roadway, creeping upon the ground, and under the low-swinging tree branches, with, as it seemed, a pre-meditated furtiveness; and then, as if emboldened by finding the way unopposed, these mists had risen up from the ground, always swiftlier, until at last they had eclipsed all. Gerald, now that he ended his talking, could see nothing palpable anywhere save the little patch of inter-mingled stone and grass immediately beneath his feet; and about him everywhere were the cool mists, lighted with a diffused gray radiancy which seemed to come from all sides.

PART ELEVEN

THE BOOK OF REMNANTS

" When *Wages are Paid, Work is Over.*"

GERALD now was wandering among thick luminous gray mists, on a gray way which led through long quieted places. It led him to a weather-beaten pavilion of badly stained and tattered cloth which once had been flesh-colored.

Within this pavilion was a masked skeleton. The gleaming bones sat upright, and in unmarred order, in a gilded chair. A fan lay in the lap of this skeleton, a fan that was painted with the gay amours of Harlequin and Columbine, which Pierrot was observing, wistfully, through a gap in a yew-hedge: and the skeleton wore a little black velvet carnival mask, which covered all the upper front part of the skull, about the eye-sockets.

And beyond that was a castle, whose exterior was overlaid with cracked and peeling black-and-gold lacquer work. This castle was empty everywhere of any inhabitant. Gerald passed through its courtyard and about many large rooms and corridors, all hung with faded, very ancient tapestries. He encountered nobody. Then he came to the inmost tower, builded of horn, and so into the room which had been the bedchamber of the lord of that castle, and he perceived the reason why not even mice nor spiders dared to dwell in that place.

Afterward Gerald came to a dragon's den. But the dragon was dead long ago, and the cupboards of that den were as empty as had been the castle of Vraidex, except for a pepper cruet and a salt cruet, both of time-blackened silver, and a light golden semi-circular crown inset with emeralds such as blonde princesses were accustomed to wear in that dragon's heyday.

Thence Gerald passed to a jousting ground, and that too was tenantless and fallen into decay. In the paved place where knights had tilted against one another lay at random nineteen broken spears and three tarnished shields. In the ladies' gallery Gerald found only a chamber pot. The hangings of this gallery were discolored and torn, but you could yet see that these hangings had been of black cloth embroidered with small rearing silver horses.

And Gerald came also to a green pasture through which flowed unruffled a deep stream of still water. This pasture was strewn everywhere with many curious objects. He noted a crozier, and a wheel, and a camel-hair shirt, and a huge gridiron, and a copper dish containing the breasts of a young woman. He found in that pasture also a porcelain box of ointment, and a great saw, and a blue hat, and a large iron comb, which like the saw had long-dried blood upon its teeth, and a palm branch, and two enormous, very rusty keys marked with the monogram S. P.

Then Gerald passed where three crosses lay overturned.

And beyond that the way was yet more murky. To this hand and the other hand Gerald could just dimly divine the ruined porticos and domes and pylons of incredibly ancient buildings: he seemed to go among obelisks and many-storied square towers. But all was very gray and dubious. He wandered now in a cloudiness wherein not anything was indisputable.

He passed across a narrow bridge beneath which showed a dark and sluggish river. In that water Gerald could see moving, many-colored figures which were not strange to him. For Evasherah was there, and Evaine, and Evadne, and Evarvan also, smiling at him now for the last time, and he could see how notably they had all resembled one another. And yet one more woman was there, a blue-clad woman in a crown just such as Maya had worn before she became his wife, but the face of this woman Gerald could not clearly discern.

And upon the farther bank of the dark river one sat among a herd of black swine, and the eyes of all these swine gleamed meditatively at Gerald through their ragged white lashes. The man arose: and Gerald saw this swine-driver was that same young red-haired Horvendile who was Lord of the Marches of Antan.

Then Horvendile began to speak.

HORVENDILE spoke of the race of Manuel, and of the joy, and the vexation, too, which the antics of this so inadequate race had been to Horvendile. And it was of Merlin that Gerald was thinking now, for it seemed to him that here was yet another poet who did not any longer delight to shape and to play with puppets, because Horvendile was saying:

"Now I abandon a race whose needs are insatiable. For tall Manuel lived always wanting what he had not ever found, and never, quite, knowing what thing it was which he wanted, and without which he might not ever be contented. And Jurgen also, after Heaven's very best had been done to grant him what he sought for, could reply only that he was Jurgen who sought he knew not what. And all their descendants have been like these maddening two in this at least, all seeking after they could not say what. Nobody can do anything for such a race! For their needs have stayed insatiable: their journeying has been, in every land and in every time, a foiled journeying: and in the end, in the inevitable unvarying end, each one of you treads that gray quiet way of ruins which leads hither and to no other place."

"Well, for that matter," Gerald said, "it seems that you too, Horvendile, have some engagement in this hog wallow."

" I endeavor, in point of fact, to become familiar with this last stretch of limbo, against the time of my own need not ever to be remembered anywhere."

" — And for my part, I came of my own choice and in self-protection," Gerald continued, with his chin well up. " For I must tell you, Horvendile, that I have had little peace since our last meeting."

Then Gerald (putting out of mind those attendant, very hungry looking pigs) related the epic of his journeying, without reserving anything out of false modesty, now that he talked with a confrère. He told of how he had descended into the underwater palace of the Princess Evasherah and of the orgies which he had shared in. He spoke, a bit contritely, of the amorous excesses he had been led into by the wives and the three hundred and fifty-odd concubines of Glaum during their master's absence. With unconcealed embarrassment he told of how the people of Lytreia had endeavored to detain him in their temple, to reign there as their tribal god, because they found his nose to be so much more majestic than the idol they hitherto had worshipped. He confessed to his dalliance with the enamored Fox-Spirit. He frankly admitted that he had not behaved well in seducing Evarvan and then deserting her after her marvelous beauty had become to him an old story. He told of how Queen Freydis had come repeatedly to him with the most generous proffers of her realm and person; and he spoke of this matter with visible compunction, because he could not deny that after three or four bouts he had repulsed the infatuated poor lady rather rudely.

In fine, said Gerald, since every man ought honestly to acknowledge his own weaknesses, he could get no real peace in the Marches of Antan. So at the last he had stolen away, into this quiet, gray untroubled place, of his own accord, just to be rid of so many persons who took unfair advantage of his over-amiable and fiery nature. . . .

And Horvendile, at the end of Gerald's repentant narrative, observed: " I comprehend. You have been, in brief, the devil of a fellow and a sad rip among the ladies."

" Oh, but you wrong me! Such a suspicion is very horrifying and quite unjust! No, it is merely that not even Fair-haired Hoo, the Helper and Preserver, the Lord of the Third Truth, and the Wellbeloved of Heavenly Ones, is immune to over-constant temptation."

And at that, Horvendile shrugged. " A god with so many fine titles is not to be argued with. In any case, do you be of good cheer, for even after all these regrettable amours, and beyond the mire that my swine delight in, the Princess still awaits you."

" But in what place? " said Gerald, " and how is she called? "

" She awaits in every place so long as youth remains — "

" Upon my word, now, Horvendile, but that is the truth, and a rather plaguing truth! "

" — However, this especial Princess is called, as it chances, Evangeline — "

" Oh, come! " said Gerald, " come now, but really, my dear fellow — ! "

" — And at your first sight of her you will be enraptured. For this Princess Evangeline is so surpassingly lovely that she excels all the other women your gaze has ever beheld — "

[294]

WHO GAVE UP THE RACE

"I know," said Gerald. "Her face is the proper shape, it is appropriately colored everywhere, and it is surmounted with an adequate quantity of hair."

"— Nor," Horvendile went on, with rising enthusiasm, "is it possible to find any defect in her features —"

"No: for, doubtless, the colors of this beautiful young girl's two eyes are nicely matched, and her nose stands just equidistant between them. Beneath this is her mouth; and she has also a pair of ears."

"In fine," said Horvendile, with his hands aflourish above his attendant pigs, "the Princess is young, she exhibits no absolute deformity anywhere, and your enamored glance will therefore perceive in her no fault, because of that magic which in the Marches of Antan the Two Truths exercise over all vigorous young persons."

"You very movingly depict a woman of extraordinary and, I have not the least doubt, resistless charm. Nevertheless, I cannot any longer be wandering about a place wherein there are only two truths, and where the magic of these Two Truths is forever meddling with my young body, for the gods of the Marches of Antan do not content me."

Then Horvendile replied: "Men have found many gods. But these gods pass. They descend into Antan, and they do not return. One god and one goddess alone do not pass. They remain eternally, if but to weave eternally a mist about the seeing and the thinking of the young, and thus to secure the existence of yet other young persons within a month or so."

"With observations to that same general effect,"

[295]

Gerald answered, " I am not unfamiliar. But let us make the thing complete! Do you now voice, here in your murky pigsty, one or another long-winded restatement of the fact that time disastrously affects all organic material. You will then, I think, have summed up the entire philosophy of the Marches of Antan. Perhaps it is a true philosophy. Nevertheless, that philosophy is a morbid materialism such as does not amuse me, who am a self-respecting citizen of the United States of America. No: I had far rather play with a beautiful idea than with one utterly lacking in seductiveness. So I prefer to think that the gods and the dreams of men pass to a noble and a worthy goal — "

It was then that Horvendile sighed, a bit despondently. " Ah, Gerald, but how may you presume to speak of such matters, who did not attain to Antan? "

" My friend," replied Gerald affably, " I was too wise to risk any such indiscretion. No: I did not enter into my appointed kingdom; and I have destroyed it. Therefore it must remain, so long as I remain, whatever I choose to imagine it. I retain the privilege of playing with a beautiful idea, in just the proper half-remorseful frame of mind which begets the most luxuriant fancies — "

" But — " Horvendile began.

" No, my dear fellow, you are quite wrong."

Horvendile said, " Still — "

" Yes, there is something in that, at first glance, yet it does not really touch the root of the matter."

Horvendile protested, " I was but going to say — "

" I know! I perfectly comprehend your argument. And I admit that you phrase it forcefully. The

[296]

trouble is that you are wrong in your underlying principle."

Horvendile said, " However — "

" Yes, but not always," Gerald stated. " For the one way for a poet to appreciate the true loveliness of a place is not ever to go to it. No, Horvendile, a poet is not to be fobbed off with facts. No matter what the surrounding facts might be, all poets from Prometheus to Jurgen have preferred a beautiful idea to play with. So a logical poet will always destroy his appointed kingdom, because in this way only can he convert it into a beautiful idea. Therefore for me, who am a poet of sorts, to have entered into my appointed kingdom would have been woefully shiftless. I would have had henceforward only one kingdom. But, as it is, I can remake the destroyed place several times a day, in my imaginings, and can every time rebuild it more beautifully. I have thus a thousand kingdoms, each one of them more lovely than the other. To-day it will be Evasherah who awaits me there, among all the splendor and the perfume and the sunlit lewdness of the most ancient East. To-morrow the sweet singing of featherylegged Evadne will summon me to a quite different Antan, which then will be a sea-engirdled, low-lying tropic island. And the day after to-morrow, far more idyllic lures will be recalling me to that pastelcolored, pastoral and rather populous Antan which is inhabited by all the many dreams that I had in youth, and is to be made my strictly personal heaven by the pure lips of Evarvan. Whereas, upon yet other occasions, — when my frame of mind takes on a more scholastic turn, — I shall know that in Antan awaits me each paragraph of the profound, wide erudition of Evaine. . . . But more often, Horvendile, I shall think of yet another woman and of a boy child, who were not wonderful in anything, but who for a while seemed mine. And I shall believe that these two wait for me, in a much more prosaic Antan; and I shall know that no magic, howsoever mightier than the less aspiring dreams of my manhood, can afford to me anything more dear. . . . For all that one needs, Horvendile, I have had. Antan could boast of nothing more desirable, to me, than that which I have had. So now not any power can ever quell my thankfulness for those illusions which have made sport with me for my allotted while. And I cry out defiantly, among your waiting swine, in this gray place of endless ruining, I am content . . . ! "

Then Horvendile replied: " A fool with so many fine words at his tongue's tip, a fool also is not to be argued with. For it is a foolishness beyond any describing, to believe that Antan can be destroyed by you or by anybody else. Ah, no! your kingdom awaited you, poor Gerald: but you faltered, you fell away into domesticity, — and you talked! Now it is the Master Philologist who, through the might of that word which was in the beginning, and which will be when all else has perished, has removed your kingdom from your reach, and from your seeing, and even from your quite whole-hearted belief, forever. Now it is your only comfort to poultice your failure with such foolish phrases. And now also it is I who tell you that for such faltering and for such failure, and for such phrases, there is possible but one answer."

Thereafter Horvendile gave Gerald a queer word of power, and Horvendile took out of his pocket a little mirror three inches square. You heard in the duskiness a flapping of small vigorous wings. Then three white pigeons stood among the swine, at the feet of Horvendile. He did what was requisite: and Gerald thus came straightway into a place which was not unfamiliar.

PART TWELVE

THE BOOK OF ACQUIESCENCE

" Candor is no More Palatable than an Oyster when Either is Out of Season."

GERALD came thus into the library in which, no more than four months ago, as it appeared to him, he had quitted his natural body. Lights burned there, but the room was unoccupied.

Nor did he perceive any marked signs of change. Most of his books were very much as he had left them. Upon the bookcases were still ranged his porcelain and brass animals and birds and reptiles. Investigation, though, revealed the addition to this diminutive fauna of a rather charming china cat, — a black cat, fast asleep, with a red ribbon about its neck, — and of a small ivory elephant, which also was black, but had white tusks.

The chairs, he saw, had been recovered, but it was with a figured stuff of much the same design and color. The rug that once had been his mother's was still underfoot; and the curtains, while new looking, were of just the same repulsive shade of green velvet that by candle light turned yellowish.

" It is a quite detestable color. I had always intended to change those curtains so soon as I could afford it, for a green with some real life in it. I can but deduce that my body has remained remarkably conservative through all these thirty years which have seemed to me only a month or two. My body has evinced commendable industry, also, for here

[303]

are dozens upon dozens of books by Gerald Musgrave."

It seemed a bit droll thus to be confronted with so much strange work performed by his own natural body, — thought out in his own brain cells, and written with his own hand, — during the time that these chattels had been entrusted to the Sylan. Yet the results were gratifying.

For here were not any folderol romances such as Gerald himself, he felt uneasily, might have perhaps contrived with those brain cells and that hand, romances which at best would have wasted his readers' time, and at worst might have incited unedifying and improper notions. Instead, these quartos were all serious and learned and scholastic works. Gerald therefore regarded these large quartos with a justifiable pride and with profound respect. Their very bindings were in themselves as incompatible with anything frivolous as were their contents with any unscientific double meanings. These books had the fine clarity of a physician in conference with a midwife. Moreover, Gerald's admiring eyes found nearly every page empedestalled upon the most impressive looking kind of footnotes: upon tall footnotes in almost illegibly small type; upon huge polyglottic footnotes, very full of Roman and Arabic numerals and of the phrases " *Ibid.*" and " *op. cit.*" and of small p's with a period after them; upon footnotes which flatteringly assumed your acquaintance with all human tongues and your possession of all printed books, so that you could be referred offhand to such and such a page of an especial edition; and upon footnotes which appeared to quote from the literature of every known language after having abbreviated the title of each cited volume into unintelligibility.

For these quartos dealt with no romantic nonsense such as the phantasms with which novels vitiate the intelligence and the morals of their readers, as Gerald observed with approval. They dealt with really worth-while ethnographic matters like the marriage customs of all lands, and the ways of male and female prostitution among the different races, and with the history, in each country, of paederasty, and of lesbianism, and of bestiality, and of necrophily, and of incest, and of sodomy, and of onanism, and of all manifestations of the sexual impulse in every era. Here, in a more imaginative vein, were the *Tentative Restoration of the Lost Books of Elephantis,* the handsomely illustrated *Seed of Minos,* the doctoral thesis upon *Lingham Worship,* the *Fertility Rites of the Sabbat,* the privately published *Myth of Anistar and Calmoora,* the *Study of Priapos,* and the various other monumental works which, although Gerald did not know this, had already made Gerald Musgrave's name familiar to the lecture halls of all universities and the pages of the more learned reviews.

These quartos were, in fine, the books which had made Gerald Musgrave the most famous and widely read of American ethnologists; and by his body's industry and erudition and broad-mindedness Gerald was properly impressed. Here seemed, indeed, to be at least one complete and scholarly treatise devoted to the historical development and the mechanics and the literature of every known manifestation of the great forces which had created all life.

" Yes, it is really edifying to note with what zeal and common-sense my body — while I was a-gypsying with over-ambitious follies, — has decorously set up as the recorder of historical and scientific truths."

Then Gerald found upon the next shelf some fourteen tall scrapbooks. They were full of what the newspapers had printed in laudation and in the most respectful criticism of the books of Gerald Musgrave. They contained, also, accounts of the academic honors conferred upon Gerald Musgrave. They were interleaved with the letters which had been written — the majority, of course, by that strange race which writes habitually to authors, but many of them, apparently, by persons of some consequence, — to Gerald Musgrave about his books.

" My body in my absence has become, thanks to my body's books, a reputable and even a looked-up-to citizen. My body is by way of being, indeed, a personage. I note, too, with that interest appropriate to the foibles of the great, that my body has also become a somewhat vain old magpie, gathering up through thirty years every scrap of paper which happens to display my name."

Next Gerald lighted on a black box with silver corners, and inside it was a time-discolored manuscript. This Gerald carried to the writing-table. And he found it that unfinished romance about his heroic ancestor, Dom Manuel of Poictesme, just ninety-three pages of it, precisely as Gerald had left it, with no word changed or added.

" There was not in my natural body sufficient power to sustain the high inspiration of my youth. So, very sensibly, my body has found other pursuits, and through them it has become a personage. I do not complain. Not every body becomes a personage.

[306]

Even so, it seems a pity to have denied to mankind
the loveliness already created in this fragment."

But it was just then that the door opened. In the
doorway stood a man in late middle life. And Gerald now for one instant regarded his natural body
and all the dilapidations which time had performed
upon that body.

And Gerald somehow comprehended the penned-
in and eventless and self-sacrificing, arduous life of
the famous scholar, the life which had been lived
so long by the natural body of Gerald Musgrave.
That blinking magpie, in this somewhat stuffy room,
— in the midst of this childish menagerie of small
cats and elephants and dogs and parrots and chickens
and camels and other imbecile toys, — day after day
compiled the valuable and interesting matter in those
quartos and the trivial magniloquence in those scrapbooks. And that, virtually, was all he ever did. Such
was his living in a world profuse in so many agree-
abilities, — to be tasted and seen, to be smelt and
heard and handled, at absolutely your own discretion,
in this so opulent world wherein anyone could live
very royally, and with never-failing ardor, upon
every person's patrimony of the five human senses.

Meanwhile, such self-devotion had paid, under
time's grasping governance, an exorbitant tax. The
impaired shrunk body was unhealthy looking. Under
each of the wavering dim eyes showed a peculiar
white splotch. The skin of the noted scholar was
pasty and seemed greasy. He had hardly any hair
except those gray and untended whiskers. Everywhere he was shrivelled and lean, except for the
abrupt, the surprising, protrusion of a large paunch.
He self-evidently had inadequate kidneys, and an

impaired heart, and defective teeth, and a sluggish liver, and approximately every other drawback to a sedentary person's late middle life.

The body of this ornament to scholarship and letters was, in fine, a quite disgusting bit of wreckage, in need of patching up everywhere; and a fallen god, when thus confronted by the work of time and of much study and of intramural living, might very well shake his red ever-busy head over the one refuge now remaining to down-tumbled divinity.

Nevertheless, Gerald spoke the queer word of power which Horvendile had given him. There followed for Gerald an instant of dizziness, of faint nausea, and of momentary blindness. . . .

Then Gerald found that it was he who stood at the door of the library peering into the quiet lamplit room. Before him waited a red-headed, slim young man in a blue coat and a golden yellow waistcoat, with a tall white stock and very handsome ruffles about his throat. And the young fellow was smiling at Gerald Musgrave with a rather womanish mouth, and in the eyes of the boy was a half-lazy, mildly humorous mockery.

Old Gerald Musgrave adored him with an ardor which was half hatred. Then he saw that the young fellow did not matter, and that Gerald Musgrave had bargained well.

"THAT is a strange and glorious word for you to be telling me," the boy began. " That is a disastrous bargain for you to be seeking. For your own will has spoken the revealing word which buys back your natural body now that your outworn crumbling body is of no more worth."

Gerald answered: " I, who have left the Marches of Antan forever, have bought freedom from the ever-meddling magic of the Two Truths. At my first sight of no other female body which is not positively deformed will I become enraptured. I have bought feet too old for errancy, ears that are deaf to the high gods, and to the heart-stirring music of great myths, and to the soft wheedling of women also, and I have bought eyes too dim to note whether or not Antan still gleams on the horizon. It is a good bargain."

Then he took up again the pages of that thirty-year-old romance. That too remains, he reflected, unfinished, like all else which I have ever undertaken. . . .

Some day it will be completed by other hands than the thin wrinkled hands before me. Somebody else, — not born, as yet, it may be, — will be writing out, — intelligibly, anyhow, — the story of Poictesme and of the Redeemer of Poictesme and of his

fine followers and many children, — but not half
so splendidly as I was going to write it. Somebody
else will, by and by, be beleaguering and entering
into — by means of the little, yet the not wholly
despicable, art of letters, — that wonder-haunted
province which — yes, that also, — was a part of
my appointed kingdom. . . . Somebody else will be
laying open the fair ways to Bellegarde and to
Amneran and to Storisende, and will be making free
these ways to every person, so that, through the
lean lesser art of letters, Poictesme may become in
some sort another Antan, — an Antan perhaps considerably abated in splendor, but graced at least with
easy accessibility. . . .

Yet not even such slight triumphs were to be won
by aged feet, and by ears no longer acute, and by
dimming eyes, and by pulses which would not be
riotous ever any more. He tore up the pages one by
one, just as, he recollected now, in the land of Lytreia, Evaine had torn up the sacred fig-leaves.
Glaum had said that the fig-leaf was the true symbol
of romance. Gerald meditatively dropped the destroyed fragments of his romance into the waste-
basket.

Gerald spoke then without any too great hope-
fulness. " Has my body, during your inhabitancy of
it, my dear fellow, escaped from Evelyn Townsend?
and gone free from the unmerited blessing of a good
woman's love? "

The red-headed boy before him replied, dis-
creetly: " Your body and the body of your Cousin
Evelyn have always been such good friends!"

And Gerald smiled. " I recognize that phrase. So
throughout thirty years Lichfield has never once

forgotten its polite formula for exorcising the inadmissible! "

" It has been generally felt," the youngster answered, " that a prominent man of letters was entitled to his Egeria. Of recent years, to be sure, your friendship has not been quite so ardent nor so frequently manifested. But there has been, to hold you two together, the boy begotten by your body upon her body. There has been the long usage to hold you two together. So your friendship has remained unshattered."

" I had forgotten," Gerald said, " the boy. Yes, I remember hearing that you had thoughtfully provided me with offspring during my absence. I know not quite how to thank you, my dear fellow, for a favor so delicate and so personal. We will therefore cough and drop the subject."

Then Gerald leaned back in the chair. He put together his finger-tips, and smilingly he looked at them with rather tired, old eyes.

" So I stay faithful to one woman, after all! I have been kept in everything a model American citizen. I have gracefully adhered to the code of a gentleman. In my private life I have evinced every proper respect for the chivalrous sacrament of adultery between social equals. In the field of my professional labors I have composed no puerile and lascivious romances, but only serious and instructive works. I am, in brief, in all respects, a credit to my native Lichfield, and, more generally, to the United States of America."

He shrugged. He spread out those old-looking, futile hands.

" Well, certainly I must not spoil the miracle. So

I submit. I yield to the demands of propriety. I accept my personal good behavior; I accept my success; and I accept also my measure of actual famousness."

Then Gerald said: " Therefore I must, so long as my life lasts, continue faithfully your work as the recorder of historical and scientific truths, since it was such truths which brought my name into famousness. Oh, yes, you may depend upon it, I shall henceforward honor these fine truths, within the limits advisable for anybody now nearing sixty. I shall serve them, that is, with my pen rather than with other instruments now perhaps more fallible. For the trained intelligence of such a famous scholar as I have become cannot deny their proper importance to those scientific and historical truths which brought him into famousness,— nor would, of course, my admirers care to have me abandoning my métier."

And Gerald said also: " Even in the private relations which you have chivalrously preserved for me, my dear fellow, one must not ask everything. Wheresoever a man lives, there will be a thornbush near his door: and I can manage well enough, I daresay, to put up with the continuance of this illicit love-affair, — in which, after all, my advanced age now protects me from being put to any frequent or far-reaching inconvenience. Meanwhile, the legend of a life-long illicit love-affair is a very splendid preservative for the fame of any writer. It would have been even better, of course, if in conjugating the verb to love, you had managed to make a few mistakes in gender. That is more piquant. That is infallible. Still, I repeat, one must not ask everything. I have my satisfying legend of private immorality, created without any least trouble on my part. Men will remember it. So all ends very well indeed. I am content with what I have found upon Mispec Moor. I am content with what I have found in Lichfield. And I shall not bother any more about Antan, wherein, for one reason and another, I have found nothing."

"Do you not be speaking lightly of Antan! For I — do you not understand? " — the young man spoke with an almost frightened elation, — " it is I who am called to reign in Antan. You have brought me the revealing word and the mighty summons of Horvendile. Antan is my appointed kingdom, into which I shall now be entering upon the silver stallion famous in old prophecies! "

"Oh, oh! " said Gerald, " so that is how it is! All ends, again, with that rather hackneyed scoring *Da capo*. And the eternal quest of Antan continues, for all that I have no part in it. . . ."

Yet the boy's joyousness and proud faith appeared to old Gerald Musgrave pitiable beyond thought. Gerald, now that he was fifty-eight, was of course not really troubled by that pitiableness, because all actual commiseration and sympathy for other persons had withered in him along with the rest of youth's over-upsetting emotions. Besides, Gerald saw that, in logic, as a plain question of arithmetic, the boy did not matter. A million or so other lads more or less like this enthusiastic young fellow were at that instant preparing for the same downcasting and failure; and by and by these lads also would be facing their own unimportance with equanimity. For, as you — howsoever suddenly, — got older, there was less bitterness, there was hardly any bitterness at all, to be derived of the knowledge that in human living very much amounted to nothing, because you saw even more clearly and more constantly that nothing amounted to very much. . . .

So Gerald said only: " You are young. At least, you are living in a young body. So do you beware! For, so long as you go about the Marches of Antan in any conveyance so perilous, the lying half-magic of the Two Truths will beset that young body, and the Princess will await you at every turn. She will encounter you under many names, for it is true that, just as you said very long ago, women do vary in their given names. She will encounter you in varying shapes. But in any case, she waits for every young romantic everywhere, as a rather lovable and as an interestingly formed and colored impediment. . . . I think it, therefore, highly improbable that you will complete the journey to Antan. I, in any case, am middle-aged. And I cry, not discontentedly, my personal farewell to the half-magic of racing pulses and of distended nerves — "

For an instant Gerald was silent. In his old eyes awoke that gleam which anybody familiar with Gerald would have recognized at once.

" You see," he continued, with large affability, " while you have been theorizing, my dear fellow, — oh, very charmingly, and with a thoroughness which does you credit, great credit, — well, my investigations meanwhile have taken a rather more practical turn. I am not, of course, at liberty to speak of my love-affairs, during my journeying toward Antan, with any real explicitness. No, here, as always, *noblesse oblige*. Still, if you only knew! If you but knew half as much as I do about that droll escapade out yonder with the Lady Sigid of Audierne and her cousin the Abbess! about what happened to me in the harem of Caliph Mizraim! about Beatrice and Henriette and Madame Pamela and Vittoria and Elspeth! about the three girls at the tanner's! or if you knew the truth as to what her Majesty and I were about that night we came so near being caught — ! "

" I see," the boy said, rather wistfully. " You have been a devil of a fellow and a sad rip among the ladies."

" Oh, dear me, not at all! " said Gerald. And the old fellow now wore the expression which, sometimes, accompanies a blush. " It is merely that I have talked a bit too freely. It is only that this rash tongue of mine was running away with me. So I can but ask you to forget every word I have uttered. Great personages ought not to be discussed with that candor to which I am far too prone. I confess it. I apologize. I shall therefore say nothing whatever about the eight other queens with whom my name has been coupled, — with how good reason I, you understand, must be the last person in the world to admit, — nor about any of the empresses either. In fact, a great deal of the scandal about my intimacy with one of them was exaggerated. No: I most certainly must not voice any indiscretions about dear Caroline. I merely point out — without mentioning any names whatever, — that my experience has been considerable. And I can assure you, my dear fellow, that in the end these half-magics produce, after all, no very prodigious miracles."

" But — " said the boy.

" No," Gerald protested, " no, really, you must not tempt me with such eloquence! It suffices that

[315]

during the thirty years that you have sat here theorizing, — and have, as it were, blossomed forth with all these delightful books, — these half-magics have led me day after day from one affair to its twin. They have led me into more or less jealously guarded lowlands, which were not markedly dissimilar. They have led then from one valley to another valley which looked and felt and, for that matter, smelt very much the same. Finally they led me to the fair breasts of Maya. And I fell away into domesticity, I went no farther. But I was wholly content there. . . . So I do not complain. I have lost through these half-magics my appointed kingdom in Antan, — or so, at least, it appears to me, in a world wherein perhaps nothing is indisputable except, of course, historical and scientific truths. Yet the losing of my kingdom has, none the less, been pleasant. I have had, under the harryings of these half-magics — always, I mean, upon the whole, — an agreeable time. To-night the half-magics whose appointed duty it is to keep all us romantics from attaining to Antan have ceased bothering about me. After to-night I am no longer formidable. I am, in a word, now that I approach sixty, almost middle-aged. It follows that Antan does not concern me any longer: and I shall think no more about Antan, wherein, for one reason and another, I have found nothing."

With that, gray Gerald Musgrave dipped his pen. He put the boy quite out of his mind. And the well-thought-of old scholar began to write, just where his natural body had left off a bit earlier in the evening, setting down decorously the historical and scientific truths as to pre-nuptial intercourse in the bedchambers of New Guinea and the Tonga Islands.

[316]

THE boy waited, looking down at this old fellow who sat there making small scratches upon paper, the most of which he presently canceled with yet other scratches, all the while with the air of a person who is about something intelligent and of actual importance. Then the boy shrugged. For, as always, to an onlooker the motions of creative writing revealed that flavor of the grotesque which is attendant upon every form of procreation.

And besides, to him for whom the silver stallion waited without, and for whom his appointed kingdom waited also, such time-wasting appeared futile. He, who was young, and who retained as yet the untroubled faith of every boy in his own abilities and in his own importance, — and who, of course, might not foresee the fate which awaited him in the arms of Evadne of the Dusk, — could not regard without impatience such time-wasting. What made it even worse was that this dilapidated remnant of a man was so plainly enjoying himself. For he chuckled as he wrote; he had self-evidently found what he considered a rather beautiful idea to play with, for now he had cocked his battered, so nearly bald, old head to one side, and that which he had just written down was being regarded by his dimmed and peering eyes with entire admiration: and it was all somewhat pitiable to the young eyes of the observer.

[317]

SOMETHING ABOUT EVE

For it did not seem possible that anybody should sit here, thus stuffily immured, and with no exercise more profitable than writing, when yonder, as all youth knew, the road lay open to the unimaginable splendors of Antan. It was, for that matter, an unthrifty wantonness for Gerald Musgrave's young observer to be lingering here, in the cold company of books and china animals, when yonder (as all youth knew) along the pleasant way to Antan were waiting so many dear, fond, loving women eager to cheer and to inspire and to trust and to give all to speed the high-hearted adventurer in that glorious journeying toward his appointed kingdom. Decidedly, the old fellow was lost. For now he was infatuated by the contentment to be got out of writing, which remained forever, in its own fashion, as bedrugging as was the contentment to be got out of domesticity. There was no hope for this preposterous, doomed, chuckling Gerald Musgrave, — who would always now be finding one or another rather beautiful idea to play with, and who must remain, so long as life remained, a fribbling poet, whose only real delight was to shape and to play with puppets. . . .

Yet it mattered very little, to any person who was already for every practical purpose a reigning monarch, that all which pertained to this Gerald Musgrave was somewhat droll, the smiling red-haired boy decided, as he passed toward Evadne of the Dusk, and out of sight of that gray-fringed bald head bent over that incessant pen scratching.

EXPLICIT

[318]

THIS tenth volume of the *Storisende Edition* of the works of JAMES BRANCH CABELL, containing SOMETHING ABOUT EVE (first published in September, 1927), was designed by William Dana Orcutt and printed and bound at The Plimpton Press, Norwood, Massachusetts. It was completed in February, 1929, after which the type was destroyed. Issued in March, 1929, by Robert M. McBride & Company
New York